**Acclaim for
Michelle Willingham's
The MacEgan Brothers**

HER WARRIOR SLAVE
"Willingham skillfully combines a cast of
wonderfully original characters with a refreshingly different,
meticulously detailed setting to create a vivid tale
of love and danger in medieval Ireland."
—*Chicago Tribune*

"Michelle Willingham writes characters
that feel all too real. The tortured soul that is Kieran
really pulled at my heartstrings. Iseult's unfailing search
for her lost child made this book a truly emotional read."
—*Publishers Weekly*

THE WARRIOR'S TOUCH
"Thought-provoking tale of love."
—*RT Book Reviews*

HER WARRIOR KING
"Betrayal, mistrust and anger fire this medieval tale about how
love finds an aching heart when that heart isn't looking."
—*RT Book Reviews*

SURRENDER TO AN IRISH WARRIOR
"Heart-wrenching and uplifting, with riveting characters and
a captivating plot. It's the story of two people devastated by
tragedy, who find comfort and healing in each other."
—*RT Book Reviews*

Author Note

When I first began writing The MacEgan Brothers series, it was born out of my love of Ireland. I've visited the country on three occasions, and each time I've found a corner of the world that holds both mysticism and wild beauty. From the ancient ruins I imagined a family of five strong warriors, fighting to carve their place in a world threatened by Norman invaders. The books in the series include (in suggested reading order) *Her Warrior Slave* (prequel), *Her Warrior King*, *Her Irish Warrior*, *The Warrior's Touch*, *Taming Her Irish Warrior* and *Surrender to an Irish Warrior*.

Readers have written to me asking about what happened to the warriors after they found their happily-ever-after, and I began to wonder about the second generation. By the time the last book was finished a few of the warriors' children were adolescents. I decided to create a series of three stories crafted around the children of my warriors. It's set during the time of the winter solstice and Christmas, and each story features a daughter or son of one of the MacEgan brothers.

I've thoroughly enjoyed revisiting familiar characters and getting acquainted with new heroes and heroines. Thank you for sharing the holidays with my MacEgans!

Visit my website at www.michellewillingham.com for excerpts and behind-the-scenes details about my books. I love to hear from readers. You may email me at michelle@michellewillingham.com or contact me via mail at P.O. Box 2242 Poquoson, VA 23662, U.S.A.

MICHELLE WILLINGHAM

Warriors in Winter

HARLEQUIN®

entertain, enrich, inspire™

ISBN-13: 978-0-373-29718-4

WARRIORS IN WINTER
Copyright © 2012 by Harlequin Books S.A.

The publisher acknowledges the copyright holder of the individual works as follows:

IN THE BLEAK MIDWINTER
Copyright © 2012 by Michelle Willingham

THE HOLLY AND THE VIKING
Copyright © 2012 by Michelle Willingham

A SEASON TO FORGIVE
Copyright © 2012 by Michelle Willingham

Recycling programs
for this product may
not exist in your area.

For questions and comments about the quality of this book, please contact us at CustomerService@Harlequin.com.

www.Harlequin.com

Printed in U.S.A.

CONTENTS

IN THE BLEAK MIDWINTER

Chapter One

Ireland—1192

The wind had turned cold in Éireann, forcing Brianna MacEgan inside the walls of her beehive-shaped stone hut. The fire had gone out, but she hadn't built another yet. The chill within these walls matched the feelings of her heart. At any moment, she expected the door to open, with Murtagh sweeping inside to steal a kiss. But he wouldn't. He'd been killed in a raid by a *Lochlannach* warrior of Gall Tír.

In her nightmares, she saw the frozen expression of shock on Murtagh's face when the spear took his life. A cry of anguish had ripped from her throat as she'd rushed to his side, heedless of danger. Never in her life would she forget the cold expression of the Viking who had killed him. In a fraction of a second, he'd ended her world.

A part of her lay buried beneath the earth at his side. Worse, she'd never conceived a child during the marriage. There would be no son with Murtagh's eyes, no daughter with his smile. The empty longing for a child ached within her, but she couldn't imagine another man taking his place.

The walls seemed to close in on her, the grief shrouding her. Though her father had pleaded with her to return to Rionallís, her childhood home, she couldn't bring herself to leave Laochre. All of her best memories were here, in this home. Inside this space, she could feel Murtagh's presence, like a ghost haunting her. And though she knew it was time to let go of the past, she wasn't ready.

A knock sounded at the door, and without waiting for an answer, her cousin Rhiannon came bursting inside. Her long brown hair was twisted into braids in a crown across her forehead, while the rest fell to her waist. 'I've been looking for you everywhere. The guards saw riders approaching. Liam has returned…and he has a woman with him!'

'He's back from the Crusade?' Brianna stood up, rubbing her arms against the cold. Their cousin had gone to the Holy Land, against his father's orders. The king had been furious to learn of it, but he'd allowed his son to stay…provided that he remained in the service of King Richard the Lionheart. 'Why do you think he brought a woman?'

Rhiannon lifted her shoulders. 'Possibly to marry her. There are wagons behind them, and more riders.' Her cousin's voice was filled with excitement at the prospect of visitors. 'I might find a husband. Pray God, there's someone handsome among them.'

The fervent prayer wasn't entirely in jest. Rhiannon's father believed there was no man alive good enough for his daughter. He'd forbidden any of their tribe to even look at her, much less ask her to marry.

'And if you do meet a handsome stranger?' she prompted.

Rhiannon sent her a secret smile. 'I won't be telling my father about him, you can be certain of that.' She rubbed her shoulders against the cold. 'Come, and let's greet Liam.'

'Go on without me,' Brianna urged. 'I'll follow in a few

moments.' No doubt if Liam was getting married, there would be feasting and celebrations for days. The very thought of making merry was foreign to her, like a long-forgotten dream.

Her cousin's face dimmed. 'You've been hiding away for weeks. If I leave you alone, you won't come.'

'I'm sorry.' The loneliness was so unbearable, she didn't know how to force herself out of her melancholy. 'It's just that…today was difficult for me.'

'I'll stand outside the door and wait for you,' Rhiannon warned. 'And you wouldn't want your best friend to die of cold, would you?'

Beneath the teasing, Brianna heard the true concern. Her cousin was only trying to help, to draw her away from the sorrow. Perhaps Rhiannon was right. A distraction might take her mind away from her grief.

Brianna reached for her husband's cloak and drew it around her shoulders. It was too large to fit, but at least she could hold a part of Murtagh to her. 'All right, I'll come.' Before she pulled the door shut behind her, her gaze fixed upon the spear standing in the corner. The tip gleamed in the dim light, the edge honed until it would slice through any man's flesh.

She was torn between destroying the weapon that had claimed Murtagh's life…or using it for vengeance.

Fifteen years, he'd dreamed of this moment. At last, to set foot upon foreign shores and visit the places he'd longed to go. Arturo de Manzano cast a glimpse back at the ship that had brought him from Navarre, and anticipation quickened his pace. All his life, he'd wanted to taste adventure, and he intended to savour every last moment. Even if it was freezing and beginning to rain.

He rode behind his sister Adriana and her betrothed husband, Liam MacEgan. MacEgan had claimed to be an Irish prince, but Arturo would withhold his approval of the marriage until he witnessed the man's rank for himself. Though they were the same age, Liam appeared far older. He wouldn't speak of the horrors he'd witnessed while on Crusade, nor would Adriana. Both of them seemed grateful to be upon peaceful shores, far away from Saracen enemies.

Behind him, servants unloaded the ship filled with his sister's dowry goods. Adriana remained at MacEgan's side, her gaze fixed upon her betrothed husband, as if drawing strength from him. Her eyes were shadowed with sleeplessness, but what concerned Arturo most was the absence of joy in her face. A bride ought to be smiling with happiness, excited about her forthcoming wedding day. But Adriana appeared troubled.

Arturo drew his horse on her opposite side. 'You look tired.'

'It's been a long journey,' she admitted. 'I'm glad to be on land again. As is Liam.'

Liam grimaced, taking a deep breath. 'Had I known that going on Crusade would mean so many months at sea, I doubt I would have gone.' He reached for Adriana's hand. 'But then, I wouldn't have met you.'

Though she ventured a smile, Arturo saw the emptiness within it. 'She shouldn't have left Navarre.' Adriana had been changed by the Crusade. He could see the shadow weighing upon her, though she would not admit it. She'd shrugged away his questions, claiming it was only exhaustion. But Arturo suspected there was more to the story than that.

'It was an honour,' his sister countered. 'The queen needed a lady-in-waiting who could guard her.' Sending Arturo a sidelong glance, she added, 'And my brothers did well enough, teaching me to defend myself.'

'A battlefield is no place for a woman,' Arturo insisted.

'Which was why we left,' Adriana finished. With a warning glance, she silently asked him to abandon the subject.

'Adriana is braver than most women,' Liam said softly. With a wry smile, he added, 'She'll have to be, to survive the ordeal of meeting my family.'

Arturo wasn't certain what MacEgan was implying by that. 'Do they know of the marriage?'

He shook his head. 'I intend to surprise them.'

Adriana eyed her intended husband with wariness. 'And what if your father has arranged another bride in your absence?'

Liam squeezed her hand. 'You are the only one I intend to marry. And I have no doubt they will come to love you.'

She tried to smile, but worry lurked within her dark brown eyes. Arturo hung behind them, watching the couple as they rode toward a vast limestone castle. Adriana had been his friend and ally while they'd grown up together. It was she who had dismissed the potential brides their mother had brought before him, revealing the greed or faithlessness she'd discovered. And it was she who had introduced him to Cristina, the woman he'd been married to for years, before she'd died three summers ago.

The loneliness was starting to abrade his mood. It wasn't simply the desire to visit new places or to experience a culture different from his own. It was the deep need to fill up the empty spaces within his life. He wanted to feel the arms of a child's embrace during the day and a wife to curl up beside him at night. The time had come to find a new woman to bring back with him to Navarre. Perhaps an Irish one, if she was willing.

He saw love on his sister's face when she looked at Liam, despite the worry. They would find their happiness, once she adjusted to her new home. And he envied them.

They continued riding toward Laochre Castle, and the air was much cooler than his native Navarre. Arturo was accustomed to sun and mountains, while this land had the greenest hills he'd ever seen. A large stone wall surrounded the fortress, and it rivalled the holdings of their own father. It reassured him that this marriage would be a strong one, and he signalled to one of the servants to join him.

'My lord.' The man bowed, waiting for his orders.

'Send word back to the Vicomte de Manzano that he and my mother should make arrangements to travel here for the wedding.' He'd wanted to confirm that MacEgan was telling the truth about his land and holdings, before they made the journey. His mother would want to be here, and surely Adriana would be grateful for their parents' presence.

After the servant departed to do his bidding, Arturo caught up to his sister and her husband-to-be. They had already entered the gates, and from the small crowd gathering, they were fascinated by her.

His sister paled at the sight of them. Arturo brought his horse up behind her and spoke quietly in Spanish. 'Don't faint, Adriana.'

'There are so many of them,' she responded back. 'And they're all talking about me.'

'*Sí*. But likely they are enchanted by you.'

'Will you not ride beside me?' she pleaded. Liam was speaking to the people in a foreign tongue, murmuring his translation to Adriana in the Norman language.

In a teasing voice Arturo refused, saying, 'I'll stay behind, to cut off your escape.' No doubt his sister was feeling lost amid all the people. He drew closer, giving her his support in the best way he could. While Liam was embraced by family and friends, the smile on Adriana's face grew strained.

He studied the crowd of people, his gaze passing over each of them, until his attention was drawn to another woman standing back from the others. She was dressed in an unadorned gown the colour of muddy water, while her hair was hidden beneath a darker mantle. A softness moved over her face when she saw Liam, but it was immediately shadowed by sadness.

She seemed reluctant to greet them, but when another woman took her hand, the two of them moved past the crowd toward Liam. Despite the mantle cloaking her features, he recognised the fragile beauty of her. After she greeted Liam, speaking quietly in Irish, she retreated from the crowd.

Arturo dismounted, giving his horse over to the stable master. When he returned to Liam's side, he asked, 'Who was that woman?'

'One of my cousins,' the Irishman answered. 'Her name is Brianna.' With a warning look, he added, 'And she's married, my friend.'

'Widowed,' another woman interrupted, switching from the Irish language into the Norman tongue. She embraced Liam, adding, 'Brianna's husband was killed after you left on Crusade.'

That explained the sadness. Arturo knew, well enough, what it was to endure the days ahead, pretending as if the grief weren't there. Even now, there were times when he wished he could speak with Cristina again, hearing her soft laugh. As he watched the woman slipping away, he sympathised with her fate.

Moments later, the king and queen of Laochre came forward. Queen Isabel threw herself at Liam, openly weeping tears of joy as she framed her son's face with her hands. 'Praise the saints, you're home.' She gripped him tightly and then scolded, 'When you left us, have you any idea how I worried about you? I'm so glad you're safe.'

'You're crushing him, Isabel,' the king said gently, pulling her back. But he embraced his son as well before turning to Adriana. 'I am Patrick MacEgan, King of Laochre.'

His sister managed a curtsy and Liam drew her forward. 'Father, this is Adriana de Manzano, the woman I intend to marry. And her brother Arturo de Manzano.'

At the mention of a wedding, the queen sent her a blinding smile and embraced Adriana. 'I bid you welcome.' Moments later, she began chattering so fast, Arturo wondered if Adriana would understand a word of it. But she walked alongside Isabel, and he supposed the queen would take good care of her.

It was clear that the king wanted to speak to his son alone, so Arturo offered to oversee the wagons. As he supervised them, bringing them into the inner bailey, his gaze returned to the hooded woman.

Brianna held herself apart from the others, and when the drizzling rain shifted into snow, she drew her mantle tighter around her. To his surprise, she caught him watching her and walked forward until she stood before him. At first, she spoke Irish, but when he shook his head, not understanding, she switched into the Norman language.

'Why do you stare at me?'

Her direct manner caught him off guard. Answering honestly, he said, 'Why do you think a man stares at a woman?'

She lifted her chin and met his eyes boldly. 'Find another woman for your attentions, Spaniard. I am not the one for you.'

A gust of wind caught at her hood, and it slipped away from her hair. It was nearly as dark as his own, and it contrasted sharply against her fair skin, making her green eyes stand out. Her features were exotic to him, beautiful in a way he'd never seen before.

'We have more in common than you know.' He lifted her hood back to cover her hair, while the snow dusted both of them. He was referring to her loss, but she remained motionless until his hands moved away.

'Turn your eyes elsewhere, Spaniard,' she whispered. He recognised the edge of grief beneath her words. If she had lost her husband, then likely she would find his interest offensive.

'I know your pain,' he said softly. 'The grief never leaves you. But time dulls it, eventually.'

He gave a slight bow, and turned back to join the others. He didn't have to turn, to know that she was now watching him.

Brianna's cheeks rushed with colour as Rhiannon returned to her side. 'Why did you tell the Spaniard I was a widow?' she accused.

Rhiannon's face narrowed with confusion. 'And so you are. Why? Did he bother you?'

She could give no reply. No, he hadn't bothered her. But the open interest had provoked a fluttering response within her stomach. The Spaniard was taller than Liam, with dark hair and dark eyes. His skin held the olive tone of a man who had spent a great deal of time in the hot sun. And his physical form was muscular, like a fighter.

Her cheeks burned at the memory of his touch upon her

hood. She hadn't missed the interest in his eyes, but it was his words that had shaken her.

I know your pain.

Did he? Then why would he dare to speak to her, as if he wanted to know her more intimately?

Her cousin was looking embarrassed, and Brianna realised how she'd overreacted. She took a deep breath and apologised. 'I'm sorry for my ill temper. You did nothing wrong.' She took her cousin's hand and tried to smile. 'He should have looked at you, if he was wanting a woman.'

'You were the one who captivated him,' Rhiannon pointed out. 'I didn't interest him at all.'

Brianna said nothing, not believing the words. 'He may change his mind. Besides, I'm not looking to marry again.'

'At least you *had* a husband once.' Rhiannon's mood darkened. 'If my father got his way, I would be a bride of the Church. He's threatened to kill any man who speaks to me.'

'He doesn't mean that.' But both of them knew how protective Connor MacEgan was when it came to his eldest daughter.

'Whether he does or not, there are no men in this tribe who will even look at me.'

'The Spaniard might, if you tried,' Brianna offered. Though she tried to pass off the suggestion in a casual manner, a sudden shyness passed over her. It had been so long since any man had shown an interest in her, she didn't know how to respond to it.

But Rhiannon sent her a secret smile. 'Not him. But your sister is putting together a love charm for me today.'

'Oh, no. You're not going to indulge her, are you?' There was no one more superstitious than her younger half-sister.

Alanna believed in faeries and magic, and was convinced that she had otherworldly abilities.

'What harm is there?' Rhiannon said. 'I'm supposed to meet her at the dolmen, and she'll do what she can to find a husband for me.'

From the amused look on the other woman's face, Brianna relaxed. Her cousin obviously didn't believe that magic could bring about a husband. 'When?'

'This evening, at sunset.'

'Whatever you do, don't drink any liquid she's brewed. Heaven only knows what's in it.'

'I won't,' Rhiannon promised. 'But whatever charm she casts, be assured of this. I won't waste my time here any longer. I'll find a husband and make my own fate.'

They continued walking into the castle and learned that Queen Isabel had taken Adriana into the solar and had sent for wine and food. Liam had gone with his father, the king, as well as the dark-eyed Spaniard, to discuss her bride price.

'I don't envy Liam's bride,' Brianna whispered as they neared the door. 'I imagine our aunt is questioning everything about her.'

'We should rescue her,' Rhiannon suggested.

'Aye.' Brianna pressed the door open, and the pair of them went inside. The young dark-haired woman was seated upon a stool beside Isabel, her hands clasped nervously in her lap. She'd removed her travelling cloak, and from the look of her expensive gown, she'd taken great care to look her best. The green silk shimmered with silver threads, while a gold necklace hung around her throat.

'Rhiannon and Brianna, you are welcome to join us,' the queen greeted them, smiling. 'I have been asking Adriana about how she and Liam met.'

Brianna exchanged a look with her cousin. No doubt Isabel had interrogated poor Adriana, hardly letting her touch the food and wine.

'Liam rescued us when the queen and I were held captive on the island of Cyprus,' Adriana admitted. 'He risked his life to free us.' A softness came over the young woman's face at the mention of her betrothed husband. 'He never left my side, even when we journeyed to Acre.'

'Were you there amidst the fighting?'

Adriana nodded, but her face turned pale at the memory of the Crusade. 'My father and brothers made certain I could fight, if necessary.' Her hand moved to her gown, and from inside the folds, she revealed a hidden blade. 'I served the queen not only as her lady-in-waiting, but also as a guard.'

The women continued sharing stories, but Brianna drifted off in a daydream. Though she had not been trained to fight as Adriana had, she imagined searching for the *Lochlannach* warrior, waiting until he believed himself alone. With the spear, she could confront him.

A dark shadow fell across her mood. She'd never killed a man before, and it wasn't an act she could take lightly. It was one matter to imagine avenging Murtagh; it was another to begin training for it.

Was it the right thing to do? Indecision warred with her conscience. No one would think it unusual for her to seek vengeance, if she were a man. It wasn't the favoured course of action, but it happened.

She rested her hand on one cheek, unsure of what to do. For so long, she'd kept the spear, until the very sight of it made her ill. The voice of reason reminded her that she ought to destroy it and simply forget what had happened.

But she couldn't. Though a year had passed, the crippling

sadness never left her alone. It pricked at her heart, leaving her raw and wounded.

She studied Adriana. In the woman's form, she saw a lean strength and a confidence. This was not a woman who would let any man threaten her. She would stand up for herself, not hiding away from the rest of the world.

It was the woman she wanted to be, a woman of courage—not cowardice.

Although she was uncertain how she might confront the raider, she supposed there was no harm in learning to defend herself or in mastering the use of a weapon. Despite the objection of the others, she could find a way to learn. And when she had mastered the skills she needed, she could make the decision then about whether or not to act against the *Lochlannach* raider.

An awareness caught her when the voices of the women broke off. When Brianna looked up, she saw that the king, Liam, and the Spaniard had joined them. She'd been so caught up in her dreaming, she hadn't noticed them entering the solar.

The Spaniard accepted a cup of wine from Isabel, and when he took a sip, Brianna's eyes were drawn to his mouth. His lips were firm, his face honed with sharp planes. So different from her husband. Murtagh had been a teasing man and a kind one. He'd treated her with affection and had been her friend as well as her lover.

But there was no friendship in Arturo de Manzano's expression. He eyed her as though there were no other women in the room. The intensity of his gaze caught her deep inside, like an intimate caress.

As a distraction, Brianna drank from her own cup, but the spicy taste of the wine did nothing to diminish the awkward feelings inside her. Did he intend to disarm her with a look?

She met his gaze openly, hiding nothing at all. Though the Spaniard might be trying to gain her interest, she had no intention of letting another man close to her. Even if he was fiercely handsome.

'Our parents will arrive within a few weeks,' he was telling Isabel. 'I think they will be more than pleased with the marriage.'

Isabel gave him a nod, and then turned back to Adriana. 'If you love my son and bring him happiness, then I, too, am well pleased. You might consider having your celebration after Twelfth Night, if their journey takes longer.'

Liam was standing behind Adriana, with his hands upon her shoulders. The young woman covered one of his hands with her own, and although there was love there, Brianna sensed another emotion from the young woman, like a hint of consternation.

It was hard to remain here, seeing the two of them with years of happiness ahead while her own marriage had been cut short by an enemy's spear. Isabel was talking about decorating the castle with greenery and holly, and Brianna excused herself, letting them continue their discussion of wedding plans. She wanted some time alone, to practise with her spear and make decisions about what to do next.

With slow steps, she crossed the Great Chamber and made her way back home. The bitter cold made her lift her hood over her hair. Glancing at the position of the sun, she had only an hour before dusk.

When she reached her house, Brianna took the spear and hid it within her cloak. She brought a gathering basket with her, in the hopes that if anyone saw her, they would believe she'd only gone to collect greenery.

She only made it halfway across the castle grounds, when the Spaniard approached. 'Would you like company on your walk?'

'No, thank you.' The last thing she wanted was for him to catch her practising with the spear.

'Then I'll keep my distance and guard you from anyone who might bother you.' He stepped back, gesturing for her to go forward.

Brianna didn't quite know what to say. She wanted to tell him no, but he'd only offered his protection. 'It isn't necessary. My uncle's guards will keep me from harm.'

As she departed the castle grounds, she glanced behind and saw that he maintained his distance. True to his word, he gave her complete privacy, and yet he remained nearby.

She frowned as she crossed over the open meadow and toward the forest. Trees were sparser in this area, but there was a small copse that would offer her a place to practise. She set down the basket and removed her cloak, letting it fall to the ground. With the spear in one hand, she gripped the wood, finding the balance point.

It was the first time she'd practised with the weapon. Even touching it bothered her, and she half-wished she'd chosen another weapon.

Memories crashed through her, of the suffering in Murtagh's eyes when the spear had taken him. It had been hours until he'd died, and never would she forget the horror of helplessness. Or the blood upon her hands and this weapon that had cut his life short.

Hot tears burned in her eyes, and she wondered how she ever thought she would have the strength to avenge his death. She couldn't even touch the spear without weeping.

You've gone weak, her mind taunted. *You can't do this.*

Her hand dug into the wood, and she sighted another tree as her target, pulling her arm back in preparation.

'So this is how Irish women spend their time?' came a male voice.

The spear fell from her hands, clattering upon the frozen ground as she spun. 'I told you I didn't need your protection.'

'Anyone could see you trying to hide a spear,' he pointed out. 'You didn't conceal it very well.'

'It's not your concern.' She steadied her voice, trying to hide her shaken feelings.

'I wondered why you would bring it so far from the castle grounds,' he continued on. 'Were you trying to learn how to use it?'

She remained silent. *Please go away.*

But instead, the Spaniard reached down for the fallen weapon, testing its weight in one hand. 'This spear is not meant to be thrown,' he told her. Turning the shaft into a vertical position, he took her hand and guided it on to the wood.

She studied his features, noting the light chainmail armour he wore and the strength of his stance. There was none of the easy-going nature of her husband, nor the light teasing she was accustomed to. Instead, he remained stoic, rather like a block of stone. His dark eyes narrowed upon her, as if questioning her purpose.

With his hand upon hers, he guided the spear to just below his chest. 'This is a spear meant for close contact. You wait until the enemy is close enough, and thrust it upward.'

The tip of the spear rested upon his chainmail armour, and she saw the intensity in his dark eyes. Standing so near to him, she murmured, 'Not into his heart?'

'The tip would get deflected by his ribs if you miss. It's too great of a risk.'

'I'll remember that.' Slowly, she drew the spear back and nodded for him to leave.

He ignored her dismissal. 'Who is threatening you, *belleza*?' His tone held warmth, but beneath it lay strength and determination.

'There is no threat to me. And even if there was, I would not ask for your help.' She set the weapon down and withdrew her knife. Grasping an evergreen branch, she sawed at it, pretending she didn't care what he did now. Yet, she was fully aware of his presence.

The hairs on the back of her neck tingled from his proximity. When he moved beside her, the top of her head barely reached his chin. Her eyes rested squarely upon his chest, and she chided herself for noticing the way his armour moulded to it like a second skin.

'Even so, I'll stay.' His voice held a deep timbre that made her suppress a shiver. When he moved beside her, he watched her work for a moment. 'Your blade is dull,' he remarked. 'Use mine.'

His hand brushed against hers, and he gave her a knife with an ivory hilt. She held it for a moment, and said, 'Has anyone ever told you that you're unbelievably persistent?'

'My sister. But usually she calls me overprotective.' He reached out for a pine branch and waited for her to cut it. When she tried his knife, the blade sliced through the slender branch easily. He took it and put it within her basket. 'You'll want to fill this before you return. So they won't suspect.'

She reached for another branch and cut several in silence. The Spaniard took them from her, one by one. Though he said nothing more, Brianna felt the need to fill up the silence. 'You travelled a long way for your sister.'

'Adriana and I have always been close.' In his voice, she

heard the affection, but a moment later, he added, 'I had to be sure Liam was worthy of being her husband.'

'My cousin will be king one day. There is no one more worthy than he.' She gathered a pile of branches and returned his knife.

'What of your own husband?' he asked. 'If your uncle is king, then was he—'

'I don't want to talk about Murtagh.' The hurt was still fresh within her, and she had no desire to explain why she had wed the miller's son. Her husband had been hardworking and honest, although her family had not been pleased by her choice to wed him. Her father had not forbidden it, but neither had he approved of the match.

'Forgive me if I brought up bad memories.' He used the knife to detach another branch, adding it to her basket. 'It was curiosity, nothing more.'

She bit her lower lip, realising how snappish she'd sounded. 'It was a year ago today that he died.'

Arturo stopped cutting the branch, the knife still partially embedded in the wood. 'You made the wrong choice to come here.'

She sent him a questioning look, not understanding, and he added, 'On the one-year anniversary of my wife's death, I drank myself unconscious.'

A hint of a smile tugged at her. 'And was it a wise choice?'

'I didn't think so the next morn. But at the time, it made it easier to bear.' He reached down and lifted up the basket of branches. 'It's not easy to let go of someone you loved.'

'No.' In truth, she felt as if she were betraying Murtagh, just by talking to the handsome stranger. But in his eyes, she saw the reflection of her own grief. Without knowing why, she confessed, 'Murtagh was killed by the *Lochlannach*. With that spear.'

'My wife died in childbirth.' Though his words were spoken without emotion, she saw the flash of pain on his face.

'And the baby?' she couldn't stop herself from asking.

He stood so still, she knew the answer before he spoke it. Quietly, he shook his head.

The echo of emptiness resonated within her, and she heard herself asking, 'Did you love her?'

'Very much.'

'Then why would you follow me here?' she blurted out.

Arturo reached out for the spear and handed it to her. 'I remember the grieving and the loneliness. When I look at you, I see myself as I was, a few years ago. I thought you might want a friend who understands.'

The air turned cooler and snow began to fall around them. It dusted his hair and cheeks, while all around them it swirled in a blinding dance.

'All I want is someone to teach me how to fight,' she said at last.

His gaze narrowed. 'For what purpose?'

'To kill the man who took my husband's life.' She took the basket from him, sending him a challenge of her own. 'Go ahead and tell me how foolish that is.'

Instead, he shook his head. 'It's not foolish at all. You're angry.'

'Yes.' She gripped the spear, feeling the rush of injustice filling her up inside. 'When I first lost him, I spent months weeping. I could hardly get through the days. And now, I feel this rage every time I think of the *Lochlannach* who killed him.'

'Killing him won't bring back your husband.'

'It would make me feel better.' She let out a sigh and handed him back his blade, exchanging it for her own. 'I need a way of filling up the hours of the day.'

A smug expression slid over his face. 'There are many ways a beautiful woman can spend the hours of her day.'

She sent him an exasperated look, knowing exactly what he was implying. 'No, thank you.'

His voice deepened as he sheathed his blade. 'I can teach you what you wish to learn, Brianna.' The seriousness on his face made her stop walking, as she realised he was no longer teasing. 'But only if you swear to me that you won't hunt this man down alone. Put your anger into the training, and you may find that it eases your grief.'

His offer surprised her. Her own father and uncles had refused to let her near the weapons. 'Why would you agree to this?'

'I spent the year after Cristina's death fighting in any battle I could. Releasing the anger is better than holding it in.'

Brianna studied his dark brown eyes and saw the truth of his words. The physical aspect of training *would* make her feel better, even if she ended up destroying the weapon. She wanted to punish herself with exertion, until at night she fell into a dreamless sleep. And then, perhaps, she wouldn't feel the emptiness.

She shivered against the winter air, and the snow had begun to accumulate around them, coating the pine branches in a frosted white. Arturo picked up the basket and nodded for her to accompany him back to Laochre. 'In return, I ask that you take me to visit the lands nearby. I want to see what I can of this country, before I return to Navarre.'

It was a reasonable request, one she could grant easily. 'All right. Until Liam and Adriana marry.'

Though he inclined his head in agreement, she worried that spending a great deal of time with Arturo was not a wise idea. Even while walking with him, a dormant part of herself stirred, as if awakening from a long slumber.

Being trained by this man would be a dangerous game indeed.

Chapter Two

The next morning, the ground was covered in several inches of snow. Brianna stood back within the inner bailey, watching the soldiers spar. Most were fighting with light colc swords, and they wore armour made from leather. All of the men, including Liam, took part in the training. But her attention was drawn to Lord de Manzano. He held a lighter sword made from Damascus steel. The blade was beautiful, and he stood speaking with Connor MacEgan, Rhiannon's father, who had already begun working with the men. Though Connor had lost the use of one of his hands, it made no difference at all in his fighting. He went from soldier to soldier, speaking to each man and offering adjustments to improve their skill.

When he spied her, Connor came forward and smiled. 'I didn't expect to see you here, Brianna. Have you seen Rhiannon this morn?'

She shook her head. 'Not yet.' But from the guarded look on the man's face, she suspected something was amiss.

'If you see her, tell her I was looking for her.'

Brianna agreed but didn't miss the way his eyes searched the fortress. Her cousin's confession yesterday, about the love charm, made her wonder if something had gone wrong.

A few moments later, she saw Liam's bride walking along the far side of the castle. The young woman's eyes held the evidence of a sleepless night, but she walked toward Brianna and greeted her.

'Are you all right?' she asked Adriana.

The woman nodded. 'I'm still getting accustomed to this place. It was just some troubling dreams.' Though she tried to smile, Brianna noted a tension in her demeanour.

'My brother said you wanted to learn how to protect yourself. I'll join you this morn, for I want to improve my own skills.' Adriana waved a hand to Lord de Manzano, who ended his sparring match and sheathed his sword.

When he strode toward them, Brianna saw the thin sheen of perspiration on his skin. The tunic he wore was shapeless, but she'd caught a glimpse of muscles within the cloth. There was no doubt the man was a strong fighter, like her uncles.

Murtagh had been competent, but his skill was in building. He'd ignored his father's wishes and had spent his days laying stone around the castle and working with the king to improve their physical barriers against enemies. Had he trained with the others, he might have been better prepared to fight during the *Lochlannach* raid.

A silent grief enfolded her mood, and she remained solemn when Arturo bade them a good morning.

'We'll move away from the others,' he said. 'Otherwise, you'll distract the men.' He led them away, pressing his palm against the small of Brianna's back. Though it was an innocent gesture, awareness of him slid through her skin. She could smell the faint aroma of soap, as if he'd bathed before dawn. His dark hair was pulled back in a cord, and he walked with an air of confidence.

'You should learn the knife first,' he suggested, 'before

the spear. If a man tries to attack you, it's the easiest weapon to seize.'

He stood before his sister to demonstrate. Adriana smiled at her brother, and when he grasped her arms, she retaliated by slipping her hands to his waist. Within seconds, the blade was pointed at his throat.

Lord de Manzano released her and beckoned. 'Now it's your turn.'

Brianna took the young woman's place and he instructed her. 'I'm going to seize your shoulders. Your task is to unsheathe the knife at my waist.'

Brianna tried, but her hands were locked at her sides. 'How? I can't move my arms.'

Adriana moved beside her. 'Men have weaknesses when it comes to women. Put your hands upon his chest, as though you want him to hold you.'

Brianna obeyed, but when she touched Arturo, she grew aware of his hardened chest and the muscles that were like stones beneath her palms.

'Slide your hands down his torso and look at him as though you are enjoying his touch,' Adriana instructed.

Brianna hesitated. She wasn't at all accustomed to using feminine wiles against a man. When she looked into Arturo's dark eyes, she didn't like the attraction that sparked between them. Slowly, she moved her palms down his body and saw the flare of interest in his eyes.

Her breath caught, and in a suspended moment, she recognised her answering response. It had been so long since she'd felt a man's touch. And God forgive her, she'd missed it.

'When you reach his waist, hold your hands there for a moment before you strike. In one motion, you'll have to take his blade and lift it to his throat.'

Arturo's hands tightened around her shoulders, and Brianna reached for the blade at his waist.

'You have to know where the knife is,' Adrianna corrected her. 'If you search for it, he'll know your intent.'

Brianna held steady and drew one hand around Arturo's back, the other hand seeking the weapon. In his arms, she felt the heat of his skin, the dark seduction of his gaze. He watched her with the eyes of a man who knew how to touch a woman and evoke her passion. As if he had all the time in the world.

Shaken by the direction of her thoughts, her hand closed upon the hilt and she forced it upward, aiming for his throat. She moved too quickly, and the blade nicked his chin.

'I'm sorry,' she apologised, lowering the blade and touching his chin. It was a shallow cut, but she felt terrible for it. 'I didn't mean to hurt you.'

He caught her fingers, moving them aside. 'It's nothing, *cariño*. Don't trouble yourself.' He leaned in to her ear and whispered, 'Unless you want to kiss it better.'

She jerked away from him so fast, he might have been on fire. But he only laughed at her while his sister shook her head in exasperation. 'Pay him no mind, Brianna. Arturo is, and always has been, a terrible flirt.'

She spoke to him rapidly in Spanish, and from her tone, Brianna suspected she was giving him a warning. His response was a lazy smile. 'Care to try it again?'

She did, but this time, she was more careful with the dagger. After several more trials, she was able to retrieve the blade without error.

Liam joined them after an hour, and he took Adriana with him for a walk. When they'd gone, Brianna thanked him, saying, 'I should go.'

'Why? Because you're afraid to be alone with me?'

'There are nearly two dozen people around us,' she countered. 'We're not alone.'

'Then keep your part of our bargain. You were going to show me the surrounding land.'

From the uncertain look on her face, Arturo suspected Brianna would search for any possible means to avoid it. Instead she thought a moment and replied, 'All right. But first, I'll get food to take along. We'll be gone for a few hours.'

Something about her quick agreement made him wonder about her intentions. She spoke to a young girl with dark brown hair, murmuring instructions. While he arranged for their horses, Brianna departed. For a time, he didn't know when she would return, but eventually she emerged, carrying a bundle of supplies. An older man and woman followed her. Arturo vaguely remembered seeing them earlier.

With scarred cheeks and streaks of grey at his temples, the older man eyed him as if considering whether or not to kill him. His hand rested upon a sword at his side, and his eyes were a familiar green.

The woman had a warm smile, and she spoke to Brianna softly before turning to him. 'I am Lady Genevieve. Brianna has asked us to accompany you this afternoon on your ride. Of course, we'd be glad to come.' Mischief brewed on the woman's face as she approached to greet him. 'She told me that you wish to see more of Ireland.'

'That is so.' Arturo bowed and took the older woman's hand. Raising it to his mouth in greeting, he added, 'It would be my honour, Lady.'

'Let go of my wife's hand, Spaniard,' came a low growl from the older man.

Arturo met his gaze squarely, but took no offence. 'I would

wager you are Brianna's father.' At the man's curt nod, he understood that this was Brianna's means of keeping her bargain without being alone with him. Did she truly feel uneasy in his company? When he'd taught her how to defend herself with a blade, they had stood almost in an embrace. Her hands had trembled as she'd touched him, moving her hands down his chest to seize the dagger. In her eyes, he'd caught a glimpse of surprise…and a softening of her features. She'd looked at him with confusion, as if she didn't understand the way she felt.

He didn't want her to be afraid of him or to distrust his intentions. Though he wouldn't mind consoling her, he understood the boundaries. She didn't want another man to intrude upon the memories of her husband, and he respected that.

Arturo kept his expression neutral, and nodded in greeting toward the warrior.

'Bevan MacEgan is my name,' the older man said. The look in his eyes added the warning, *Don't even think about touching my daughter*.

Arturo squared his shoulders and stared back at the man as if to say, *Your warning is not needed*.

'I thought the four of us could ride together,' Brianna suggested. 'My father and Lady Genevieve can answer almost any questions you have.' She walked forward and took the reins of the mare Arturo had brought. 'If you don't mind waiting for their horses.' She took the small bundle of food and secured it to the saddle. Arturo offered to boost her up, and she accepted his assistance.

'You could go on ahead of us and ride along the coast,' Genevieve suggested. 'Show him the island, and we'll meet you there.' She turned to Arturo and sent him a wink.

Already he decided he liked Lady Genevieve. Though there

was no need to play the role of matchmaker, she was riling her husband's temper—and well she knew it.

'They can wait,' Bevan countered, his eyes hard.

Arturo lifted his shoulders in a shrug before he swung up on his mount. 'It is for your daughter to decide.' He deferred to Brianna, never taking his eyes from the older warrior's face. He sensed that he was being tested, but there was no reason for it. His intentions toward Brianna were nothing more than friendship.

It was better this way, he supposed. She could show him Ireland, and when he returned home, there would be nothing binding him here.

Brianna hesitated, eyeing first Lady Genevieve, then her father. 'It's only a short distance to the southern coast,' she said. 'I suppose there's no harm in letting you see the island.'

She nudged her mare forward through the snow, and Arturo followed until they were outside the gate, moving toward the open expanse of land. In the distance, white-covered hills rose up from the landscape, and a well-worn path led up to a higher peak.

'At the end of harvest, during Lughnasa, we walk up the path leading to the top of the hill and bury ears of corn as an offering to the gods,' Brianna explained.

'You keep to the old ways?' He drew his horse up alongside hers, curious, for he'd seen evidence of a church within the castle grounds.

'We've always celebrated both. My father and his brothers are superstitious. They'd rather keep everyone happy.' The slight smile playing at her lips suggested that she humoured them in their beliefs. 'Besides, it gives us an excuse to eat and drink too much.'

'I don't suppose there's harm in that,' he admitted. 'I heard them speaking of a celebration at the solstice.'

'*Meán Geimhridh*, it's called. My uncle Trahern will tell stories, and we'll decorate the donjon with greenery. It's a smaller celebration of the solstice before Christmas.' Brianna tucked a strand of dark hair behind one ear, and it drew his eyes to the slender line of her jaw. Her lips were full, the pale pink of morning. He found himself noticing the curve of her chin, the hollowed cheeks and the fresh beauty of her face.

Green eyes stared at his in a moment of confusion, before she quickened the pace of her horse, riding toward the sea. Almost as if she were trying to run away from him.

Arturo rode behind her, and when they neared the edge, she dismounted, letting the horse graze upon the tall grasses. The sea was grey, the tide swelling in rough waves against the rocks. Across the narrow channel, he saw an island with a wooden fortress and a smaller circle of huts.

'My great-grandsire dwelled on the island Ennisleigh,' she said. 'He was a wood carver and later, he founded the MacEgan tribe, in honour of his brother.'

'Who lives there now?'

'Other members of our tribe. Sometimes the king and queen will go off together and spend a few nights alone.' She glanced down at the ground, as if realising what she was implying.

He ignored the remark and replied, 'It's a strategic location. I imagine it's useful if enemy ships approach.'

She nodded, her face flushed. When she started to return to their horses, he stopped her with a hand. 'Brianna, you needn't be afraid of me.'

'I'm not.'

'Liar,' he whispered. Reaching for her cold fingers, he

warmed them in his palm. 'You get nervous every time I look at you.'

When she said nothing, he drew his thumb over her palm. 'I admire what I see. You're a beautiful woman.' He tilted her chin up to face him. 'But I also know that you grieve for him.'

'I feel guilty,' she confessed. 'And confused.' She pulled her hand free, letting him glimpse the apprehension in her face. 'It's too soon for me.'

'I won't be here for more than a few weeks,' he said. 'I'll have to return to Navarre and to my father's lands, where I am guardian.' His time here would be brief, only long enough to see Adriana settled. 'But before that, I want to experience this land, which is so different from my own. I would like to see it through your eyes.'

'I am the wrong person to ask,' she protested.

'You wanted to find a means of using the hours in your day,' he pointed out. His gaze shifted up, for her parents were approaching. 'If you want me to hold my distance, I will do so.'

She let out a slow breath and nodded her assent. Arturo leaned in to murmur against her ear. 'Or if you want a distraction from your grief, I can grant you that, *belleza*. No one would begrudge you a winter night spent with me.'

'It would be a betrayal,' she said, shaking her head. 'I could not do it.'

'The decision is yours. I would never coerce you into anything that would make you uncomfortable.' He drew back, resting his forehead against hers. 'But I do know what it's like, lying awake at night. The loneliness can be unbearable.'

She could give him no answer at all. But neither did she pull away from him. For a long moment, she leaned against him, the thoughts silent within her. Arturo waited, and then stepped back to regard her.

He could see the storm of thoughts churning through her. She would think about his offer. But the choice was, and always would be, hers.

Brianna led the small group toward her father's castle at Rionallís. Though it was an hour's journey, she felt a sense of comfort riding through the familiar landscape. It was the only way of steadying the trembling within her. Arturo had cast a spell upon her, until she hardly recognised herself. With the faintest touch of his thumb upon her palm, he'd roused an unexpected response within her. The gentle caress had sent blood coursing through her skin, hardening her breasts and reminding her of the intimacies between a man and a woman.

He was right. She did miss the closeness of falling asleep naked in a man's arms, her arms and legs intertwined with his. Against her will, she imagined Arturo's body upon hers, and it was not unwelcome. His whisper, that he knew of the loneliness, had reached past her shield of guilt.

No, he would not remain in Éireann for long. But she didn't know how long she could resist the invitation he'd offered. She did long for a way of silencing the despair that caught up to her at night.

It was best to refuse the temptation. Her purpose now was to avenge Murtagh's death, to bring justice to the *Lochlannach* who had killed him. She had to prepare herself for what lay ahead, and when the men of her tribe faced another raid, she would be ready to seek out her enemy and wield the spear against him.

When he was dead, it might finally heal the scar within her heart. Then, perhaps, she could look toward a future.

Her gaze shifted back to the Spaniard. The blood of no-bility ran through his veins, but she drew comfort from the fact that her father was still glaring at the man, as if he could read Arturo's mind.

He'd disapprove of him even more, if he knew of your thoughts, her mind chided. The invitation, to spend a night in Arturo's bed, shook her senses apart.

Brianna broke away from all of them, changing their di-rection toward the round tower. From beside the church, it rose nearly a hundred feet in the air, like a guardian. It was a unique structure, with a narrow diameter, the size of a small hut. A rope ladder hung ten feet down from the raised door. At the top of the tower were several bells, which could be rung in times of need.

'Have you seen towers like this in Navarre?' Genevieve was asking Arturo.

The Spaniard shook his head and smiled at her. 'Not like this. Our castles are similar to yours, though.' He drew his horse to a stop and stared at their surroundings, his gaze rest-ing at last upon Brianna.

'In the northeast territory, we have mountains the colour of sand, almost like a desert,' he told them. As he wove stories about his homeland, he never took his eyes off her. Brianna listened, while her father asked questions about their lands.

'I assume you'll be returning home, after the wedding?' Bevan ventured. His veiled hint was quite clear.

'I will, yes. Unless there is a reason to stay through the spring.' Arturo's eyes rested upon her, like a physical touch.

Before her father could say anything more, Genevieve in-tervened. 'This morn, I saw you teaching Brianna something. There was a knife, I believe?'

'What reason would you have to train my daughter in the

use of a weapon?' Bevan demanded. Once again, she heard the disapproval in his voice.

'I asked him to help me,' she answered, but her father didn't seem to hear her.

'Don't you believe that women should be able to defend themselves against an attacker?' Arturo countered, facing her father with a challenge of his own.

'And what would you know of weaponry?' Her father was staring at the Spaniard as if he were itching for a fight.

To her dismay, Arturo dismounted and unsheathed his sword. 'Care to spar, Irishman? Unless you've forgotten how…?'

'What are they doing?' Brianna whispered to Genevieve while Bevan got down from his own stallion. 'They're not going to fight, are they?'

Her question was cut off when her father withdrew his own weapon and attacked swiftly. Arturo deftly parried the blows, watching every move as if learning his enemy's methods. The snow slowed their footwork, but both held their balance.

'Stop them,' Brianna protested, starting to intervene, but Genevieve pulled her back.

'No. Let them fight.'

'But why? There's no purpose for it at all.' She was aghast when her father swung hard at Arturo's head, only to be deflected and pushed back the other way.

'Your father is testing his abilities. They won't hurt each other.'

But the fight continued longer than she wanted, until at last, Arturo attacked. He sliced his sword hard, putting all his strength into the fight until Bevan's weapon blocked his next blow. The two men pressed hard against each other, trying to force the other to yield. A bead of sweat rolled down Arturo's face, but he refused to back down.

In her father's eyes, she saw a subtle shift, until at last, he admitted, 'I see that you do know how to fight.'

Arturo sent him a slight nod. 'I guard those under my protection. And I demand that my men train until they can defend our holdings.'

The two men stepped back at the same time, both sheathing their weapons. Genevieve went over to her husband, while Brianna wondered what would happen now. Arturo eyed her for a moment, and then walked over to the church yard, where there was a well. He retrieved water and splashed handfuls upon his face, dampening his hair. The afternoon light haloed his dark hair, and when he stared back at her, Brianna felt the hunger of his gaze. It moved over her face and down her body with unveiled interest.

Without a word, without touching her at all, he made her feel vulnerable. Were she to share his bed, she had no doubt that he would spend endless time touching her, until she surrendered to pleasure.

She closed her eyes against the confusing feelings, forcing herself to lock them away.

'Bevan and I want to ride toward the outer perimeter of Rionallís,' Genevieve explained. 'You may wish to take Lord de Manzano inside the tower and lead him up to the top. The view would let him see the landscape better.'

'Will Father Angus mind?' Brianna asked. The young priest had only recently taken over the church after the older priest had died.

'I should imagine not. So long as you do not disturb the treasures within the round tower.' The older woman sent her a warm conspiratorial smile, as if her matchmaking plans had come to fruition.

Startled, Brianna turned to her father. But he, too, seemed in agreement with his wife. 'We'll return within the hour. You should eat without us,' Bevan said, lifting his wife back on to her horse.

From the way his hands lingered upon her waist and the look shared between them, Brianna suspected that they intended to do more than talk. Pushing that errant thought away, she told Arturo, 'Come with me, and I'll show you the inside.'

He held the rope ladder for her as she climbed up to the door, balancing the bundle of food between her arms. When they were inside, it took a moment for their eyes to adjust. Sunlight entered through the open top of the tower, and she began climbing the endless stairs toward the single bell at the top. Arturo followed, but before they reached the third landing, he reached for her hand.

'A moment, if you will.'

Brianna paused to catch her breath, setting down the food while Lord de Manzano stood on a stair below her. She waited for him to speak, and he said, 'I wouldn't have harmed your father during that fight.'

'That's what Genevieve said.' She sat down on the stair with him just below her. 'It's why they left us alone. You gained his approval.' It was a strange thought to imagine, for she'd never believed Bevan would permit it.

Somehow, Lord de Manzano had earned respect from the older warrior, though her husband, Murtagh, never had. Was it truly that Bevan believed sword fighting was more important than affection? Or was it the desire to keep his daughter protected?

'I like your father,' Arturo said. 'He seems like a good man. And he's a strong fighter, despite his age.'

'He is.' A smile curved over her face in the darkness.

Arturo took her hands and drew her to stand up. When he moved closer, it brought him closer to her face. At the nearness of him, Brianna started to let go of his hands.

'Stay?' he asked quietly. Moving closer, she felt his cheek come and rest against hers. 'If things were different, I would take a kiss from you now.' His words were warm against her face, and every part of her body seemed to respond to him. 'I would hold you close and taste your sweet mouth, *belleza*. But I suspect that it would only feed the hunger I feel for you, instead of sating it.'

'You know it's too soon for me,' she whispered.

'I know. But there is no harm in speaking words.'

He was wrong. His words were invisible weapons, slicing through her defences, and reawakening her. The darkness enfolded them, and in her mind, she struggled against the memory of her last kiss. Murtagh had been affectionate, and she'd enjoyed making love with him. So much, that she understood what Lord de Manzano was offering—the freedom to take him as her lover, to fill up the emptiness inside her broken heart.

Desperately, she struggled to find the willpower that was slipping away. Arturo's hands moved to her waist, pulling her close until her hands rested upon his chest.

'It's your choice, *belleza*. If you want me to kiss you, you'll have to make the first move.'

Chapter Three

Brianna hesitated, and with every second that passed between them, she sensed the caged sensuality of him. Slowly, her hands moved up his chest, to the powerful shoulders, and then to rest upon his face. She drew her fingers over his lips and was rewarded with a light kiss upon her skin.

Inside, she was quaking. She wanted him, despite all the reasons it was a mistake. What he offered was only temporary. He was going to leave and nothing between them could last. He'd offered her an escape from the loneliness. But what lay broken inside her couldn't be healed by one man's touch.

'Not yet,' she whispered, holding his face between her hands.

The words hung between them in a promise she didn't know if she could keep. Or if she should even try. She let go of him and picked up the bundle, continuing up the winding spiral stairs, until at last they reached the top. The wind was stronger here, and her hair whipped against her face. Arturo came up beside her, his hands resting upon the stone edge. He didn't look at her, but she saw the tension in his posture.

When he saw the landscape before him, there was an invisible shift. He stared at the mottled green and snowy-white hills that shifted into flatland, down to a grey sea. The faint smile upon his lips stole her breath away.

When he turned back, his dark eyes held hers captive. 'It's beautiful. Like nothing I've ever seen before.'

She nodded, but couldn't answer his smile. His earlier words resonated within her: *You'll have to make the first move.*

Confusion spiralled inside her, wondering why he'd conjured up these lost feelings. It had been so easy to ignore the advances of other men of her clan. They were like brothers to her, kind men, but she couldn't imagine being with one of them.

Not like Arturo de Manzano.

It must be because he had also lost someone. There was a bond between them, of facing the death of a loved one. The only difference was that he'd managed to lock away his grief and live again. The way she longed to.

She heard herself telling him of the different tribes that lived here. Of the Ó Phelans who had been an enemy when her father was young, and of how the MacEgans had grown stronger against the Norman forces.

'They married their enemies,' she said. 'My father wed Genevieve, by order of King Henry.'

'You speak of her as if she's not your mother.'

Brianna shook her head. 'No, she isn't. My mother stole me away from my father when I was a young child. I didn't understand what happened at the time, but she made choices she regretted. In the end, she took her own life, from her sadness.'

An unexpected flare of hurt gripped her heart. 'I was alone for a time. I couldn't understand what I had done wrong, that my mother would rather die than be with me.'

Arturo came up beside her, resting an arm over her shoulder. 'You were just a child.'

'I know. And Genevieve took me in, becoming my mother in all but blood.' She accepted comfort from his presence, leaning her head against him.

'You were fortunate to have your family,' he said. 'And they care a great deal for you.' He reached for the bundle of food and opened it. She tore off a piece of bread and they sat down to eat, while she told him about the other places nearby.

'Where is the Norse settlement?' he asked.

The question jolted her from her mood and she pointed out the area near the woodlands. 'It lies a half-day's journey from Laochre. At one time, my great-grandfather's sister wed one of them, and there was peace between us. Even when the Normans attacked, the *Lochlannach* kept to themselves.'

She faced him, keeping her voice steady. 'But during the last few years, it's been difficult. There have been raids on several occasions.'

'Without success?'

She nodded. 'King Patrick's men kept them out. Last year, they attacked the homes on the outskirts.' A chill came over her, and she gripped her shoulders. 'Murtagh was…not a good fighter. He was the son of a miller, and though he was strong, he'd never had any training.'

Fixing her gaze away from him, she refused to let the dark feelings intrude. With her throat aching, she added, 'One of the men stood apart from the others. Murtagh mistakenly thought he was the leader, and he went to challenge him while I stayed behind.'

In spite of her best efforts, a tear broke free. 'I begged him to stop, but he charged the raider. The man's spear caught him in the stomach, and it took hours for my husband to die.' A harshness coated her voice. 'I went to kill the *Lochlannach*, but the soldiers from Laochre held me back. The king drove them away, and they haven't returned since.

'A few days later, they sent gold as a body price for my husband's death.' Bitterness swelled within her, and she shook her head in disgust. 'As if that would bring him back.'

'Killing the Norseman won't bring Murtagh back, either.' His hand rested upon the small of her back, warming her.

'Would you have waited at home, if an enemy had slain your wife?' she questioned. 'Or would you have avenged her?'

His silence was the answer she wanted to hear. Reaching for the flask of wine, she took a drink and passed it to him. His mouth rested upon the place where she'd sipped, and once again, she found herself watching him.

The wind rushed through the narrow space again, moving against the bells. She shivered at the cold and stood up. Arturo removed his own cloak and set it across her shoulders.

'You don't have to do that.'

'It gives me a reason to hold a beautiful woman,' he teased, drawing the cloak over her arms. He let his hands linger upon her, and the spicy scent of his skin quickened her blood. For a time, neither spoke, and she drew comfort from the heat of his body.

If she closed her eyes, she could almost imagine it was Murtagh standing behind her. That it was his arms upon her shoulders and not a stranger's. The nearness of him, and the instinct to touch, was dragging her away from reality.

When Brianna turned around, Arturo moved his hands on either side of her. In his sienna eyes, she saw the cloaked desire. He spoke to her in Spanish, words she didn't understand. But his voice drew her in, blurring the lines she'd drawn around her life.

His hands rested upon the stone, waiting for her decision. Her body already knew the answer, though her mind was crying out for her to stop.

The endless days alone had weighed down upon her, making her no longer feel desirable to any man. But to Arturo, none of it mattered. He'd suffered the same losses she had, and he understood what she didn't want to admit—that she craved human touch.

Without speaking a word, she went into his arms, resting her cheek against his broad chest. His mouth drifted against her hair in a light kiss. 'I know, *cariño*.'

Did he? Did he truly know how difficult it was to reach out to another, feeling as if the ghost of her husband were watching?

'He wouldn't have wanted you to live like this. Admit it to yourself.'

She closed her eyes, knowing he spoke the truth. As she tried to pull away from his arms, he held her trapped for a moment. 'Thank you for showing me this land of yours.'

She nodded, and he released her. As he bent to help her put away the food, he stopped to ask, 'Were you curious?'

'About what?' She tied up the bundle and held it in one hand.

'What it would have been like to kiss a man who wasn't your husband?'

She faltered, but then steadied herself, recognising it as a teasing invitation. 'No.'

'Liar. I can see how you're sacrificing yourself to his memory,' he said softly. 'Not allowing yourself to feel any happiness at all. You wear clothes without colour, and you don't smile. You might as well take a step off the edge of this tower, for you seem intent upon letting the rest of your life slip away.'

Anger rushed through her, that he would dare accuse her of this. 'You don't know anything about me.' The bundle slipped from her hands, and the flask of wine spilled upon the stones.

'You won't let anyone know you any more. You lock yourself away, don't you? Because you feel guilty that you're alive. And he isn't.'

'Yes, damn you.' The anger raged from a place so deep inside, she struggled to control it. And when he dared to pity her, to rest a hand upon her cheek, Brianna was determined to prove him wrong.

She lifted her mouth to his, kissing him hard. Did he think she was a hollow shell with no feelings of her own? The salt of her tears mingled against their lips, but Arturo wasn't about to let her use him to prove a point. Instead, he softened the kiss, capturing her mouth. Sensual and firm, he commanded the kiss, forcing away her broken memories until she was consumed by him. She let herself fall under his spell, opening to this stranger and finding the parts of her that needed him.

Her arms came around him, and she slid her tongue against his mouth, feeling the rush of heat when he answered her call. He took his time, savouring her mouth, his hands moving up her spine and down to her body. With the softest nudge, he drew her against the heated ridge of his arousal, and she couldn't stop the shudder of answering desire.

In her mind, she imagined them naked, and what it would be like to be touched by him. To lift her leg over his hip and feel the sweet rush of his body entering hers. To forget the pain of the past and escape all of it for a single night that belonged only to him.

Arturo broke away, his dark eyes feasting upon her. She couldn't catch her breath, and she sensed that the barest touch

from him would send her over the edge, into the release she
wanted so badly.

Her lips were bruised, swollen from his kiss. And she hated
herself for feeling this way.

Arturo didn't press Brianna any further, for both of them
had the answers they'd sought. He'd sensed that she was a
passionate, fierce woman, and he'd not been disappointed.
But he wouldn't push her. There was still hurt and anger inside her, from her husband's death. He wasn't going to take
advantage of her, not when she was grieving.

He said nothing as they descended from the round tower.
When they climbed down the rope ladder, her parents had returned from their own ride. Bevan took note of his daughter's
flushed face and swollen lips. While he made no remark, Arturo knew that there was a silent warning to tread carefully.

'You'll dine at Laochre this night, won't you?' Genevieve
asked. 'The feast is in honour of Liam and Adriana.'

'Of course.' When he bent to help Brianna on to her horse,
this time, he lifted her up by the waist. He let his hands rest
there for a single moment, and her green eyes flared with
caution. Second thoughts had already taken root within her,
and he respected her wishes, turning back to his own horse.

Throughout the remainder of the day, Bevan and Genevieve guided him throughout their lands, showing them their
estate at Rionallís.

'Do all of your brothers live nearby?' he asked Bevan. 'It
seems that you've claimed a great deal of land in this region.'

'Three of my brothers live nearby,' Bevan agreed. 'But
Connor's holdings lie further west. He often visits with his
wife and children.' He shielded his eyes against the late af-

ternoon sun, watching over Genevieve and Brianna as they rode ahead.

When they were out of earshot, Bevan drew back to speak with Arturo privately. 'If you hurt my daughter in any way, you'll answer to me, Spaniard. She's been isolating herself for the past few months, and this is the first time I've seen her leave Laochre. I won't have you making her miserable.'

He met the older warrior's penetrating gaze with his own steadiness. 'She is a beautiful woman, and we understand each other.' He saw the darkening disquiet brewing, and he continued, 'I won't deny that I wouldn't mind taking a new wife back to Navarre. But the choice is hers. If she does not care to be courted, I won't ask for more than she's capable of giving.' The words seemed to reassure the man, and he said nothing more.

They arrived back at Laochre Castle after nightfall. More people had arrived, and seeing the vast crowds, Arturo didn't envy his sister. So many of the MacEgan tribe members were speculating about their wedding, and he knew Adriana loathed being the centre of attention.

Bevan and Genevieve went to speak with the king and queen, while Arturo gave their horses over to a young boy to be stabled. Brianna started to walk home, when he caught up to her. 'Will you attend the feast this night?'

'I don't know,' she hedged. 'It's been a long day and I'm tired.'

He lowered his voice. 'I won't apologise for kissing you earlier. But I vow that I won't press you any further.'

'It felt wrong,' she whispered, opening the door to her home. The interior was dark, and after she lit an oil lamp, her breath clouded in the night air. Outside, a few sparse snowflakes drifted upon the wind. Brianna laid a few ever-green boughs over the hearth, and the heady scent of pine filled the room.

He didn't know what to say. To him, the kiss had been deeply arousing, and she'd responded with her own passion.

'You were the second man I've ever kissed,' she confessed, her gaze turning downward. Arturo kept his distance, waiting for her to continue.

'I gave in to temptation, and I lost myself in it. In that moment, I forgot about everything I intended to do. I betrayed his memory.'

'He's dead, Brianna.' The words were cold, he knew, but he wanted to lash out against the pedestal she'd set her husband upon. 'He can't blame you for wanting to live again.'

'I know it.' Her voice came out in a whisper. 'Murtagh was a kind man. But sometimes I can't sleep at night, thinking of how he died.' She crossed the room to stand in front of him. 'You said you loved your wife.'

'I wouldn't have minded growing old with her.' He rested his hand against the door. 'But as the years passed, I knew she wouldn't have wanted me to be lonely and never have children of my own.'

Brianna was listening to his words, and within the golden light of the lamp, her face grew pensive. 'Perhaps.'

He moved toward her and tilted her face toward his. Leaning down, he brushed a light kiss upon her lips. 'I won't apologise for that, either.'

She caught his hand before he could leave. Though she looked embarrassed and a little nervous, she held his palm, as if pleading with him.

I need more time, her eyes seemed to say. Arturo studied her, wondering if the two of them could possibly heal the loneliness in each other.

* * *

Brianna sat in the dim light of her hut, with a small fire burning within the hearth stones. She touched her fingertips to her lips, the confusion filling up inside her. Ever since Arturo de Manzano had come to Ireland, he'd shaken her life apart. She hadn't wanted to be attracted to the handsome stranger, but she was drawn to him in ways she didn't understand.

The kiss had evoked sensations she'd forgotten, making her stare at the lonely bed with regret. Her thoughts confused her, tearing her apart with longing for a husband and children…and wanting to avenge Murtagh's death.

She rose from her seat and donned a mantle, pulling the hood over her hair. A walk was what she needed right now. A chance to clear her head and breathe in the frigid night air.

But when she reached the inner bailey, she found utter chaos. Connor MacEgan was gathering up a group of men. His face was lined with worry, and his wife, Aileen, stood nearby with her hands gripped together.

'What's happened?' she asked.

'It's Rhiannon,' Aileen confessed. 'She went out on her own yesterday and still hasn't returned. I pray nothing has happened to her. I can't imagine anything worse than finding her hurt or…' Her voice trailed off with fear.

Connor barked an order to a group of soldiers, commanding them to search the different parts of Laochre.

Brianna recalled her cousin's enigmatic words, that she planned to seek her own husband. 'Have you spoken with my brother and sister? They were with her yesterday.'

Connor nodded. 'They were separated during the snowfall and thought she returned last night. We've sent out small groups to search, but haven't found anything.' In his eyes, she saw the unfathomable fear for his eldest daughter.

'What about the island? Could she have gone there?'

'We searched there already.' He shook his head, his face turning grim. 'Now, we've sent men to Gall Tír.'

A cold chill spiralled into her stomach. 'She wouldn't go there.' The idea of her cousin seeking shelter among the *Lochlannach* was unthinkable.

'I'll search every last blade of grass until she's found,' Connor said. His brothers Patrick and Bevan joined his side.

'There was no sign of her along the coast,' the king said. Placing his hand on Connor's shoulder, he said, 'We're postponing the feast tonight until Rhiannon is safely home with us.'

'We'll find her,' Brianna said softly. 'I'm certain of it.'

'I pray you're right.'

A few hours after dawn, Rhiannon returned. Tired and silent, she would not say where she'd gone, but that she'd found shelter on her own. Her father, Connor, had raged at her for causing them worry, but not a word would she say.

Not to them.

But when Brianna met her cousin alone, while they hung greenery around the castle, she whispered, 'I'm so glad you're all right.' With a pause, she predicted, 'You met someone, didn't you?'

Her cousin froze, holding a pine bough. Instead of sharing the secret, Rhiannon looked stricken. All she would admit was, 'I was lost in the forest, and he rescued me. It was too dark to find my way back, so I stayed with him.' But she wouldn't meet Brianna's eyes, as if consumed by guilt.

'Was he handsome?' she prompted again, trying to understand what had happened.

'He was…like no one I've ever met before.' A mask of determination came over Rhiannon's face. 'I'm going to see him again. I don't care what anyone says.'

'I'll give you my help, if you'll tell me who he is and where you were.'

Rhiannon reached for another pine branch, sadness spreading over her face. 'I can't tell you. You wouldn't approve of him. Nor would anyone else.'

'Then why risk it? You only just met him.'

'Sometimes a few nights is all it takes.' Rhiannon finished with the greenery and added, 'He needs me. Like no one ever has.' A flush came over her cheeks, and she sent Brianna a soft smile before returning outside.

Arturo entered the donjon, casting a glance at Rhiannon before he greeted Brianna. 'They found her, I see.'

She nodded, noticing that he was wearing chainmail armour again. The silver links outlined his muscular form, and she tried to push away the traitorous thoughts. But when her gaze slipped up to his mouth, the shield of her willpower began to crack apart. His lean, tanned face held a bristled texture from not shaving. 'If you keep staring at me like that, *belleza*, I'll forget the reason I came to see you.'

'What was it?'

'Did you still want a lesson in fighting?' He eyed her manner of dress, as if it were unsuitable for what he'd planned.

'I do, yes.'

'Then come.' Arturo extended his hand, and Brianna left her basket of greenery behind. Outside, the sky was heavily clouded, an omen of more snow. He led her through the grounds until they reached the training area.

To her delight, she saw her Aunt Honora, dressed in light-weight armour. Beside her stood Uncle Ewan and their two children.

Brianna welcomed them and complimented the little girl's miniature *léine* and overdress, trimmed with ribbon and silk. The child curtsied prettily, then walked demurely off to join the other children.

'I believe the faeries switched my daughter by mistake,' Honora remarked. 'Lora has no interest in fighting, but spends all her time sewing and behaving like a lady. My sister's daughter hates gowns and cut her own hair with a knife, pretending to be a boy.'

Glancing at Honora's armour, Brianna offered, 'I suppose Lora doesn't want to learn to fight.'

'No, but my son does.' Her hands rested on the boy's shoulders. 'Kieran has begun his fostering, and I believe he'll be a strong warrior one day.'

'Like his mother,' Ewan teased, kissing his wife. He greeted all of them and then said, 'I'll leave you ladies to spar with one another.' Taking his son's hand, he departed the grounds.

While Honora led her through a few training exercises, Brianna was intensely aware of Arturo watching. She moved, feeling the heat of his gaze upon her.

'He's a good match for you,' Honora murmured, adjusting Brianna's hands upon the spear. 'A Spaniard, is he?'

She nodded. 'But we're just friends.'

Honora sent her a sidelong glance and murmured, 'He wants to be more than that, from the way he's watching you. But is that what you want?'

Colour rose over her face. 'I don't know.'

'The solstice will be celebrated in a few hours,' Honora

reminded her. 'The night will be longer than usual. And you know what that means.'

She did. After spending most of the afternoon and night in darkness, the wine prompted men and women to spend time in each other's arms. It loosened inhibitions, and often wicked games were played on that night. Many believed that a woman was more fertile, more open to conceiving a child upon the winter solstice.

Brianna shivered, unsure of whether she wanted to join in or not. A part of her wanted to cast aside the past and spend one night without the burden of sadness. She wanted to be like the other women, celebrating the midwinter with joy. But if she succumbed to Arturo's invitation, she knew it would not ease her grief. It would only tempt her more.

She forced her attention away from the thought. Grasping the spear, she practised thrusting it into the bag of sand, over and over. In her mind, she imagined the cold eyes of the Viking, and promised herself that if he ever set foot upon Laochre again, it would be his last moment alive.

The longer she practised, the more her body grew warm with perspiration. She was conscious of the way Arturo was eyeing her, and she quickened her pace to try to block out the distraction of him.

'You've done enough,' Honora pronounced, reaching for the spear. 'Go and prepare yourself for the celebration.'

Arturo was waiting, and he held out a flask of cool wine. Without a word, he gave it to her, and she drank, tasting the sweet fermented grapes while he watched.

'Will I see you tonight?' he asked.

She nodded, her hand brushing against his as she gave back the wine. Already the day was waning, the night moving ever closer. He shadowed her as she returned home, and when she reached the door, she stopped for a moment. 'On this night, we sometimes exchange gifts.'

'There is one I brought with me from Navarre,' he said. 'I believe it will please you.'

'I have nothing to offer in return,' she said. 'I fear that—'

Leaning in against her cheek, he murmured, 'There is only one gift I want from you, *belleza*. And you already know what it is.'

A night in her arms. She couldn't suppress the tremble that fired within her skin at the thought. He tempted her more than he should. And she suspected, if she were to ignore the voices of reason, claiming one night to fight against the loneliness, it would change her for ever. She would want more from him.

When he departed, she closed the door and lowered the bar across it. The fire had burned low, and she added peat to it, the bitter aroma filling up the room. She set a kettle of water to heat, and pulled out a gown she'd not worn in many years.

The overdress was dark green, the colour of evergreen branches with a gold *léine* meant to be worn beneath it. Made of the finest silk, Brianna had put it away after her marriage, for it only reminded Murtagh of the difference in their status. She'd thought about selling it but never had.

Tonight, it seemed fitting to wear it. She didn't know what decision she would make about Arturo, but she wanted to look her best.

While the water was heating, she removed her clothing until she stood naked before the fire. She sat upon a low stool and brought the bucket of warmed water beside her. With a sea sponge, she dipped it in the water and began to wash.

The droplets slid lazily over her skin, puckering her nipples. She washed away the grit and sweat, and with the cleansing, her mind fell into a greater turmoil.

Arturo was right. Murtagh wouldn't have wanted her to bury herself away from life. He'd have wanted her to seek happiness.

She wept openly as she drew the sponge over her naked skin, grieving for what she'd lost. For her husband and the love they'd shared. For the child she'd never conceived. And for the woman she'd let herself become.

When her bathing ritual was finished, she walked naked across the room and reached for a small wooden box, given to her by Rhiannon's mother, Aileen. Inside it lay healing herbs and a few vials of oil. She reached for one and poured a few droplets on to her fingertips. The soft fragrance reminded her of summer wildflowers as she anointed her throat, sliding her hands over her bare skin.

The solstice was here, and outside she could hear the sounds of her kinsmen celebrating. She pulled on her shift, followed by the golden *léine* and the emerald overdress. Reaching behind her, she struggled with the laces of the outer gown. Last, she unbraided her hair, letting it slide across her shoulders in waves, falling just above her waist.

With a last glance at the spear resting in the corner, she steadied herself for the night ahead.

Chapter Four

The castle was filled with candles. Arturo stepped inside the Great Chamber and saw nearly fifty hollowed-out turnips with beeswax candles burning brightly. Greenery and holly were hung throughout the room, and mistletoe sprigs were tucked within the boughs. Lady Genevieve and another woman nearly the same age, were both seated upon the dais, playing a lilting tune upon their harps.

Someone handed him a cup of mead, and he spied a group of people sitting on the floor near a giant of a bard who was telling stories with a small boy on his lap. Adriana stood on the far side of the room, wearing a gown the colour of silver. Although the feast was in her honour, she seemed less nervous around the guests. Liam kept his arm around his bride, and wonder spread over her face at the sight of the festivities.

The gleaming candles cast a spell over the night, transforming it into a hallowed magic. Arturo's gaze passed over the people, searching for Brianna. When at last he spied her, she stole his breath away. Dressed in green and gold, the gown outlined her curves, while her black hair was crowned with a wreath. Her cheeks were rosy from the warmth of the room, and a smile played upon her mouth as she looked around at the decorated chamber.

The queen passed through the crowd to greet her, and she tucked a sprig of white berries into Brianna's wreath. The young woman laughed and embraced Isabel, giving Arturo the chance to approach them.

'I have gifts for both of you,' he said, bowing before the queen. Isabel drew back and merriment glimmered in her eyes.

'Something from Navarre?'

He nodded. 'There is a special wine I've brought with me. As well as these.' Opening the small bag he carried, he showed them the oranges.

Isabel reached for one, fascinated by the fruit. 'I've never tasted one before.'

'Remove the peel with a knife,' he advised. 'You'll find the fruit sweet and filled with juice.' The queen thanked him for the gift, and he took one orange back, before handing the remainder to Isabel.

When they were alone, he gave the last orange to Brianna. She held the sphere in her palm, studying it with interest. 'Am I meant to try this now?'

Arturo took it back. 'Later, I'll share it with you.' He took her hand in his and brought it to his lips. 'When we're alone.'

A slight moue of worry creased her lips. 'Perhaps.'

With their hands joined, she led him through the Great Chamber, introducing him to her extended family. He came to understand that she had five uncles, and all of them were married with sons and daughters of their own. The MacEgan tribe spread throughout southeast Ireland, and three of the five men were married to Norman brides.

As the night continued, they feasted upon beef that had

been freshly slaughtered the day before. There were platters of roasted geese and boiled goose eggs, as well as fish, eels, and tart apples. He chose food for Brianna, offering her the best portions. As they ate and drank, he saw her beginning to relax and enjoy herself.

'Is it always like this?' he asked.

'Usually. Last year I didn't celebrate with them,' she admitted. 'I couldn't bear it.'

'And now?'

'It still hurts to be here without Murtagh,' she said. 'But it's easier to bear it with a friend.'

Arturo squeezed her hand, though he didn't want to be her friend this night. The kiss she'd given him had haunted him all last night and this day. He didn't know where it would lead, and already he was letting his mind spin off with ideas of bringing her back to Navarre. But he didn't know if she would want to leave her home and family.

The music ceased after a time, and several couples had left the Great Chamber. From the over-bright faces of the men and women, many had enjoyed the wine he'd sent. The king moved to the centre of the dais and lifted his hand. Several men raised a knee as a gesture of respect, and the crowd drew back, forming a small space in the front of the Chamber.

'It is time for the competitions,' Patrick declared. 'All men wishing to join in, should come forward.'

Arturo sent Brianna a questioning look, and she nodded in encouragement. While he wasn't certain whether the competitions involved fighting, he felt confident in his abilities. The other MacEgan men joined him, as well as Liam. Turning to the man beside him, he asked, 'What must we do?'

'You'll see,' Ewan replied.

One by one, the women approached. He saw Brianna

and Adriana, as well as Honora and the other wives. Several women began adjusting their skirts, using ribbons to tie them to their ankles. It wasn't until the first contest began that he realised what was happening. The women were competing for the right to choose a man.

'What happens if the wrong woman chooses you?' he asked Ewan, who stood beside him.

'My wife is the strongest fighter among them,' Ewan countered. 'She'd bring down any woman who dared to ask for me.' Sending him a teasing look, he added, 'And would you really complain if a beautiful woman asked you to be hers for the night?'

Arturo shrugged in answer, but he wasn't so certain. Brianna wasn't nearly as strong as her opponents, and he didn't know if she was willing to fight for him. Though the MacEgan wives chose their husbands, he saw several unmarried women eyeing him. One winked as she faced off against Adriana. His sister struggled against the woman, trying to fight in a more womanly manner. But when the maiden rolled Adriana to the ground and sat upon her, his sister grasped the woman's hair and yanked hard, jerking her away. A smile crossed Liam's face as his bride began fighting with more aggression, until she held the woman pinned to the dirt.

After the fight ended, Adriana moved to Liam, who claimed her in a fierce kiss. The cheers resounding in the Hall showed their approval of his choice of a bride.

Arturo paid little heed to the next fight, for he didn't know either of the women. But to his startled surprise, the winner of the match came forward and took his hand. A roar of laughter resounded from the men.

The woman was quite young, possibly seventeen, with braided red hair. If she knew that his choice was Brianna, she didn't seem to care. With mischief in her eyes, she started to lead him away.

'Choose another man, *cariño*,' he told her.

'You don't have a choice.' She wrapped her arms around his neck and said, 'I claim a kiss as my reward.'

Baffled, Arturo looked back at the other men. They were laughing at him, offering no help at all. Brianna had disappeared from the crowd, and he didn't know where she'd gone.

The others were waiting for him, and the maiden had her lips puckered, waiting for the kiss. Arturo cupped her face, lifting it up. All were watching him, and when he pressed a kiss upon the maiden's forehead, she challenged, 'Is that how the men kiss in your country?'

'You didn't say where the kiss was supposed to be,' he pointed out, and she sent him a furious glare. He hadn't really intended to embarrass her, but she'd taken away Brianna's opportunity.

A young girl cleared her throat, interrupting them. 'My sister Brianna went home,' the girl informed him, 'but do not fear. I put a charm in her wreath that will make her love you.'

There was seriousness in her face, and Arturo bent down. 'I thank you for your assistance.' At the girl's warm smile, he found himself amused by her belief in magic.

'You are the one for her,' the girl promised. 'I know it, for it was in the bones I cast.'

In answer, Arturo lifted her hand to kiss it. 'Then I should go after her, shouldn't I?'

The young girl's eyes widened, and she hurried back to her parents. Arturo moved through the crowd and after searching the inner bailey and the castle grounds, he found her walking amid the snow.

'Brianna,' he called out.

She stopped, but didn't turn around. Gripping the long sleeves of her gown against the cold, she stood in place until he reached her side.

'Why did you leave?'

She didn't answer at first, and when he saw her shudder from the cold, he drew his arm around her. It encouraged him that she didn't pull away. 'Not out of jealousy,' she said. 'You've the right to choose any woman you please.'

'And if I've already chosen?' He slid his arm around her waist.

The words hung between them, and she gave no answer for a long time. 'If it's a new wife you're wanting, you should choose one of them. Someone who will add joy to your life.' She stepped away from his arms, walking slowly toward one of the other homes.

He didn't like the direction of this conversation. It sounded as if she'd already given up. 'And you felt nothing at all when you kissed me yesterday?'

She let out a heavy breath. With a hand, she tucked a strand of hair behind one ear, beneath the wreath of greenery. 'I did. And that's what bothers me.'

He wanted to go to her, but she had to make this decision on her own. Instead, he held back, watching over her. Amid the drifting snowflakes, there came the cry of an infant. Nothing at all unusual, but the sound stilled him. He heard the sounds of a mother soothing the child, and regret tightened within him.

Had Cristina lived, he might have held a son or daughter of his own. He might have taken the child upon his shoulders, soothing its cries.

Brianna turned and seemed to read his thoughts. The infant continued to fuss, and she glanced toward the sound. 'Are you all right?'

His expression tightened, but he nodded. From a fold of his cloak, he held out the orange to her. 'Take it, and go home, Brianna.'

But she made no move toward the fruit. She drew closer, studying him. 'You said your wife died in childbirth.'

The edge of grief closed upon him, the cries of the infant grinding against his memories. 'She did.'

'Was it a son or a daughter?' She moved closer, and if she knew what her questions were doing to him, she made no effort to stop.

'I never knew.' He shook his head, for the babe had died inside her. Often he wondered if he'd made the right decision not to let the healer cut into Cristina. They'd known that the babe was already dead, and he'd not wanted to desecrate his wife's body.

Brianna caught his wrist and held it. Whether she was offering her sympathy or something more, he couldn't tell. 'Why do you ask me these questions, Brianna?'

She lifted her shoulders in a shrug. 'I'm trying to understand you.'

He took her face between his hands. 'I grieved for them until it nearly destroyed me.'

The sorrow in her eyes mirrored what he'd felt over the past few years. Even so, her hands came to rest upon his chest in silent understanding.

'I know what you have suffered,' he continued. 'And if you wish it, I would try to ease your pain. For however long I remain in Ireland.'

She stared at him, the indecision etched upon her face. 'I

know what you want from me, Arturo. But I can't change what I feel inside.'

His hands came to rest upon hers. 'Do you want me to stay?'

For a time, she didn't answer. The intensity in his eyes allured her, making her want to set aside the past and begin anew. Already she knew the taste of his kiss and the soft swirl of desire that reached into her heart, offering a night to forget.

Even so, her courage faltered.

'If you stay, I would be using you to forget my grief,' she confessed. 'You don't deserve that. You should be with a woman who can give you the love I can't. There's nothing left within me.'

'*Belleza*, are you afraid of me touching you?'

'I'm afraid of the way I feel in your arms.' She sensed that he would take her to a place where her mind would have no voice, where she would forget everything except the devastating pleasures of her body.

He lifted her hands to his mouth, and she felt the warmth of his breath upon her fingertips. 'Then I'll take you home.'

A wisp of regret slipped beneath her defences. This man confused her, offering her glimpses of a life she wanted. But she didn't know if she had the courage to reach for it.

With their hands joined, he led her back to her hut while snowflakes spun upon the wind, coating her lashes and hair. In the darkness, they walked in silence until they reached her home. Arturo raised her hand to his mouth in farewell and turned to go.

'Wait.' Her voice came out in the smallest whisper. She reached out and touched his shoulder, so very frightened of what she was about to do. 'The orange,' she reminded him.

In answer, he held out the fruit to her, his expression

shielded. She fully understood the consequences of her actions. But if he walked away, her regret would be greater.

'Will you come inside…and share it with me?' She accepted the fruit, waiting for his answer.

'*Belleza*, you know what will happen if I do.' In his eyes, she saw the shielded desire, of a man who wanted her.

She did. But within her home was nothing but emptiness and shadows. Tonight, she'd wanted to be like the other women. She'd taken care with her appearance, trying so hard to enjoy the solstice.

Last year, she'd huddled within this bed, crying as if her heart would break. Tonight, she wanted to leave that broken woman behind. And though it terrified her, the way Arturo made her feel, he understood her in a way no one else ever could.

She opened the door, raising her eyes to his. 'Please.'

Arturo built a fire, filling the interior of the cold hut with heat. When he stood, he touched the evergreen boughs she'd bundled and laid upon the mantel.

'They make it smell like Christmas,' she admitted. 'I've always loved pine in winter.' The genuine smile upon her face put him more at ease, and he crossed the room to sit across from her. In her hands, she held the orange.

Arturo took it from her and withdrew his knife, cutting a small segment. Holding it to her, he said, 'Taste it, *mi amada*.'

She took the orange and bit into the flesh. Her face showed surprise, and she said, 'It's sweeter than I thought it would be.' A drop of juice slid from her lips and he touched it with a fingertip, tasting it.

Colour rose to her cheeks, but she brought a second piece to his mouth, offering it. He captured her hand and tasted

the fruit. The taste of orange was delicious, but there was
another taste he wanted.

Reaching out, he plucked the white mistletoe berries from
the wreath she wore and held them above her head. Leaning in, he watched closely to see if Brianna would change
her mind. He touched a new segment of fruit to her mouth
and then bent to lick the juice from her lips. A dark sigh escaped her, and she kissed him back, offering a seductive call
he couldn't resist.

'I'll stop at any moment you ask,' he swore, letting the
mistletoe fall to the ground. It had been a long time since
he'd wanted a woman this badly, but there was more to this
moment than physical pleasure. He wanted to reawaken her,
to show her that there could be glimpses of happiness amid
the shadows.

'I don't want to stop,' she murmured. 'Make me forget.'

He understood that she wanted the escape of lovemaking,
to be taken by him, surrendering to his touch.

'Look at me.' He drew her hands to his tunic. 'I won't deny
that I want you, Brianna. But you're not going to use me as
a substitute for him.'

She held his gaze, nodding her assent. 'I won't.' Her hands
moved over his chest in a caress that flooded him with heat.
'But it's been a long time for me. I may not…please you.'

Her anxiety only strengthened his resolve to show her how
much he desired her. He removed his tunic, moving her hands
over his bare skin. Drawing her fingertips to his pulse point,
he said, 'Do you see how you please me already, *mi cielo*?'

Her hands moved over his skin, exploring the texture.
There was interest in her eyes, and when his hands moved
to loosen her overdress, she reached back to help him. Arturo
helped her lift it away, followed by the *léine*, until she stood

in a thin shift. Her breasts tightened against the linen, firm buds that intensified his hunger for her.

She placed her hands upon his face, standing upon tip-toe. With her mouth close to his, she admitted, 'I've been so lonely, Arturo.'

He took her mouth, kissing her and releasing his own years of solitude. She was different from Cristina, more tentative in her touches. But as he entered her mouth, sliding his tongue against hers, he coaxed a stronger response. Her bare arms came around his neck, holding him tightly as she kissed him back. He felt the nudge of her hips against his rigid arousal, and she surprised him when she pulled his hips to hers.

Nestled against her, his hands dug into her waist when she rubbed against him. 'Is it wrong, for me to have missed this?'

'No.' His hands moved up her waist and over her ribs. He filled his palms with her full breasts, watching her face soften with the flush of desire when he stroked her nipples. She trembled against him, her head arching back as he stimulated her. The shift slid from one shoulder, and he lowered it to her waist, revealing her pale breasts.

'Will you kiss me—?' Her plea was cut off when he bent his mouth to the taut nipple. With his tongue, he slid over her flesh, suckling her.

She nearly drove him past the edge when her hand cupped his erection without warning. He stilled as she loosened his trews, moving her fingers down to his shaft.

Arturo discarded the rest of his clothing and stood motionless while she touched him. She explored the length of him, squeezing him in her palm. Though he didn't want her comparing him to her husband, neither could he grasp his thoughts as she began to caress him, gently stroking him until he fought to regain his control.

In answer to her torment, he drew his hands between her thighs, toward her centre. She gave a cry when his fingers found her damp opening, sliding deep inside.

'Is this where you want me?' he murmured, stretching her with a slight penetration.

Brianna could hardly breathe as his hands found a rhythm, causing her body to bloom with needs she'd forgotten. 'Yes,' she breathed, leading him back to her bed.

His eyes were hungry as he continued to fondle her, capturing her mouth in a ruthless kiss. She grew pliant against him, meeting his tongue with her own. He stripped away the last barriers between them, and the touch of his hardened chest against her breasts felt so good, it started to conjure up the guilt once more.

She'd enjoyed sharing her bed with Murtagh, but it had not been like this. Second thoughts were clouding her mind, and she pleaded, 'Come inside of me now.'

'Not yet, *belleza*.' He returned to pick up the forgotten orange and cut another segment from it, bringing it close. Brianna wondered what his intentions were, but a moment later, he drew the cool fruit down her neck. He replaced the wetness with his mouth, drinking from her skin and sucking the droplets away.

'You're not ready for me yet,' he murmured against her skin.

'I am,' she protested, guiding one of his hands to the wetness between her legs. She was aching for him, wanting so badly to silence the guilt rising within her.

'Not until I've watched you come apart,' he answered. With the orange, he slid the cool wetness over her nipple, tantalising her with the sensation. The duelling sensations of hot and cold made her body quicken to his touch. He reversed them, drinking and suckling the juice from her other breast, while his hands drew the fruit over the opposite swollen nipple.

Arturo took his time, savouring every inch of her body, while the sensations of arousal intensified. Tearing the orange away from its peel, he placed it in his mouth and fed her the other half. She was lost in a frenzy as his hands stroked and caressed her skin, moving over her stomach until he cupped her damp heat.

Once again, she reached for him, trying to guide him inside her. But he would not allow it. He pulled her to the edge of the bed and knelt before her. Spreading her legs wide, he placed his mouth between her legs.

Her body jolted when she felt the first touch of his tongue against her. 'I can't bear it,' she moaned.

With both hands, he stroked her breasts, while his tongue swirled over the hooded slit above her entrance. 'Do you want me to stop?'

'No. I—I need—' Her words broke away when he found the spot he'd been searching for. In answer, she arched against him, holding his head to her body. Her breathing quickened, and a sob escaped her as he suckled against her mound, the pressure intensifying. Her body was straining while he tasted her, his tongue drawing a response that went deeper than anything she'd ever known. Her release was there, so close, her hands dug into his shoulders in a wordless plea.

It came in a rush, her body convulsing against him as she rode out the intense crest of pleasure. Her cheeks were wet with tears, and he drew his shaft between her legs, gently lifting her hips.

'Now, *mi cielo*,' he promised. The heated ridge of his erection slid over her and she guided him to the place where she needed him.

'Inside me,' she commanded.

The expression on his face revealed a man who was fighting to maintain control. He fitted himself to her, slowly sliding within her tight entrance. The heady sensation of their joining made her press against him, until he was fully sheathed within her. He drew back, touching her while he entered again.

She was slick with need, on the brink of another release. With his hand, Arturo coaxed her further, angling himself until she could feel the edge of pleasure once again.

The pressure of his hand and the counterpoint of him filling her, was all it took. Her breath shattered, her body bucking against him as another blast of relief claimed her. She was wet and hot, clenching him as he penetrated her in swift strokes.

He moved her on to her stomach, still inside her, and the new position guided him deeper. She trembled with the erotic thrusts, her body revelling in the dark passion.

Grasping her hips, he withdrew and filled her, panting hard. She backed against him, cries escaping her as he thrust. There was no choice but to surrender, letting him conquer her.

'I want to see your face,' she demanded, forcing him to withdraw again. She moved to her back in another position, lifting her knees in invitation. 'I want to see you when you find your release.'

Her encouragement was what he'd needed. He drove hard within her, doubling his pace in his own agonised frenzy. Her body arched violently as he invaded and withdrew.

She couldn't grasp another thought as her legs tightened around his waist. He pumped against her until finally, a growl ripped from him as he finished within her, his body spasming atop hers.

Never, in all the years of her marriage, had she experienced lovemaking such as this. A heaviness built up within her, that Arturo had given her something so beautiful, a gift that made her shiver against him with aftershocks.

And when her gaze drifted over to the spear in the corner, she closed her eyes, trying not to weep.

When he awakened the next morning, Brianna was gone. Arturo rose from the bed and stretched, feeling uncertain about what he'd done. It had been an impulse, to share a night with a beautiful woman. But he'd wanted to kiss her awake, to feel her warm skin against his. Instead, she'd fled.

Did she regret what they'd done? It was possible. He got dressed and studied the interior of her home. Although most of the hut was clean and organised, one part of the room lay untouched. There was a man's tunic resting upon the ground with a belt beside it. A cup stood upon a shelf, along with an eating knife. These must have belonged to her husband. Arturo reached for the cup, studying the simple carved wood.

'What are you doing?' came a voice from behind him. Brianna wore a shapeless dark gown with a length of wool wrapped around her head and shoulders.

'I wondered where you'd gone,' he said, but before he could say anything else, she took the cup from him and put it back.

'Please,' she said quietly. 'Don't touch anything. Leave his cup alone.'

His gaze drifted back and he realised that she'd left them as they were on the day Murtagh had died. As if she could somehow hold on to him by keeping everything as it was. He couldn't fault her for it. He'd done the same with Cristina's belongings, until Adriana had quietly removed them one day.

It had helped, strangely. Lifting the invisible burden, giving him the freedom to go on with his life. But he didn't know if Brianna was ready to let go yet.

He set down the cup and faced her. 'Before we eat, I've something to ask you.' In his mind, he'd already imagined what he was going to say. But Brianna's mood had altered, and now that he'd dared to touch the altar of her husband's belongings, he questioned the wisdom of speaking at all.

She lowered her hood, and her cheeks were rosy from the cold outdoors. Raising her green eyes to his, she waited for him to speak.

'In another month I'll be returning to Navarre,' he said, taking her hand.

She nodded. 'You needn't worry about me. What happened last night was…'

He stilled when her voice drifted off. She was going to say it had been a mistake, wasn't she? She was going to make excuses, that she'd never planned to share the night with him.

For him, it had been wondrous. It had been so long since he'd touched another woman, and Brianna's unrestrained responses had made him want to drag her back to bed and make thorough love to her again. The last thing he wanted was to hear that she regretted the time they'd shared together.

She wouldn't come back to Navarre with him, if he asked. He knew it instinctively, but held his silence, watching her. Hoping for some sign that he was wrong.

And when she stole another look at her husband's cup, he knew.

'Thank you for last night' was all he could say. He lifted her hand to his mouth and kissed the outer edge of her thumb.

She nodded, tightening her lips, her eyes blurred with tears. A tightness locked up in his chest as he opened the door and walked away. But he had his pride. He wasn't going to beg like a dog, hoping for a sign of affection.

Frustration darkened his mood as he strode toward the stables. He considered going out for a ride, when he saw a group of a dozen men arriving. Dressed in armour with weapons, they had the look of Norsemen, from their height and stature. Arturo reached for the sword hilt at his side, prepared to alert the king. But then, as he drew closer, he saw that they came bearing gifts. The tall bard from last night came to welcome the visitors with enthusiasm.

Strange. The man looked as if he belonged among the Vikings, but he spoke Irish well enough.

When the king came forward and greeted the Vikings, Arturo overheard the name Trahern. He realised the tall bard was one of the king's brothers. While the men were distracted, talking with the visitors, Arturo's attention was drawn to a woman slipping inside the gates. It was Rhiannon MacEgan, and from her secretive manner, he could only guess that she'd travelled with the men.

She caught his gaze and sent him a pleading look, not to tell anyone. Arturo kept his expression neutral, making no promises. But neither did he alert the others to her presence.

He walked forward and joined the men. It was Ewan MacEgan who explained why the men had arrived. 'They've come to share Christmas with us. It was Trahern's idea, after the fighting last year.' He pointed toward the tall Irishman, adding, 'He has a bit of *Lochlannach* blood in him, and he's spent time living among them with his wife and son.'

It was then that Arturo spied a young boy with his father's features, a solemn expression on his face. When he saw Trahern bring the boy forward, resting his hands on the lad's shoulders, the sting of regret lashed through Arturo. He wanted children of his own and a wife. His thoughts drifted back to Brianna, and the feeling of sleeping beside her at night.

She'd been passionate and loving—everything he'd hoped for. And though he wanted to spend more time with her, he'd been fully aware of what last night was…a shared moment of pleasure. Nothing else. He couldn't allow himself to soften, for she wasn't at all ready to be with him. It was too soon for that.

As if in answer to his thoughts, Brianna emerged from the hut. A stricken expression came over her face as she stared at the Norsemen. There wasn't a doubt in his mind that among them she'd seen the man who had killed Murtagh. A renewed vengeance sparked in her eyes, and she started to move toward them.

The men had come here for a celebration, to renew the peace between them. But Arturo strongly suspected Brianna had other ideas.

Chapter Five

She'd nearly reached the men, when her cousin Rhiannon cut her off. 'Don't,' she pleaded.

'Don't what?' Brianna countered. 'Don't face the *Lochlannach* who murdered my husband?' Fury seethed through her, that the man had dared to show himself again. She wanted to seize a weapon and end his life. To watch him suffer in death as Murtagh had suffered.

Her grasp upon rational thought was slipping away, and she tried to break free of her cousin's hand.

'It's not what you think,' Rhiannon said. 'He came to make amends.'

'There's nothing he could ever say or do to make amends. He killed my husband, and that, I'll never forgive.'

'They didn't come here to fight.'

'Do you think I care why they came?' She was blinded by anger, even as she struggled to regain control of her senses.

Rhiannon looked as if she wanted to say more, but in the end, she held back her words. Misery darkened her face, and she could only squeeze Brianna's hand before she left.

Brianna returned to her hut and walked over to the corner and seized the spear, staring back at the door. Wild thoughts of vengeance flew through her mind, though she could not give in to impulse. Instead, her fingers curled upon the spear in a fierce grip.

Worse, she spied the tangled sheets where she'd slept in Arturo's arms last night. Was that not a greater betrayal? She'd let herself forget the love she'd felt for her husband, in order to experience pleasure with another.

The spear clattered from her hand and she sank down to sit upon the low stool beside the fire. He'd thanked her for last night, and it had made her feel so small, so angry with herself. The night she'd spent with him, touching his muscled skin, had been wonderful.

Moreover, it had been her choice. Arturo hadn't forced her into anything. But his reminder, that he would be returning to Navarre, had been the caveat she'd needed. He wasn't a man who would stay in Éireann indefinitely. He'd come for his sister's wedding, and afterward, he would leave. Likely he didn't want her to form any feelings for him, since it would only hurt her in the end.

She took a deep breath, then another. From the ground, she retrieved the spear and vowed that she would spend the remainder of the day practising. If Fortune smiled upon her, she would have her chance for revenge. And when it came, she would be ready.

'Please. You have to stop her.'

Arturo glanced over at Rhiannon MacEgan, whose face was pale with worry. The young woman nodded toward Brianna, who had seized a spear and was practising with Honora, stabbing a bag of straw with it.

Though he had every intention of doing so, there was

something more beneath the surface of Rhiannon's plea. 'Why does it matter to you?'

'She'll be hurt. She can't possibly attack a trained warrior, especially a *Lochlannach*.'

Though it was true, he saw the way the young woman's eyes fell upon one of the men. Tall and strong, the man set himself apart from the others. He held a spear in his hand, and from the threatening expression on his face, only a fool would approach him.

'That's the one, isn't it? The man who killed Brianna's husband.'

Rhiannon's face coloured, but she nodded. 'It was an accident.' Her lips tightened and she added, 'You don't understand. He's not like the others. He can't—'

'You're in love with him.'

From the terrified look of anguish on her face, Arturo saw that he was right. It was known to all that Rhiannon had gone missing a few nights ago. And this morn, she had slipped back into the ringfort with them.

'Don't tell my father,' Rhiannon pleaded. 'Please. He would never understand.'

Arturo didn't doubt that. Not only was she defying her father's will, but she loved the man who had killed Brianna's husband.

'I'll protect Brianna,' he promised. 'But if my silence interferes with her safety or yours, I won't hesitate to tell Connor.'

She looked stricken, her eyes filled with fear. 'I'll tell him myself. When the time is right.'

After she'd gone, Arturo crossed the grounds to stand near Brianna. Her face was flushed with exertion, but she continued to practise with the spear. When he came nearer, he saw anguish in her eyes, as if she were physically hurting.

'Brianna,' he interrupted, 'I want to speak with you alone.'

She withdrew her spear and regarded him. 'What is it?'

'Not here. Meet me in the grove where you cut greenery the other day.' He didn't wait for her to argue, but walked toward the gates. He spoke with one of the guards and borrowed a spear. Though it didn't bother him that she wanted to practise with weaponry, now that her enemy was here, he didn't trust her not to seek vengeance. And there was one way to convince her not to fight—by showing her how ill prepared she was.

Arturo waited for her within the grove for half an hour before she finally appeared. She'd washed her face, and her hair was damp around the temples. In her palm she held the spear. 'Why did you ask me to come?'

'Because I wanted no one to see us.' He adjusted his grip on his own spear. 'I saw the way you were watching the Norseman.'

'I'm not a fool, Arturo. I know how to bide my time and wait for the right moment.'

'He's far bigger than you are. If you attack him, he'll kill you.'

'He might.' Her voice came out in a soft tone. 'But then, what sort of coward would I be if I just let him go?'

Arturo stood opposite her. 'You're not ready for that fight, *cariño.*'

Her eyes glittered with anger. 'I disagree.'

Without warning, he lunged forward, pressing his spear against her throat. 'You'd be dead within seconds. You weren't fast enough to defend yourself.'

She pushed the spear aside. 'I wasn't ready.'

'And do you think he'll simply wait until you are? If you

attack him, you'll find his spear buried in your flesh. And I'm not about to let that happen.' He circled her, watching as she grew more alert, her own spear prepared. 'Try to stab me,' he ordered.

'I don't want to.'

'I didn't say you had to succeed.' He held the spear with both hands, watching her. Waiting for her to make a move. When she thrust her spear forward, he seized it and twisted the shaft, forcing her to let go.

'You can't do this, *belleza*. Face the truth.' He reached for her fallen spear and cracked the dry wood apart, splitting it over his knee. Tossing the pieces aside, he was unprepared for her attack.

She threw herself at him in fury. 'What have you done? I needed that spear.'

He caught her wrists, watching the play of emotions over her face. 'No, you didn't. You're not the sort of woman who could kill a man in cold blood.'

'You don't know that. After what he did—' Her words turned from anger into grief. She released the outpouring of tears, and he pulled her into an embrace. Around them, the wind cut through the evergreen trees, the bitter cold sweeping through the air.

'He took my husband from me, and I had to hold him while he suffered.' Devastation filled up her voice. 'Murtagh died in my arms.'

Brianna clung to him as she wept. Arturo held her close, knowing her pain. He'd endured every second of it himself, knowing the helplessness and the grief that had stolen his soul. As her body merged against his, he felt the need to bring her comfort. To show her that the scar could heal, in time.

Her arms gripped him tightly, and he bent down to kiss her as if he could mend the wounds within her heart.

Against her lips, he voiced the words he'd been wanting to say. 'Marry me, Brianna. Come back to Navarre as my bride.'

She stiffened in his arms, drawing back to look at him with tear-stained eyes. 'I can't. You know that.'

'Because you'd rather martyr yourself for your husband? Are you trying to die by the spear?' He broke free of the embrace, watching the myriad of emotions on her face.

'I have to finish this. I have to face him.'

'Face him? Or kill him?' he pressed.

When she didn't answer, he picked up the spear he'd borrowed, taking a step backward. 'You're not a murderer, Brianna. Talk to the Norseman if you must. But know your weaknesses.'

'Arturo?' she whispered, her eyes downcast upon the fallen spear. 'Why would you want to marry me?'

'Because I care for you. And I want a wife and a family.' The thought of spending each night with her, loving her until she conceived a child, was a longing that filled up the loneliness inside him. Brianna would make a good mother; he had no doubt of it.

He returned to stand before her and tilted her chin up to face him. 'You must choose, Brianna. Between vengeance and death…or marriage and life.'

When she returned to the castle, it was late afternoon. Arturo's words played over in her mind again and again. She watched as the men competed in sword fighting and foot races. Her brother won a match, using a quarterstaff, while she spied her youngest sister sitting with a group of *Lochlannach* women, staring intently as the women told fortunes over runes.

Arturo's proposal had taken her by surprise. She'd refused him without thinking, for she didn't believe she could be a good wife for him. And yet, being in his arms had closed off the hurt. He'd showed her that there were feelings left inside her, though they were well buried.

Across the inner bailey, she saw the *Lochlannach* murderer leaning against the wall, his expression empty. He didn't appear to be watching any of the competitions, as if they bored him.

Her feet began moving forward, as if directed by an invisible force. One after the other. Although she didn't know what she would say to him, the need was too strong to ignore.

When she reached the man, his posture altered when she came within a few feet. But he didn't look at her. 'What do you want?'

His voice held a deadly air, as if he'd sooner kill her than speak to her. For a time, Brianna studied him, noting the bruises upon his face and arms. He looked as if he'd been in more than a few battles. Icy blue eyes stared past her and she wished she'd armed herself first.

'You killed my husband a year ago,' she accused.

A tightness formed upon his mouth. 'I've killed many men. Especially those who attack me first.'

There was no regret or sympathy in his eyes—only the fierce stare of a man who didn't care. It reopened the wounds inside her, and a dark tightness closed over her heart. 'You were among those who raided Laochre. When my husband attacked you, he was trying to protect me.'

A hardness came over his face. 'And you've come here to kill me now. Is that it?' He took a step closer and unsheathed his blade, offering it to her hilt-first. 'Take your vengeance, if that is your will. But know this—'

His eyes held emptiness, fury glittering upon his face as he turned to her. 'I am already cursed and have been, since I was a child. If you kill me, it will end my suffering, granting me what I deserve.'

Arturo searched for Brianna among the crowd, and when he saw her, he broke into a run. She stood before the Norseman, a blade in her hand.

He didn't think but shoved his way past the people to reach her. If she dared to strike out at the man, she would die. Blood roared in his ears as he raced toward her. He heard a woman screaming and he unsheathed his own sword, hoping to God he could protect Brianna from the man.

He'd watched one woman die, and he wasn't about to lose another. The image of Brianna's blood pooling upon the ground, her green eyes sightless, was one he never wanted to see. He'd sooner give up his own life than let her be harmed by the raider.

Arturo didn't hear the cry that escaped his own mouth, as he raised up the sword and reached for Brianna, meaning to push her out of the way. Nor did he see the flash of the blade as the Norseman seized Brianna and used her as a shield.

He was too late to stop his momentum, and when he reached the woman he loved, cold metal slid into his flesh. Shock froze away any pain as he saw the horror in Brianna's eyes, his blood upon her hands.

And when his vision blurred, he sank into darkness, hearing nothing more.

Chapter Six

'Brianna, no!' came the cry from Rhiannon.

She barely heard her cousin, for she'd dropped to her knees in front of Arturo. He was bleeding, and the knife had stabbed him on the right side of his ribcage. Her mind was faltering, and all she could say was 'Find your mother. We need a healer quickly!'

'It wasn't his fault,' Rhiannon insisted. 'Kaall didn't do this.'

When Brianna turned, her cousin clung to the Viking. Icy rage sharpened in her mind when she realised that Rhiannon had feelings for this man. Her cousin had been leaving each night to spend time with the one who had taken Murtagh's life.

The dagger might as well have been sheathed within her own heart. 'How could you?' She couldn't breathe from the anger that roared through her.

'He's blind, Brianna.' Rhiannon helped her cut through Arturo's tunic to stanch the blood flow. 'I promise you, he had no intention of killing Murtagh. It was an accident. A terrible one, but I can't hold him to blame for it. Kaall defended himself from a man he couldn't see.'

When Rhiannon held pressure upon the wound, her voice grew quiet. 'Forgive him, I beg of you. And me.'

Brianna couldn't answer. Right now, all of her concentration was focused upon Arturo. He was barely conscious, his face tight with pain. She reached out to touch his cheek, and his dark eyes centred upon her. 'I never meant for this to happen,' she whispered. He didn't speak a word, but simply accepted her answer.

Inside, her emotions were a tangled war of fear. If he died, she couldn't live with herself. For she was to blame for the wound. Revenge had conquered her sense of reason, and now a man she cared about had been hurt.

'Stay with me, Arturo,' she told him, framing his face between her hands while they waited for the healer. His dark eyes closed, though his hands came up to take hers. It tore her apart to see him like this. In the past few days, he'd given her so much. He'd brought her out of her sorrow, giving her a reason to smile. A reason to put aside her grief and look toward the future.

She didn't want to lose him, not now when she'd come to care for him.

'Will he live?' came a gruff voice.

She glanced up and saw the Viking staring with an empty gaze. Though his posture remained defensive, regret lined his tone.

'I hope so.'

Slowly, with uncertain steps, he came closer. Dropping to one knee, he admitted, 'Rhiannon didn't mean to betray anyone. I know what I am and what I've done over the years. I deserved to lose my sight.'

'Kaall, no.' Rhiannon reached out to him, and in her cousin's eyes, Brianna saw the anguish.

'She needs to know.' The man tried to turn toward her. 'There was a time when I could see blurred shapes. But when I raised my spear to defend myself that day, I never saw your husband.' His blue eyes turned to frost. 'I can see nothing. Not even her face.'

The bleakness in his words underscored his own suffering. Confusing thoughts of anger and hurt collided in Brianna's mind, for he was right. No curse could be greater than the one he lived with each day.

'I believe your words,' she said at last. 'Perhaps we might… talk later. I need to tend Arturo now.'

Rhiannon let out a sigh, as if Brianna had given her reassurance. But right now, she needed her own strand of hope. As she held Arturo's hand, she forced herself to look at him and not his wounds. She'd locked her feelings away, shutting him out when he'd tried to help her escape the grief she'd lived with for so long. In his presence, she'd felt alive again, like a woman given a second chance.

'I won't let you die,' she told him. 'I watched one man I loved die in my arms. I'll not let it happen a second time.'

His eyes flickered, as if he were fighting to stay conscious. 'Are you in love with me, *belleza*?'

She didn't know. The words had slipped out without her realising it. Never had she thought her bruised heart was capable of loving another man. But there was no doubt that Arturo had slipped within the crevices, helping her to leave behind the shadows of grief.

She squeezed his hand and bent nearer to him. 'You'll have to stay with me to find out.'

The healer Aileen arrived, and the matron lifted the cloth away to examine the wound. 'We need to bring him inside, so I may tend him. But it appears the blade hit his ribs and didn't go in too deeply.'

Several of the MacEgan men helped lift Arturo while Aileen kept pressure upon the injury. He lost consciousness when they moved him above stairs to one of the bedchambers. Numbness filled Brianna's heart, consuming her with fear.

The minutes seemed to stretch into eternity while Aileen cleaned the wound and stitched it shut. She mixed a blend of herbs into a paste and created a poultice to draw out any poison. When they wrapped the bandage around him, the bleeding had stopped, but his complexion was pale.

Adriana arrived, with Liam following behind. Her expression was filled with worry and she bent to take her brother's hand. 'Will he be all right? How did this happen?'

'The wound wasn't deep,' the healer said. 'It's possible that he will be fine. But there is the risk of a fever.'

'I'll stay with him,' Brianna said, meeting Adriana's gaze. 'He was wounded because of me. He thought I was in danger.'

It was an accident, just as her husband's death had been. And though she hated the thought of Rhiannon loving the *Lochlannach*, she now understood why her cousin wanted her to let go of her hatred.

For so long she'd blamed the man for taking away her husband. She'd allowed the anger and sorrow to consume her, dissolving the rest of her life in endless grief.

But this man, Kaall Hardrata, hadn't committed murder. He'd sensed Murtagh's attack and had wielded the spear to fight an enemy he couldn't see. She didn't know how to respond to this new revelation.

The healer stood from Arturo's side and said, 'He needs rest and time for the wound to heal. I believe Brianna should stay with him alone. The care of a woman can often bring a man back from the edge of death.' Aileen reached for a flagon of wine and mixed a blend of herbs within it. 'This will help him to sleep.' After she poured a cup and set it near Arturo's side, she rose and went to the door. Then she signalled for the others to leave.

Adriana looked uncertain, and Brianna promised, 'You have my word. I won't leave his side until he's healed.'

'I should be the one—'

'No.' Brianna cut off her words. 'I care about him, too.'

The young woman assessed her with a sharp eye, unsure of what to do. But Arturo stirred at the sound of their voices and said, 'Brianna should stay.' When his sister appeared disappointed, he added, 'I've had worse injuries, Adriana.'

She leaned down to kiss his forehead. 'I will keep you in my prayers.'

After she'd gone, Arturo turned to Brianna. 'Will you help me to sit up?' Upon her face he could see the terror, and he wanted her to know that he wasn't as badly injured as she feared.

'No. It will reopen your wound.' Instead, she moved to sit with him and lifted his head to rest in her lap. She drew her hand over his bristled cheek, studying his face. 'I truly am sorry for what happened.'

The pain from his wound did hurt, but he was more interested in the thoughts veiled within her face. He saw the worry for him, but he wanted it to be more than that.

'I've no intention of dying over this,' he said. 'It's a shallow cut.'

'Stop trying to be brave,' she chided, staring down at him. 'You bled a lot.'

His hands moved up to cover hers. 'I heard what you said to my sister. That you cared for me.'

She nodded, and within her green eyes, he saw the warmth mingled with her fear. 'I do.'

Her whispered words made him reach up to touch her hair. 'There's one thing you can do for me, *cariño*.'

'What is it?'

His hands slid against her dark hair, drawing her closer to him. 'Kiss me to make it better.'

The words were spoken in teasing, but she obeyed, drawing her lips to his. Against the gentle touch of her mouth, he countered with his own warmth. Coaxing away her fears, convincing her that he wasn't going to die.

He had many reasons to live, and she was one that he didn't want to lose. 'Marry me, Brianna,' he murmured against her mouth. 'Let me take you back to Navarre, to a place where you will be mistress of your own household. You'll sleep in my bed at night and let me give you children.'

He didn't give her the chance to answer, for he poured everything he had into the kiss. She needed to understand that he was the best husband for her, a man who understood her better than anyone. Their breath mingled, and at last she pulled back.

'You haven't allowed me to answer.'

'Because I don't want you to say no.' He saw the flush upon her cheeks, the swollen lips, and fire in her eyes. Already she'd refused him once. It was possible she still wasn't ready to let another man into her life.

'If you don't let me speak, I can't say yes, either,' she replied.

He waited, holding her face near to him. 'If you say yes, then this wound was worth it.'

'Don't say such a thing. I can't tell you how terrible I felt when I caused this.' She drew her hand over his hair, closing her eyes at the thought.

'Then give me the answer I want, *mi cielo.* Share your life with me.'

She took a breath and opened her eyes. 'For the past year, I lived with my pain, and I never imagined there would be anything else for me. But then you came to me.'

His hands laced with hers, and he waited for her. 'Can you put away the past, Brianna?'

She braved a smile. 'As long as my future is with you.'

Epilogue

It snowed on the morning of her wedding, but Brianna didn't care. So much had changed, and she was eager to begin her life again with the man she'd come to love.

Rhiannon stood before her, lifting a crown of holly and ivy into her hair. 'You'll take Arturo's breath away when he sees you,' she pronounced.

Brianna squeezed her cousin's hand and smiled. Though she would always bear the scar of losing Murtagh, she couldn't wait to start a new life with Arturo. The Spaniard had helped her to put the past behind her.

'Are you ready?' Rhiannon asked.

Brianna was nervous about the crowds who had gathered to witness her marriage but nodded. 'I still wonder if we should have waited for Arturo's parents to arrive. Adriana and Liam have not yet wed, because of it.'

'Let them have their own celebration,' Rhiannon said. 'And I imagine it's because Arturo doesn't want to wait any longer for you.'

Brianna's skin tightened at the thought. Though she had already shared his bed, he'd whispered his plans for other wicked intentions this night.

Outside, the torch lights gleamed against the snowy sky. Brianna walked through the throngs of people to find Arturo waiting. His dark eyes warmed at the sight of her, making her feel beautiful as he guided her toward the chapel within the castle.

Inside the small space, her parents, aunts, and uncles gathered around with Adriana and Liam on the opposite side.

'Our mother will be angry with you for not waiting,' Adriana warned.

Arturo tightened his hold on Brianna's hand. 'I don't want my bride to change her mind.'

In the glow of candles, she made her vows a second time. Her heart was filled with hope and love. When she looked into Arturo's eyes, she saw a man who had stood by her in the darkest of times. He'd opened her heart to forgiveness, bringing her to a new life.

And there was no greater joy.

* * * * *

THE HOLLY
AND THE VIKING

Prologue

Ireland—Spring 1192

It took three men to subdue him. Kaall Hardrata strained hard, fighting against the strong arms that had dragged him back.

'Father!' his daughter, Emla, shrieked, sobbing as the others took her away. A female voice tried to soothe her, but he couldn't see if she was reaching for him. His heart was tearing apart at the thought of losing her.

'Why would you do this?' he roared at the faceless strangers. 'Never once has she come to harm.' Fury blazed through him, that they would dare to take her away from him.

'You're not capable of caring for her,' came the voice of his father, Vigus Hardrata. 'We allowed it for a short time, but it's time for her to be fostered with parents who will see to her needs.'

Words caught in Kaall's throat, with a thousand reasons why it was wrong to take Emla away. She was all he had left of Lína, and he'd done everything in his power to see that the child was content.

'It's because of the MacEgan man I killed, isn't it?' he predicted. From their silence, he suspected it was true. Although it had happened last winter during a raid, it had been an accidental death when the MacEgan man had attacked him. He'd only defended himself as was his right, but Kaall knew there were those who wanted him dead because of it.

'I sent the body price,' he reminded them. Though it had stripped him of nearly all his wealth, Kaall had done what was required of him to support the man's widow.

'And because of it, you hardly have enough to support yourself, much less a child,' Vigus said. 'Emla will be given to a good family.'

'She's mine,' he insisted. 'You've no right to take her away.'

'Don't make this more difficult than it already is,' came the voice of his mother, Jódís. 'If you let her go now, she'll come to love her new family.'

Her hand touched his shoulder, but he shrugged it away. 'Where are you taking her?'

'It's better if you don't know,' Vigus responded. 'Rest assured, her new family will love her.'

He wrenched himself free of the men, stumbling forward until he crashed to the ground. 'Emla!' he called out.

But there came no answer from the young girl. Before he could run, they seized him again. Vigus gripped his arm. 'I've no wish to have you bound, Kaall. Let her go, and face the truth. You were never capable of caring for her.'

Hatred rose through him, for they believed it. It didn't matter that he'd made a home for Emla, provided her with food, and tucked her into bed each night as he told her stories. They saw only a broken man, not one with a father's love.

'Bring her to me,' he said quietly. 'Once more, before she goes.'

'It wouldn't be wise. It will only make her cry again.'

'I deserve the chance to say farewell to her,' he said, gritting his teeth at their patronising tone. 'Grant me that at least.'

But they refused. And when at last, they let him free, the child was already gone.

Chapter One

Winter 1192

I'll cast a spell for you, cousin. And on the winter solstice, I promise you'll find love.

Rhiannon MacEgan highly doubted that a twelve-year-old girl could conjure up a man, particularly one who would fall in love with her. But Alanna firmly believed in the Old Ways. Perhaps Druid blood ran within her veins, or perhaps her Uncle Trahern had told her too many faery stories. Regardless, there was no harm in walking out to the stone dolmen that lay halfway between Laochre Castle and Gall Tír, the Viking settlement. Her cousin could cast whatever enchantments she wanted, and Rhiannon wouldn't stop her.

The sky brooded with heavy clouds, and the air was so cold, her breath hung in misty circles. Frost crunched beneath her feet, and she drew her cloak tighter as she neared the dolmen. It resembled an ancient altar with two parallel stones at the base and a slanted stone table. Alanna waited near the Druid burial site, while beside her stood Cavan MacEgan. He looked annoyed at having to shadow his younger sister.

When Rhiannon reached them, Cavan sent her a dark look.

'I cannot believe you agreed to her foolish superstitions. It's freezing and about to snow.'

'It's not foolishness,' Alanna protested. 'I promise this will work.'

Cavan rolled his eyes, but Rhiannon sent the girl an encouraging smile. 'What must I do?'

'I'll need a lock of your hair.' The girl produced a bundle containing a blend of birch bark, and herbs, while Rhiannon used her knife to cut a small lock from the underside of her hair. Alanna wound the dark hair around the bundle and set it upon the dolmen. 'Now we'll light a fire, and I'll cast the spell.'

Cavan withdrew flint and held it out to Rhiannon. She hesitated. 'Perhaps you should light it. I'm not very good with striking a spark.'

'No,' Alanna protested. 'If he does it, then the love spell will fall upon him.'

'And we wouldn't want that,' her cousin commented drily. Rhiannon took the flint, holding it over the bundle of herbs.

'As you strike the flint, clear your mind and I shall conjure up the face of the man you will come to love. We'll burn the charm and you'll inhale the smoke.'

'Burning hair smells terrible,' Cavan pointed out. 'She'll probably choke.'

His younger sister sent him a furious look, but he only grinned, standing back with his nose pinched. 'Go on, then, Rhiannon.'

It took several tries, but finally she managed to get a spark to land upon the small pile. It died instantly, sending up a tiny flare of smoke.

'Quick, breathe it in,' Alanna commanded.

Rhiannon gave a sniff, laughing as she did. 'You're right, Cavan. It does smell awful.'

'I think we should go back to Laochre for a hot drink,' her cousin suggested, glancing up at the clouded sky. 'Before we're buried in snow.'

'Not until I've finished.' Alanna squared her shoulders and commanded, 'You must burn the love charm. And don't forget to think of your lover's face. It's important.'

Rhiannon bit her lip to hold back the laughter. It was silly, but she understood that this meant something to Alanna. So many of the others had made fun of the gawky girl, teasing her about her beliefs. And she knew from her own experience, how painful it was to be ridiculed.

The young men avoided Rhiannon as if she had leprosy, because of her overprotective father. She'd never been kissed, nor had any suitors at all. Connor MacEgan had sworn to kill them if they so much as looked at her. And when one friend had dared to hold her hand during the feast of *Bealtaine*, her father had raged at the young man, threatening to cut off his fingers.

Though Rhiannon had more than enough female friends, she'd watched them marry one by one. She'd left her home in the west of Éireann and travelled to her uncle's castle at Laochre, hoping to find a husband. But although a few had smiled at her, none had dared to court her. Her father's interference continued to shadow her, and though she didn't truly believe in love charms, she was running out of other ideas.

Striking another spark, she coaxed it to life with the warmth of her breath. The malodorous blend of herbs burned brightly, until it died to coals and finally ashes.

'There. It's done now,' Alanna pronounced. 'Did you see the face of your lover?'

'Yes,' Rhiannon lied, though she hadn't thought of anyone. The wind tore into her cloak, making her shiver. 'Let's go back and we'll see if it worked.'

Her cousin appeared troubled. 'Of course it will work. But only if you believe in it.'

The weather shifted, and the first few flakes of snow drifted from the sky. It was growing darker, and Cavan took his sister's hand. 'We should go back while it's still light.' They started to run, racing one another, while Rhiannon followed behind at a walk. They had to cross through another forest, and she wanted a few moments to herself.

But as the minutes passed, the storm worsened. Blinding white flakes swirled, and she pulled her cloak tighter, her eyes stinging from the wind. Cavan and Alanna had run so far ahead of her, she could no longer see them.

She held fast to her cloak, hurrying toward her cousins, but the clouded darkness made it impossible to see more than an arm's length in front of her. Though she knew the direction of Laochre, the forest stretched out for half a mile. The trees did little to cut through the wind, and the ground quickly transformed from dark brown into snowy white.

Leaning against the wind, she kept her head down for the next mile. At any moment, she hoped to catch up to them. But as time stretched on, the coldness sinking into her skin went beyond the frigid storm—it was a darkening fear that she might not find them. That they had become lost, while the frozen night descended.

Her teeth began to chatter, and she picked up her skirts, running hard. 'Cavan!' she shouted into the storm. 'Alanna!' When there came no answer, her heart quickened. Were they hurt? Or so far ahead that they couldn't hear her?

The pragmatic side to her tried to remain calm. Her uncle's castle was only a few miles away—less than an hour's walk.

If she made it through these trees, surely she would see the clearing that led the way toward Laochre Castle. She might even see torches gleaming, to light her way.

She scanned the snow for her cousins' footprints, but the rapidly falling snow had masked any trace of them.

What if you don't find them? came the voice of fear. Though she tried to dispel the thought, it taunted her mind with a tangible threat. *You could die in this storm without shelter.*

Again, Rhiannon quickened her pace, but a hidden tree root caught her footing, and she stumbled to the frozen ground. Her hands sank into several inches of snow, and she grimaced. The furious blizzard swirled around her, making her disoriented.

Just keep walking. She stood up and brushed herself off, trying to ignore the rise of tears in her eyes. Being afraid and cold wasn't going to get her home any faster. Once again, she called out to her cousins. And still, there was no reply.

Rhiannon sent up a silent prayer for their safety. Never had she seen a storm like this, not in all her years of living in Éireann. She stopped walking, and turned around to reassess her whereabouts. She bit her lip hard, forcing back the rise of panic as she left the trees and entered the open clearing.

As soon as she saw it, her heart sank. It wasn't the long stretch of land leading toward Laochre. Instead, it was a hilly terrain that curved southeast, a few miles away from the *Lochlannach* settlement of Gall Tír.

Somehow, when she'd had her head down against the wind, she'd gone the wrong way. Frustration welled up inside her, and she made her way back into the forest. Why hadn't she kept her head up? Why hadn't she paid more attention? Now she had to walk all the way back in the opposite direction.

Her hands were starting to go numb, for she hadn't brought

any hand coverings. Rhiannon tried to wrap them in her cloak, but her feet, too, were starting to lose feeling. As a healer, she knew what that meant. She couldn't risk the walk back home or even to Gall Tír. She needed to find shelter until the storm ceased. Even if she couldn't build a fire, she could at least massage some warmth back into her hands and feet.

Right now, she was wishing she hadn't given Cavan back the flint. What she wouldn't give for the warmth of a fire and dry clothes. Through the trees she walked, shivering hard as she searched for something. Anything to shelter her from the storm. But there were only endless rows of trees, the snow rising higher above her ankles.

Her teeth chattered, and she kept walking through the woods. A strange scent caught her attention…something that seemed like smoke. Was it a fire? Or better, someone who could help her? She continued toward it, hurrying as fast as she could, until a feral growl stopped her in her tracks.

The grey wolf stalked her, his fur dark against the snow. A low snarl came from his muzzle, and he bared his teeth at her.

Rhiannon froze in place, for any sudden movement might cause it to attack. She gazed around for an escape or a weapon of some sort. There was a fallen branch not too far away. But she feared that if she reached for it, the animal would spring upon her, tearing out her throat.

She held her breath and stared at the animal, not knowing what to do. Its ears were perked up, its body crouched low. One matter was certain—she couldn't remain like this for much longer. Her heart was beating so fast, she could hardly bring herself to move. But there was no other choice.

Steadily, she inched toward the branch, hoping she could defend herself with it. Or at least have more time to run.

Another step…closer…

'Who's there?' a man's voice demanded. The wolf growled toward the sound, and the distraction was just enough for her to seize the branch. A tall, shadowed man had emerged from the trees, a torch in one hand, a blade in the other. When the wolf darted toward him, Rhiannon cried out a warning. 'Watch out!'

She didn't think, but ran after the wolf, cracking the branch against the animal's head. It snarled, diving toward her in fury.

She had no time to scream, but threw up the branch to protect herself. Before it could sink its teeth into her, the man waved his torch at the animal, singeing its fur. She rolled away, unable to breathe when the wolf sprang up at the man. He let out a grunt of pain when the predator bit into his arm. Blood stained the white snow, and a moment later, the animal's snarl was cut off as it dropped to the ground.

'Are you all right?' she whispered, stepping closer.

The man didn't answer, but cleaned his weapon in the snow before drying it and sheathing it. His arm was raw and bleeding as he lifted the torch toward her. And when the light of his torch illuminated him, she saw a face she knew…the face of a murderer.

Kaall Hardrata could smell the woman standing there. Her scent was faintly feminine, like a blend of herbs he didn't recognise. He didn't know what had brought her here, but he wanted her gone so he could tend his wound. The beast he'd slain had dug its teeth into his arm, and he clenched his jaw against the pain.

'I've seen you before,' she murmured. 'Last year, during the raid.'

Then she was a MacEgan. Kaall gave no reply but stepped

back four paces until he was near the hidden entrance of his cave. He shoved his sleeve down, hiding the bloody gash. 'You should know better than to wander out alone,' he said in the Irish language. 'Go back home to your family.'

'I was trying to. But the snow made it to difficult to see.'

A dark smile crossed his face with the irony of her words. 'And you sought shelter with me?' Of all the places to go, his dwelling was the worst place for sanctuary. He might have defended her from one beast, but it didn't atone for his past deeds. Most of the others believed he deserved to live away from the rest of the tribe.

She didn't answer for a long moment, and he sensed her fear. 'I don't have much of a choice, do I?'

The snow was still falling rapidly, and the droplets struck his skin, melting against him.

'You could stand out here and freeze to death.'

She said nothing, as if she were considering it. Then her quiet accusation struck. 'You killed my cousin's husband.'

Kaall let her words linger for a time, choosing his words with care. 'So I did.' He didn't apologise for it, or offer any excuses. He hadn't wanted to kill anyone and truthfully had questioned the wisdom of going to Laochre that day. He'd believed he could help his father stop the raid, but he'd failed in the attempt.

'Are you sorry for it?' she asked curiously.

'Should I have stood there and let him kill me with his spear?' His words came out with the frustration he'd held inside over the last year. His soul was already damned, for because of that death, he'd lost everything of value to him. Not only his wealth, but his daughter.

That had been the worst penalty of all—that the others had used his mistake as a means of taking the child from him.

Despite everything that had happened, he was determined to get Emla back. He would prove himself to them...somehow.

Kaall clung to the thread of hope, even knowing how hopeless it was.

Rhiannon let out a breath. 'No, I suppose you had no choice but to defend yourself.'

Though it was a grudging comment, at least they understood one another.

He didn't want the woman here, intruding upon his solitude. But the freezing air held the promise of continuing snow for the next few hours. Though he'd rather she left, she might die of exposure. He was a heartless bastard, but not that cruel. Beckoning for her to follow, he lifted aside the hide covering the hidden cave.

'I'm going back to the fire,' he informed her. 'You can warm yourself for a few minutes and then go on your way.'

Entering a cave alone with a murderer wasn't a good idea. Rhiannon knew it, but the alternative was worse. She kept her distance from the man, though she was glad the interior was warm from the fire and stone walls.

Had he told the truth, when he'd claimed to be defending himself? Or was it a lie, meant to lure her into trusting him? There was no way to know. For now, she would remain alert and pray that the storm would stop quickly.

She stepped closer to the fire, the heat almost painful against her freezing hands and feet. The scent of peat filled the space, the smoke rising toward the top where crevices allowed it to escape.

'My name is Rhiannon MacEgan,' she offered.

The *Lochlannach* didn't offer his own name, though she

hadn't expected him to. Instead, he moved behind her and closed the hide curtain that veiled the entrance of the cave.

While she warmed herself, she saw the pain upon his face as he held pressure against his bleeding arm. The animal bite would likely fester and cause a fever. Perhaps worse.

Leave him alone. He killed Murtagh and isn't worth your time.

Her cousin would say that, she knew. But this man had claimed he was only defending himself. Rhiannon didn't know what to believe.

In the light of the fire, the Viking's dark gold hair gleamed. It hung past his broad shoulders, making him seem more like an ancient barbarian. He was so tall, she had to lean back to look at him, and his physical body was honed like a steel blade. And yet…she found him compelling, beneath the fierceness. His stark blue eyes were unusual, like none she'd ever seen before.

In many ways, he reminded her of a wounded predator. Being here with him wasn't at all safe. She'd escaped from a wolf, only to end up in the lion's den.

But this lion was in a great deal of pain because of her—and it was impossible for her to watch a man suffer without wanting to do something about it. A good healer treated every man—rich or poor, sinner or saint. It was part of who she was, and if nothing else, he *had* protected her from the wolf and granted her shelter. Even if he did terrify her, she owed him something for saving her life.

Reluctantly, she took a step closer. Her gaze passed over his wounded arm as she considered what to do. Blood was seeping into his tunic, but the greater risk was that his blood would become poisoned from the bite.

'How is your arm?' she asked.

'An animal tried to bite it off. How do you think it is?' Though his words held bitterness, she sensed he was trying to keep her at a distance. Whether it was pride or pain, it was working. She had no desire to go any closer. Fear and uncertainty heightened, her pulse pounding in her veins.

'Don't waste your breath on me, *kjære*.' His low voice was rigid, without a trace of softness in it. 'If the storm has stopped, and you're warm enough, then leave.'

'I should,' she admitted. 'My family will be searching for me.' She desperately wanted to return home, where her family and friends would keep her safe. But an invisible hand seemed to hold her captive here.

He gave a shrug, as if that didn't surprise him. 'Go, then.'

Kaall turned his back, waiting to hear the sound of her footsteps. As he'd expected, a moment later, he heard her lift back the heavy hide. She would leave, and he could then try to treat the festering wound. Right now he wanted to plunge his bare skin into the snow—anything to rid himself of the fiery ache.

'The storm is worse,' she called out. 'I can't see anything but white.' The draft of cool air was sealed off when she lowered the drape once more. Regret coated her voice as she admitted, 'I'll have to stay longer.'

It wasn't at all what he'd wanted to hear. The last thing he needed was to spend the night with a woman who loathed the sight of him.

'You can share my shelter,' he said in a low voice, stepping back, 'but stay away from me.'

'Believe me, I'd rather not stay, either,' she told him. 'I wish I knew what happened to my cousins. If they're out there—' Her voice broke off, as if she couldn't bear to think of it.

'There's nothing you can do,' he told her.

'I know you're right. But it doesn't make it any easier.' She approached him, and he stiffened, wondering why she would want to come nearer. His arm was burning with pain, and he wanted to be alone.

'If I have to stay here, then at least let me look at your arm,' she urged. 'It was my fault you were hurt.'

He backed away until his shoulders rested against the wall. The idea of her touching him, even to treat a wound, brought a warning flare through him. Her soft scent held the sweetness of youth and the maturity of a woman unawakened. It had been years since he'd had a woman, and his mind filled up with unholy images.

'Leave it.' The words came out half in a growl, but instead of obeying him, she pulled back his sleeve.

Stubborn, wasn't she? When her fingers reached his arm, Kaall reversed their positions, pressing her back against the stone cave. She was at his mercy, trapped within his arms. He wanted to frighten her away, so he chose words deliberately intended to wound.

'You don't understand, do you, *søtnos*? I'm not a good man, like your MacEgan cousins, who will watch over you. Touch me again, and I'll take far more than you're offering.' His hands moved up her ribcage, as he anticipated her flight. She would tremble with fear, and the moment he released her, she would go to the furthest corner of the cave, leaving him alone. She'd be glad to be rid of him in the morning.

The familiar coldness slipped within him, freezing out all emotions. He knew what he was. Why no woman wanted him. This woman would be no different from the others who had kept their distance.

Instead, her hands came up to touch his arm. 'Stop trying

to frighten me. I can see that you're in pain and you're too proud to ask for help.'

He cut off her words, taking her face between his palms. Her hair, like dark silk against his fingertips, held a hint of curl. Her breath warmed his fingers, and he sensed the goose bumps upon her flesh.

'Run away, little girl,' he warned.

'I'm—I'm not a little girl,' she whispered. In her voice, he heard the tremulous fear.

He moved his hands on either side of her, against the wall. 'If you stay here in my arms,' he murmured, 'I'm going to kiss you.'

The threat was meant to push her away, to send her back to the other side of the cave where she would count the minutes until she could go. He didn't want her sympathy or worse, her pity.

At last, she shoved her way past him. Good. If she had any sense at all, she'd leave him alone. He heard the slight rustle of her movement nearby and turned toward the warmth of the fire. Before he could sit, her hand caught his in a firm grip while she pushed back his sleeve.

A soft cloth wiped his forearm, gently stanching the blood flow. Kaall froze in place, as Rhiannon wrapped the linen over him, forming a bandage.

'There,' she breathed. 'I really need to clean it, but at least the bleeding will slow.'

The act of compassion angered him. She'd called his bluff, not believing he would act upon his threat. So be it.

'You were warned.' Then he leaned in, his mouth seeking hers.

Chapter Two

Blood pounded in Rhiannon's veins when the Viking cupped her chin, his mouth claiming hers. His lips kissed her hard in a storm of heat, demanding a surrender from her. She was stunned by it, unable to think or breathe while he conquered her.

She'd never been kissed before by any man, and whatever she'd imagined, it wasn't the molten sensation of drowning against his sensual mouth. His warm breath stole hers away, quickening her heartbeat as she struggled to make sense of it.

Without warning, her body began to respond to the onslaught of sensation, her skin growing hotter. Her breasts tingled, and an invisible thread of desire slipped downward, until she found herself clenching her legs against the unfamiliar ache.

It made her angry, for this was not what a first kiss should have been. She'd wanted to kiss a man who liked her, not one who was trying to prove a point. By the holy Virgin, if he believed she would stand by and be frightened by him, he knew nothing about her.

As if to fight back, she returned the kiss, echoing the fierceness of his lips, her hands coming up to touch his face.

She poured herself into it, meeting his force with her own aggression. He seemed taken aback by her actions, as if he'd expected her to surrender to his conquest. Or to be more afraid.

Instead, she chose to prove her own point—that he would never bend her to his will. She slid her hands into his hair, and from the moment she touched him, he softened his mouth upon hers, no longer punishing. But he didn't stop.

He slowed down, taking his time. The difference devastated her, for now he kissed her as a lover would. His lazy mouth nipped at hers, tasting her lips and coaxing her to open her mouth. She did, and his tongue slid inside while his hands moved up her ribcage. Against his mouth, her lips were swollen while he aroused her. Between her legs she grew wetter, and her breathing quickened. His hard body pressed close to hers, and when he drew her hips close, she felt the length of his own arousal.

He was lean and muscular, a warrior in every sense of the word. His mouth was fearless, demanding that she yield to him, while his hands moved over her hair and face, learning her by touch.

When he drew back, his thumbs moved across her lips and down her chin. She imagined his hands moving lower over bare skin and warmed to it.

In the light of the fire, his dark gold hair was haloed, his blue eyes shielded against any words she might say. She stared at him, wondering why he was so isolated here, with no family or friends. Was it by choice, or had he been driven out?

She didn't speak, allowing her heartbeat to calm while she watched him. Though he was undeniably handsome in a fierce manner, there was something else troubling her. Not once had he looked into her face. He seemed to look past her, and she stared into his clouded eyes once again. They were gazing at the wall behind her as if...

She frowned, a sudden thought making her wonder.

When he let her go, she stepped backward, watching his face. She lifted one hand and moved it slowly in front of him, but his eyes showed no sign of seeing it. Again, she moved a different hand, but his eyes never tracked the motion.

'Don't come near me again,' he ordered. 'Unless you want to finish what we started.'

'You're blind,' she blurted out. 'Aren't you?'

There was an immediate change in his visage. He closed the distance between them, his expression rigid. 'I don't need sight to recognise who's before me. A MacEgan princess, pampered and given everything she's ever wanted. You live in a castle with servants to tend you. And these hands have never known work.'

His sudden attack revealed the fierce pride of a man who loathed this weakness. He was taunting her, trying to make her hate him.

In the dim light, she narrowed her gaze. Upon his arm, she saw the evidence of heavy bleeding through the bandage, his face tight with discomfort. Like her father and his brothers, this man would not admit to weakness, and the kiss had done nothing to distract him. He needed a respite from his pain more than all else.

With this amount of bleeding, the wound might need to be stitched shut. The problem was gaining his consent to be treated. And she lacked the healing herbs she needed to prevent swelling and fever. Animal bites rarely healed easily.

'I need to clean and treat your arm,' she informed him calmly, ignoring his angry words. 'If you allow me to tend it, I promise I'll leave at first light. Or if you insist on being stubborn and proud, I'll continue to stay here.'

'Don't you want me to die, *kjære*?' He lowered his voice, adding, 'I deserve it.'

'You probably do. But not right now.' She seized his hand and led him back toward the fire. 'Sit down and let me clean it.'

She could tell he didn't want to, but she'd given him no choice.

'Do it quickly, then.' He sat down before the fire, holding out the arm. She took a wooden bowl and went outside to scoop snow. She would melt it and use the water to clean the animal bite.

All the while, she was trying to recall the best ways to ward off fever and swelling within the wound. Garlic bulbs, archangel, harebell roots—but none of those herbs were here. Nor could she find any herbs in the forest during winter.

When she returned, she set the bowl of snow near the fire to melt. He hadn't moved from his position, but from the tension in his posture, he knew she'd returned. Rhiannon reached for his forearm and unwrapped the bandage. 'I'm melting snow for water,' she said. 'It's the best I can do to clean it.' She didn't tell him the danger he faced from fever or poison within the wound. The next few hours would be the true test.

When the water was ready, she scooped handfuls over his skin, wiping away the dried blood. 'Have you been blind all your life?' As she spoke the words, she watched the shielded anger cross over his face.

'If you're too proud to answer, I'll assume the answer to my question is yes,' she continued. The ragged flesh wasn't as bad as she thought, and she wrapped the bandage tighter, putting pressure upon it.

'Do you enjoy pretending to be a healer?' His voice held mockery, as if he didn't believe her capable of it.

'I *am* a healer,' she countered. 'And if I had my herbs, I'd make you a poultice or a sleeping draught. Something to improve your mood.'

'This is one of my better moods. I liked kissing you.'

Her face brightened, for his voice had grown husky, as if he wanted to touch her again. 'You shouldn't have.'

'You kissed me back.' His words held a hint of disbelief as if he couldn't understand why.

She didn't know the answer. It had started as her own rebellion at being kissed against her will...but it had transformed into a dizzying desire. Wounded or not, he'd offered her a taste of sin. It shamed her to know that she'd liked his hands moving up her back, losing herself in the raw sensations.

The unexpected longings he'd conjured were nothing but a betrayal to her best friend. This man had killed Brianna's husband, leaving her heartbroken.

'It won't happen again,' she vowed. Right now, she needed to put distance between them. The space had grown intimate, and she no longer knew if he could be trusted to leave her alone.

She needed a distraction, something to keep her hands busy. Her stomach ached, for it had been hours since she'd eaten last. 'Is there any food?' she ventured. 'I could prepare a meal for both of us, if you're hungry.'

'There are supplies over there.' He pointed toward the back of the cave.

Rhiannon crossed the space and studied his belongings, which were in disarray, as if he'd been searching through them. Nothing was organised or in any sort of order. Though she knew she shouldn't concern herself with his possessions, she couldn't simply leave everything on the ground. Everything needed to have its own place, and she couldn't stop herself from the intrinsic need to bring order to the mess.

Quietly, she began sorting through them, putting clothing in one stack, weapons in another, food in a third. The sacks of food contained stale bread and venison of an uncertain age. But the frigid air had kept the meat cool, so it might serve well enough.

She took out a knife and began trimming off the questionable parts of meat. Her hands were shaking, and she tried to push back the nerves that had crept up once more. It was just a meal, she reminded herself. Nothing to fear.

Yet, she studied the man sitting beside the fire, his knees drawn up. Though he was blind, he showed no trace of weakness. He'd fought a wolf, without being able to see. It was startling to even imagine that kind of courage.

Why, then, was he living here alone?

Rhiannon speared a chunk of venison on to a stick and brought it with her as she approached. 'I don't know how long you've been living here, but your belongings were spread out everywhere. I suppose you couldn't find anything at all.'

She stoked up the flames, adding a chunk of peat, and then set up a makeshift spit to hold the meat over the fire. 'I organised them for you.'

His expression turned furious. 'Why would you do this? I knew where everything was.'

'You had bags of food mixed in with weapons and clothing.'

He stood up and advanced upon her. 'You had no right to move my belongings.'

'It will be easier for you to find them without stumbling over everything.'

'I could find everything right where it was!' He reached out and groped for her wrist. 'Put it back. All of it.'

'I couldn't do that if I wanted to.' She tried to pull away, but he held fast. 'If you'll stop treating me like a barbarian, I'll show you where everything is.'

'I don't want your interference,' he warned. 'You shouldn't have moved anything.'

She reached out to take his other hand. Gently, she pulled at him, guiding him into the darker space. 'The food is here.' She drew his hands down to touch the sacks, which she'd set against the wall. 'And your clothes behind that, and last, the weapons.'

'So if we're attacked, I'll have to sort through food and clothes before I can find my weapons?' His voice held both anger and scorn. 'Should I tell the wolves to wait outside while I find what I need to kill them?'

'You have a blade at your waist,' she pointed out. 'And if you want me to move the weapons closer to the front, I will.'

'I don't need you to do anything for me. I was fine before you came here.'

'And before that?' She didn't know what possessed her to argue back, but she couldn't see what harm there was in trying to help him be more organised. 'Did you live among the others, snarling at anyone who tried to help you?'

'I didn't need any of them,' he fired back. 'I could live well enough on my own.'

'You're making it harder on yourself.' She reached out and touched a dark spot on one cheek. 'I imagine you have many of these bruises from walking into trees or walls.'

'Did you want to see my other bruises?' he countered. His

voice resonated through the space, sliding beneath her skin in a challenge. She imagined his bare skin, golden in the fire-light, a temptation she didn't want. From the tight muscles that stretched against his tunic, she had no doubt that his body would be ridged with strength.

'No, of course not,' she answered. But it didn't deter her imagination.

Rhiannon continued turning the meat, though she cast a glance at his blue eyes and the way his blond hair hung down over his shoulders. He stood with his back to the wall, his immense height towering over her. His fists were clenched, his face shadowed with pain. This was a man who fought hard for everything he wanted. A proud man who wanted no one to see him as weak.

'Don't feel sorry for me, *kjære*. I don't need your pity.' He stepped away from her and went to examine his belongings, running his hands over them to mark where they were, before he moved the weapons to the front.

'How long do you plan to stay here?' she asked. 'When you run out of food—'

'I'll hunt,' he finished. 'And if I can't provide for myself, I don't deserve to live.'

She didn't believe he would truly stay here that long. No man could live alone without companionship. 'Surely you must have parents or family at Gall Tír.'

'The only person who would ever miss me was taken away because they believed I couldn't take care of her.'

'Taken?' Had the tribe members stolen a loved one from him? How was that possible? 'Was it your wife?'

'My daughter.'

The words were so quiet, she could sense the pain in his voice. In that moment, she saw the crack within his shield, the feelings for his child. She simply couldn't imagine how terrible it would be to have a daughter taken away. Likely they didn't believe a blind man could care for the girl.

'Will they ever give her back to you?'

He gave no answer, and the silence was damning. She knew, as he did, that they would not. They judged him by what they saw—a man without sight. And he was already condemned for it.

The injustice bothered her. This man was holding back anger and pain, but she saw the softness toward his daughter. No one had the right to separate a father from his child.

It brought to mind her relationship with Connor MacEgan. It had been years before she'd known he was her father, but she had memories of him taking her on long walks, showing her the hidden treasures in the woods. Sometimes it was a flower bud about to unfurl or a squirrel's nest high in the trees. When she was a girl, she'd felt beloved and protected by her father.

It was only within the past few years that their bond had deteriorated. Connor's overprotective nature had driven a rift of resentment between them. But despite her frustration, she still loved him.

Just as this Viking loved his own daughter.

'Where is your daughter now? Is she living at Gall Tír?'

He shook his head. 'But I will find her.'

The vow was spoken softly, but beneath it, she heard the determination. He wouldn't stop searching until he knew she was safe. Just as her own father would search for her, once he learned of her disappearance.

'I hope you do.' The meat was done, and Rhiannon divided it between them, spearing the other half for him.

She reached for his hand and guided it to the skewer. 'I

fear it won't be seasoned properly, for I haven't any herbs or salt. But it should be good enough.'

He took the offering and bit into the meat. Rhiannon did the same and though it was somewhat bland, at least she hadn't burned it.

'You never told me your name,' she said at last.

'Kaall Hardrata,' he admitted. 'I am Vigus's son.'

She stilled at the mention of the chief. 'I didn't know he had a son.'

'He didn't want to acknowledge me.'

Though his words were spoken in an indifferent tone, undoubtedly he felt the sting of his father's rejection. She was beginning to understand why he lived apart from his family. Perhaps he didn't want to live among those who saw him as different.

But there was another person he hadn't spoken of. From his bitterness, she suspected the worst. 'What of your wife?'

His unseeing eyes regarded her, and an expression of harsh amusement rested at his mouth. 'Why would you think a woman would wed a man like me?'

There was no good answer to that question, but she pressed on. 'What became of the woman who bore your daughter?'

Kaall tossed the stick toward the fire, his face growing shadowed. 'She died a year ago.' Though he said nothing else, the grim expression revealed that the woman had meant something to him. And a part of her sympathised with him for the losses he'd endured.

'I'm sorry.' The fire was beginning to die down to coals, and Rhiannon added more fuel to bank it for the night.

Kaall rested his hands upon his knees, turning his face toward her. Though he couldn't see her, his presence raised the hairs on the back of her neck. 'Have you a husband who will search for you?' he asked. In his voice she heard another un-spoken question: *Is there a man who has laid claim to you?*

Her cheeks warmed, and self-consciousness overcame her. The idea of sharing this space with him was suddenly intimi-dating. 'No. But my father will search, once he learns I didn't return with the others.' She sent up another silent prayer that Alanna and Cavan had made it back safely.

'Why were you so far from your home before the storm?' he asked.

'It was my own foolishness,' she confessed. 'I allowed my cousin to cast a love charm upon me, so that I might find a husband.'

Abruptly, she stilled when she realised what had happened. She *had* met a man this night, one who had saved her life. A handsome man, albeit one who wasn't at all tame by nature. And he'd kissed her. To distract herself, Rhiannon picked up a few stones from the ground, sifting them in her hand.

'The charm didn't work,' he warned.

She was fully aware of the warning in his voice and reas-sured him, 'I never expected it to. But I saw no harm in in-dulging her. She's been teased enough by the others.'

'And you like to champion those less fortunate?'

There was an accusation in his voice, as if he believed she was patronising him. 'Sometimes.' The stones in her palm spilled to the ground.

'Were you planning to throw those at me?' he asked.

'How did you know what I had in my hands?'

'I have ears, *kjære*. I hear everything.' He stood up, skirt-ing the fire until he hunched down beside her. His nearness unsettled her, and she started speaking to cover her nervous-ness.

'When I was a girl, my cousins and I used to tell fortunes

with stones.' She rested her hands against her skirts, keeping her gaze fixed to the ground. 'I suppose you never played games.'

'I gambled with dice,' he admitted, 'and always won.'

'And why is that?'

'Because I could feel the dice in my hand and cheat.' Though he didn't smile, she sensed the diminishing anger. 'The others refused to play against me, after a time.'

She could understand why, given his unique abilities. But she'd played games numerous times with her cousins, all of whom were bloodthirsty opponents who loved to cheat.

'I could beat you,' she predicted.

He raised an eyebrow. 'Don't wager with a blind man, Rhiannon. You'll always lose.'

The confidence in his voice made her want to try it. She reached for a stone that was smooth on one side, rough on the other. 'Are you certain?'

His smile turned wicked. 'And what would you want from me if we had a wagering game?'

A flush came over her face, for he'd made her remember what it was like to kiss him. The carnal images that flooded through her mind were completely forbidden…made worse by the knowledge that, after tomorrow, it was unlikely she would see this man again.

Anything could happen. Or nothing at all.

She shivered, torn about what to do. In the end, her conscience prevailed.

'I would like honest answers,' she admitted. 'To any question I ask.'

Kaall's mouth twisted, and he opened his hand to reveal the stone. 'Don't wager with me, Rhiannon. You'll lose.'

'I'll toss the stone for you, and you'll call rough or smooth before I catch it. Will you promise to give me the truth?' She reached for his hand and pressed the stone within it.

'Only if you give me what I want in return.'

She heard the sensual invitation in his voice, and her traitorous imagination envisioned another kiss. 'What do you want?'

'Nothing you're not willing to give.'

She eyed him, and saw the interest in his face. Here, in this isolated dwelling, she was at his mercy. At any time, he could have forced his attentions on her…but he'd pulled back, letting her free of the kiss.

'Then I can refuse, if it's not something I wish to do?' At his nod, she released a slow breath. 'I want to believe you're a man of honour. Can I trust you?'

He said nothing at all, but placed the stone in her palm. 'Try it and see.'

Kaall sensed her nerves tightening. Though he'd given her every opportunity to stay far away from him, she'd refused. Honest answers, she'd claimed to want. He couldn't imagine what sort of questions she would have, but he decided to let her win a few matches, to find out.

'Call it,' she ordered. 'Rough or smooth?'

He'd placed the stone rough side down, and the weight of it was slightly askew. Odds were, it would land with the smooth side facing up. 'Rough,' he told her. As she made her toss, he moved away from the fire, for it was growing warm within the space. His arm ached from the wolf bite, and he could feel the tightness of his skin as it swelled. In truth, he was grateful for this distraction, for it would be a long night.

He heard the sound of Rhiannon catching the stone.

'Smooth,' she told him, bringing his hand to touch it. 'And now you'll answer my first question.'

Kaall took the stone from her, and heard her pause as if trying to find the right words.

'My question is about men. My...father would never allow me to speak to men or become friends with them.'

Kaall hid his smile, for he could understand exactly why Rhiannon's father didn't want her around men. He'd felt the same way about Emla, though she was hardly more than a young girl. The idea of any man courting her was reason enough to lock her away until she was five and twenty. Or older.

'What is it you want to know?' he prompted.

'I've never had any fortune in finding a husband,' she confessed. 'My father threatened any man who dared to even look at me. What should I do?' In her voice, he heard the embarrassment, as if it pained her to ask the question. And yet curiosity had won over her pride.

'Smile at a man who interests you,' he replied. 'If the man returns the interest, he'll come to speak to you.'

'And then what?'

'You'll have to win another toss of the stone before I answer that.' This time, he intended to win a prize of his own. Adjusting his palm, he widened the space and ordered, 'Your turn.'

'Smooth,' she predicted.

With a shift of his wrist, he flipped the stone so that it would land rough-side up. 'My win.'

She made no response, and he knew she was expecting him to demand a physical favour. Instead, he voiced his own question. 'Tell me what you look like.'

From her silence at first, she seemed taken aback by his question. 'I have brown hair and—'

'No. More than the colours.' He set down the stone and reached out until he touched her hair. 'I haven't seen colours since I was very young. Brown means nothing to me.'

She took his hand and guided it over the silken mass of her hair. 'It's like the earth, after a rain. Not quite as dark, and there are hints of gold in it. As if the sun were warming the earth. It falls below my waist.'

'And your eyes?'

'They're green and grey, depending on the light.'

'Like water or ice?'

'Like a running river,' she answered, 'and the moss that grows upon the stones.'

'Other men call you beautiful, don't they?' His hand moved over her face, touching the soft cheeks, feeling the slender line of her nose.

'Some do.' Her voice was soft, but he didn't care that he'd made her uncomfortable. In his mind, he was beginning to form a vision of Rhiannon. And he liked what he saw.

'Your turn.'

He heard her lift the stone into her hand and as she gripped it, he expelled a slow breath, fighting against the pain of his arm. He could feel his skin growing hotter and knew what that meant. But first, he would get through this night.

'Smooth,' he predicted.

'Rough,' came her answer. When she brought it for him to touch, he wondered if she had flipped it over. He wouldn't put it past her to cheat.

'I shouldn't ask this, I know. But I—I want to know. When you kissed me earlier, it was the first time for me. I did a poor job of it, and I was wondering, how does a man want a woman to kiss him? Soft or firm or—'

Kaall clamped his mouth shut to stop from laughing at her. She was serious in her questions and after a brief hesitation, he managed to answer. 'Any way a woman kisses a man is welcome. It's impossible to do it wrong.'

He claimed his next turn, already knowing the forfeit he would claim. Again, he used the weight and surface of the stone to cheat, and successfully won the toss.

'What is it you want from me?' she whispered.

'I think you know that answer.' Kaall reached out and found her hand, following it up her arm until he located her face. He threaded his hands into her dark hair, imagining the spill of it over her creamy skin. Her hands remained at her sides, and he ordered, 'Put your hands on my shoulders.'

She did, and the coolness of her fingertips against his neck revealed her fear. His body heat was rising hotter from the wound, but he said nothing, for it would only upset her.

'Put your mouth upon mine and kiss me,' he said, waiting for her. 'I'll teach you what you want to know.'

Rhiannon didn't move for a long moment. 'I don't know if I should. It's really meant to be between two people who have feelings for one another.'

'It's a lesson, Rhiannon. I'll show you what a man wants. Nothing more.' He didn't want her imagining anything else between them. It was a way of tasting her mouth once again, giving him a memory to take with him.

She held back for long moments, making him wonder if she would refuse. And just when he'd given up, he felt a closed mouth descend on his with the barest kiss.

'More,' he commanded. 'This time, open your mouth slightly. Let me kiss you back.'

This time, when she lifted her mouth to his, the warmth of her breath spilled into him, tender in her innocence. He returned the kiss, keeping it slow and deep. Making no demands, only offering her a taste of him. Against her mouth, he murmured, 'Is this a better first kiss?'

'Second kiss,' she corrected. Drawing back from him, he sensed that she was intrigued but shy.

'Or did you want this?' He took her face between his hands again, kissing her hard. With his tongue, he slid against her mouth, demanding that she open. When she did, he invaded her warmth, feeling the tremor of her pulse as his hands moved to rest near her throat. He withdrew and moved his tongue within her mouth, imitating the sexual act.

She was both innocent and passionate as she matched his kiss. He grew aroused by her, wanting to spend this night discovering why a woman like her would bother kissing a man like him.

But as she did, the darker memories rose up. Of Lína, whom he'd adored. He'd wanted it to be like this between them, but she'd turned from him. Her kindness had never been desire, and that knowledge had dug into his heart. She'd been right to choose another man to wed, though he'd have laid down his life for hers.

Women didn't want men who couldn't protect them, who were less than whole. Especially not beautiful women who could have any man they chose.

He tore his mouth away, realising that he was trying to use Rhiannon in place of Lína. And that wasn't fair at all.

'I'm sorry,' she whispered. 'I never should have—'

'Forget it happened.'

Rhiannon hadn't known what she was doing, while he'd taken advantage of her. He wasn't at all a man of honour, like she'd believed. Frustration flooded through him, and as he returned to sit by the fire, a wave of dizziness passed over him.

Now that he'd regained his awareness, his arm ached as if someone were trying to saw it off with a dull blade. Kaall took slower breaths, trying to blot out the pain.

'Your skin is warm,' he heard her say. She returned to his side and touched his forehead. 'This is a fever.'

He captured her wrist, holding her cool palm to his skin. Right now, he'd much rather distract himself from the pain by kissing her again. Or by letting her touch him. With reluctance, he let go of her hand.

'I won't die from a fever.' He started to move away, breaking the spell between them. 'We should both get some sleep, and it will be better in the morning.'

'Not always,' she warned. 'How far away are we from Gall Tír?'

He could see where this was leading and put an immediate stop to it. 'Too far.'

She took his hand, insisting, 'You can't remain here without any further treatment. If I have the right herbs, I can—'

Kaall pressed her back against the wall. 'The longer you stay with me, the more danger there is to you, *søtnos*.'

She didn't move, and he bent nearer to her, speaking against the soft column of her throat. 'I've kept my hands to myself. But don't pretend you didn't enjoy that kiss. Don't tell me you didn't want more.'

Goose flesh rose upon her skin, revealing her own sensations. He'd released her, but she didn't move away. Which made it dangerous for both of them.

'I don't know what I want.' Her voice was a whisper, filled with indecision. 'Only that this is forbidden.'

His mouth slid over her throat in silent invitation. 'If you don't want me to touch you again, you'd better move away, Rhiannon.'

She said nothing for a moment. But when he moved his hands to cup her face, she lost her courage and fled. Her footsteps trailed away until he heard her lift the hide away. The freezing air blew within the warmed space, cooling his desire.

'It's stopped snowing,' she offered. 'I could help you return to Gall Tír. It's not so very far.'

There was little point to it. It was the middle of the night, when the temperature would be coolest. 'No. But if you want to return to Laochre, I won't stop you.'

The hide dropped downward again. 'What kind of a healer would I be if I left a wounded man alone, suffering from a fever? It could worsen tonight, and then I'd never be able to move you.'

'I don't need to be moved,' he snapped. 'Let it be, Rhiannon.'

'It's not a sign of weakness to seek help. This wound is getting worse, and I know you're in pain.'

'It wasn't so bad a few moments ago.' When she'd kissed him, he'd forgotten all about his arm.

But he heard the rustling noise, and a moment later, he felt her arrange a fur coverlet over his shoulders. 'I'm taking a torch, and we're going to Gall Tír. I need herbs to treat your fever, and it can't wait until morning.' She took his hand in hers. 'Unless you're not strong enough to walk there.'

He had no desire to walk outside into the freezing temperatures. Especially given the danger from animals and with only Rhiannon to lead the way. But his arm was burning with pain, and she was right; there was nothing more she could do for him here.

'I can't lead you there,' he warned.

'I know how to get there, now that the snow isn't blinding me.' She lit a torch and drew back the hide covering the entrance of his cavern. Reaching for his hand, she led him forward into the night.

Chapter Three

His hand was warm, and though Kaall followed her, Rhiannon saw how the fever weighed upon him. In the forest, their feet sank into the snow past their ankles. The night was freezing, and she huddled close to him for warmth.

As soon as she did, she realised her mistake. Getting closer to this man would only unravel another thread of her willpower.

He lowered the fur covering over her shoulders, resting his arm around her. It was a simple gesture, nothing other than a friend might do. But her mind was spinning off other visions, as if more would happen between them.

Each time he'd kissed her, she'd been unable to refuse. His touch disintegrated her naïve ideas, drawing her toward temptations she should avoid. She didn't deny that she took pleasure from the warmth of his body, just as she'd enjoyed his kiss.

And he was utterly forbidden to her.

'What is the fastest way to reach Gall Tír?' she asked, as they moved further away from the cave.

'It's about two miles east of Laochre. Keep the forest to your right side and keep walking. You'll find it.' Though he trudged beside her without complaint, he was guarding his arm, holding back the pain.

'How did you get to the cave alone?' she wondered.

'Trahern MacEgan is a friend of my father's. He brought me to the shelter when I asked for his help.'

'But why would he—?'

'Help a man like me?' he finished. 'Trahern knew Vigus and I were trying to stop the raid.' There was tension in his posture, and he added, 'I've lived here since last spring.'

Half a year, then. His daughter must have been taken away just before that. 'How old is your daughter now?'

'Emla will be four in a few months.' He adjusted the fur coverlet over them as she led them outside the forest and into the clearing.

She continued talking, wanting to distract him from any pain. Keeping a swift pace, she guided him east.

'It's almost the winter solstice,' she remarked. 'Did the two of you decorate your home with greenery in the past?' She imagined a young girl helping with freshly cut pine branches.

'Her mother, Lína, died on Twelfth Night, and I saw no reason to celebrate.'

She reached out to touch his hand, understanding that his pain had not faded. 'Perhaps one day, when you're together, you can find a way to honour Lína and pass on your memories to Emla.'

When they reached the clearing, she saw the dim flare of lights from Laochre Castle to the west. Ahead, a single rider moved closer toward the forest, a torch in his hand. Rhiannon shielded her eyes and recognised the young man.

'Wait here for a moment,' she said to Kaall. 'There is someone I need to speak with.'

He remained in the shadow of the trees, holding on to his

arm while Rhiannon picked up her skirts and hurried forward. When the rider spied her, he moved in fast.

It was her cousin Cavan. 'Thank God,' he breathed, dismounting from the horse. 'When we didn't find you, I went back to search.'

'I am fine,' she admitted, embracing him. 'I found shelter.'

'Come on, and I'll take you back,' he offered.

For a moment, Rhiannon hesitated. Although they were closer to Laochre, it wasn't a good idea to bring Kaall there. After he'd killed Brianna's husband last winter, the young woman hadn't abandoned her quest for vengeance. Bringing him among her family would only result in more danger.

'No. I can't.' She shook her head. At her cousin's incredulous look, she said, 'I promise you, I have a place to stay. But there's a wounded man who needs my help. I'll come home in a day or so.'

She couldn't consider abandoning Kaall. Not now, when he needed her.

'You can't just disappear,' Cavan argued. 'Your father will turn over every stone looking for you.'

'Please,' she begged, 'don't tell him I'm gone. I can't tell you where I'm staying, but I promise I'll return. Just give me one day.'

The young man eyed her with the greatest reluctance. 'The only reason we haven't told Connor already is because I promised Alanna I'd find you.'

'And you did.' She took his hands in hers. 'It's all right. I'll return before anyone else notices I'm gone.'

'What am I to tell Connor if he asks where you are?'

'Tell him the truth. That I've gone to tend a wounded man.' She saw the doubts on the young man's face and asserted, 'If anything happens, I will take the blame for it.'

Though her family might discover her absence, the greater concern was caring for Kaall's wound. She couldn't leave him now.

Because you don't want to return home, her treacherous mind warned. *You want to stay with him.*

Turmoil and confused feelings warred within her. She was consorting with an enemy she hardly knew.

But you want to know him, her conscience continued. *Even though it's wrong.*

A moment later, she turned at the sound of footsteps crunching through the snow. Kaall stood at the edge of the forest, making his presence known. In his hand, he carried a blade.

Cavan started to protest, but she silenced him. 'He's only protecting me. It's all right.'

'Do you know him?'

'Yes,' she replied.

Her cousin eyed her with wariness, but finally relented. 'Only until the morrow. If you're not back by nightfall, they'll come after you.'

'Thank you.' By then, she would know if Kaall's wound had worsened. Yet, it was not enough time for him to heal… nor was it long enough to make sense of her troubled feelings.

With a farewell to Cavan, she returned to the woods. The outer crust of snow had frozen, and her footsteps made a crunching sound as she approached. When she reached Kaall's side, he pulled the fur coverlet across her shoulders, drawing her close. She didn't protest, though the heat of his skin worried her. She needed to brew him a tea to bring down the fever and help him to sleep. It would also make it easier for him to fight off the poison rising in his blood.

They walked for long moments and the torch made it possible to light the way. About halfway through the journey, she felt his body beginning to tremble. 'Are you all right? Can you finish the walk?'

'I'm cold,' he admitted, though his skin burned to the touch.

'We're closer now,' she said. 'I promise you, when we arrive, I'll take away your pain. You'll sleep and feel better.'

He gave no response, and she continued talking, trying to take his mind off his injury. 'When I was a girl, I lived near Banslieve, with my mother and father. It's northwest of here, far away.'

'Why did you travel here?'

'Most of my cousins and other family are nearby. I thought I would marry someone from this region, but my father travelled here when I was seven and ten and forbade it.' She supported Kaall as he walked, adding, 'He made it impossible for me to find a husband.'

The *Lochlannach* stopped walking a moment and regarded her. The moon had slid out from behind a lacy cloud. 'He wants you to have a strong protector. A man who would fight for you, no matter what he faced.'

'No man was willing to stand up to him. When my father threatened them, they stayed away from me.' She leaned in closer, keeping out the frigid winter air. 'I hated him for that.'

'Then those men were weak.' His sightless eyes stared past her. 'When I wanted Lína, I did everything in my power to win her. I wouldn't have cared what her father said or did. But she didn't want me.'

Rhiannon took his hand in hers. 'If she spurned you for your blindness, then she was weak.'

Kaall didn't respond, but neither did he release her hand. For a brief moment, she allowed herself to daydream, to imagine this man confronting her father. There were a hundred different reasons why Connor would object to the match, especially with Kaall's blindness.

But then, such imaginings were foolish. His heart belonged to the woman he'd lost a year ago. And though he'd kissed her, both of them knew it meant nothing.

Then why did you stay with him? her mind taunted. She had no answer for that.

Just ahead, Rhiannon saw the torches on either side of the gate. The *Lochlannach* settlement of Gall Tír had been here for hundreds of years. Once, it had been the home of Viking raiders, but gradually they had intermarried with the Irish over time. Yet they still kept the Norse customs, holding on to their own traditions.

'We're here,' she said. Tension tightened within Kaall's posture, as if he didn't want to be. His complexion was feverish, his gait unsteady.

There were men guarding the longphort, and when they saw her, their expression turned wary. They spoke in the Norse language, and from their angry tone, she suspected they weren't glad to see him.

'I am taking him to see Vigus,' she interrupted, stepping between them. 'He's been wounded.'

'Vigus won't see him,' one said in her language. 'He's an outcast.'

Their declaration startled her, for Kaall had led her to believe he'd chosen to live apart from them. Regardless of the truth, their blatant prejudice irritated her. 'I am a healer, and I brought him this far so I can treat his wounds. How can you deny shelter to a man who needs it? I thought you were his kin.'

They said nothing, and she took Kaall's hand, pushing her

way past them. The men didn't stop her, but neither did they offer their assistance.

'Where can I find your father's house?' she demanded.

'Take me to the house furthest from all the others, near the outer wall.'

She frowned, for the dwelling he'd mentioned was small and looked abandoned—not at all a house she would expect a chief to live in. They crossed the space, and when they reached the hut, she suspected it had once belonged to Kaall. Why would he bring her here, instead of seeking help from his family?

Pride, no doubt. She decided it didn't matter. When she knocked on the door of the hut, as expected, there was no answer.

'Just go inside,' Kaall told her. 'Build a fire and we'll spend the night here.'

She bent before the hearth stones and found some wood and peat which she built up, along with tinder. Within a few minutes more, she had a small fire burning.

'I'm going to find your tribe's healer,' she protested. 'She may have the herbs and medicines I need to brew you a tea.'

'This was the home of our healer before she died,' he said quietly. 'You should find what you need among her belongings.'

A sudden realisation came over her when she saw the shielded pain in his expression. 'Your healer was Lína?'

He nodded, his hands moving across the table until he found a pallet against one wall. Rhiannon gave him the fur coverlet, and he shivered hard, clinging to it. The dim light of the fire made it difficult for her to find what she needed, but within a wooden chest, she found an iron pot and a box containing various herbs, along with dried mint, chamomile, and willow bark. First, she would give him a mild brew to take away the pain and help him sleep. Then she planned to make a stronger poultice to draw out the poison from the wound.

As she worked, she kept an eye on Kaall, not knowing how far the fever had progressed. The short journey had taken its toll, and she hurried to make the tea. When at last it was ready, she brought it to him, easing him up to sit while he drank.

'This should help your fever,' she said. 'You'll feel better in the morning.'

He finished the cup and set it aside. Before she could return to make the poultice, he caught her hand and held it. 'You didn't have to go to such trouble.'

'You're welcome,' she whispered, though he was wrong. She couldn't have allowed him to suffer through the night, not when she could do something to prevent his pain.

His hand squeezed hers and he drew it slowly to his mouth. The light kiss was wholly unexpected, as if she meant something to him. A piece of her heart seemed to break away as he lay down and closed his eyes. But he didn't let go of her hand.

Rhiannon held it for a time, not knowing how he'd managed to slip past her defences and lay siege to her feelings. This man needed her. He'd given her shelter, saving her life, and she could do no less for him.

But more than that, he'd revealed a truth to her—one she'd never guessed. Her father hadn't prevented her from finding a husband. He'd prevented her from finding the wrong husband.

She released Kaall's hand and settled down to clear her mind. If she wanted a man to share her life, he needed to be strong enough to fight for what he wanted. And if he wasn't willing to fight for her, there was no hope for such a match.

In the darkness, she blended garlic with other herbs, making a poultice for his arm. She bound it over his wound, and though he was conscious of her actions, he said nothing, keeping his eyes closed.

When at last she'd done all she could for him, she lay beside him. Kaall's body heat mingled with hers, and she drew comfort from his presence.

It was dark when Kaall awakened, and the fire burned low. Though his skin still felt warm, it was no longer the harsh burning fever he'd known last night. Rhiannon slept beside him, and from the scent of her skin, he felt the sudden ache of what it would be like to have a wife. To awaken with a woman in his arms, one he could hold in the darkness.

The thought disappeared as quickly as he'd imagined it. It would never happen.

He sat up on the pallet, trying to gain his bearings. He'd known Lína would have the herbs Rhiannon wanted. Upon his arm, he felt the remnants of whatever poultice Rhiannon had given him, and he discarded the herbs to examine the wound with his fingers. The swelling had receded, and though his arm was still sore, the pain was more bearable.

Slowly he stood, feeling his way with the wall to guide him. When he reached the far side of the room, his knee cracked against a table, and he let out a curse.

'Kaall?' came Rhiannon's sleepy voice. He tried to move toward her, staying clear of the fire's warmth, but then he walked into one of the support beams. The blow caught him across the cheek, and he slammed his fist against the wood, furious at his blindness. He couldn't even walk across a room without harming himself. What hope did he have of getting Emla back?

'Is it dawn?' he demanded. The winter nights were long, and he couldn't tell if it was day or night.

'Almost.'

He heard the soft footsteps coming toward him, and her hands reached out to touch him. 'Your knuckles are bleeding.'

'Do you think I don't know that?' he snarled. His fury was hanging by a thread, at the frustration of being unable to complete the smallest task. 'It's nothing I haven't done before. The bruises and cuts will fade.'

His humiliation went deeper than that. He'd wanted to show Rhiannon that he was more capable than this. That he could be like other men. No doubt she saw what everyone else did, that he was worth nothing at all. That he couldn't take care of himself, much less a child.

But Rhiannon reached out to touch the bruise forming upon his forehead, her hands moving down his face. 'How is your arm?'

'Better.' She made him feel like an ungrateful beggar for lashing out at her when she'd tried to help him. He gathered control of his temper, but her fingers were moving over him, examining his skin. She tempted him in ways she didn't understand.

'I'm starved,' he admitted. He'd slept hard, vaguely remembering moments when she'd changed the poultice, spooning tea into him.

'I'm not surprised,' she told him. 'You slept through all of yesterday until your fever broke last night.'

An entire day gone? He could hardly believe it, but when he felt the bandaged arm, it did seem much improved.

'When the sun rises, you should go back to Laochre,' he said. Her family would likely be beside themselves with worry since she hadn't returned.

'Is that what you want?'

No, that wasn't what he wanted. In these few days, she'd

given him a glimpse of another life. One where there was someone to talk to, someone to help him cook a meal. A slight respite from the endless hours without Emla, easing the loneliness. If he were a different man, he'd ask her to stay a little longer. Perhaps get to know her better.

He sensed her moving closer and ventured, 'What would you have me say? We both know it's better if I leave you alone.'

'Is it?' she murmured. Her words allured him, making him wonder what she meant by that. Though he'd given her every opportunity to leave, her hands rested upon his chest, over his heart. The light touch sent his pulse racing, for he was entirely aware of her. He wanted nothing more than to pull her hips against his, to taste her skin and feel her come apart as he penetrated her body with his.

But he knew, even if she didn't, that to imagine anything more would only cause complications.

'When it's light, I'll ask my father to escort you home.' He pulled back from her, and the cold winter air drifted against the dying fire. There was no reason to prolong her departure, not when his wound would now heal on its own.

'I suppose you'll be glad to be rid of me. It's what you wanted, wasn't it?'

Disappointment hung within her words, and he found himself unable to agree with her. 'It was once.'

She let out a slow breath, as if she'd been holding it. 'And now?'

He had no answer for that. Interminable minutes passed, but the only answer he could give was touching the side of her face. Letting the physical caress speak the words he couldn't say.

Rhiannon held his hand to her cheek, and ventured, 'I'll ask Vigus about where they took your daughter.'

The promise caught him like a blade within his stomach. It was as if she'd seen past his blindness, offering him the thing he wanted most. Bringing his daughter home again meant everything. And yet, he couldn't involve her in this. Her family would never allow it.

'You needn't trouble yourself on my behalf,' he said quietly. 'I'll speak to my father and ask.' Whether or not Vigus would answer was impossible to know.

Rhiannon tossed another brick of peat upon the fire, and he heard it catch with the flames, hissing in the silence. 'Why did they call you an outcast when we arrived here?'

'I chose to exile myself from them.'

'But why would you want to leave? Were you giving up on Emla?'

'I never gave up. I did it to prove I was capable of caring for her. I lived alone for half a year, with no one to help.'

Her silence was damning, as if she didn't believe it was a good idea at all. 'If you chose to isolate yourself and let her go without a fight, then I suppose that was your choice.'

'This was never my choice!' he lashed back. 'Do you think I wanted to lose her? Do you think I wanted to lose my sight?'

'No,' she murmured.

'I wasn't born blind,' he told her. 'I saw this place as a boy. And as the years passed, my sight grew worse until it was gone. You can't imagine what that was like.'

'My father was a master swordsman,' she said quietly, 'until his hand was crushed by an enemy. He thought he would never fight again, but he overcame his wounds.'

'I'll never see again, Rhiannon. It's not a wound that will heal.'

She reached out and took his palm. 'But you can still

fight for your daughter and prove yourself. Walk with me a moment.'

With his hand in hers, she guided him toward the door while counting paces. 'Five,' she finished. 'Five paces from the doorway to the back of this space.'

She opened the door, and the cool morning air blew over his face. 'It's not quite dawn,' she told him, 'and in another day, it will be the solstice.'

'The longest night of the year.'

'Yes.' She kept his hand in hers and added, 'Which dwelling belongs to Vigus?'

'We're not going there.'

'Oh, yes, we are.' She tightened her hold upon his palm. 'You weren't a coward before, so don't start now.'

'I have nothing to say to him.'

'We'll find out what happened to Emla. Now count the paces with me.' She wasn't at all listening to him, and her obstinacy intensified his bad mood.

'What are you trying to do, Rhiannon?'

He felt her cool fingers brush over his eyes. 'You're right that I can't heal these. But there are other parts of you that are hurting. You want your daughter back, and you have the right to know where they took her.'

'Why would you want to help me?'

'Because a father and daughter shouldn't be apart.'

He squeezed her hand in silent thanks. Her fingers threaded with his, and he sensed a connection with her. As if she understood the hollowness he'd lived with for the past few months.

Rhiannon continued counting aloud, leading him past each of the homes. Though he didn't know if anyone was watching them, they had barely reached the centre of the longphort before she stopped suddenly. Her hand tightened in his in a silent plea for help.

'Have you found a new pet to take for a walk?' a man taunted.

Kaall recognised the voice of Hromund, one of the men who had instigated the raid last year. Without a word, he drew Rhiannon behind him. 'Leave her be, Hromund. She's returning to Laochre.'

'I'd be glad to escort her back.'

In the man's voice, he heard the tone of interest, and Kaall suppressed the possessive rage that rose up inside him. 'You won't come near her.'

He unsheathed the battleaxe at his waist, all instincts on alert. Hromund held a high opinion of himself and relished a fight. Every instinct warned that this wasn't a good idea. The last time he'd tried to fight, he'd killed the Irishman without meaning to.

But Rhiannon's hands pressed against his back, and she whispered, 'He's standing to your right.'

Kaall had guessed as much, from the sound of Hromund's voice. But he didn't know what sort of weapon the man had, nor what his intent was. He didn't want Rhiannon caught in the middle, if Hromund dared to attack.

'Step away,' he ordered, pressing her back.

She ignored the command, as if trying to guard him. 'Your arm isn't fully healed,' she whispered, 'and I don't trust this man.'

Neither did he. And for that reason, he wanted her nowhere near Hromund. She wasn't safe in the man's company, and if it meant being cruel, he'd do what was necessary to protect her.

'I don't need to hide behind your skirts, Rhiannon.'

As he'd hoped, her hands fell away, though he could guess

at how his words must have hurt her feelings. Her footsteps crossed behind him and to the side.

'I've not seen this one before, Kaall. Were you hiding her in the woods, letting her warm your bed?'

The insult was meant to provoke him into a fight, but he held steady, knowing it was what Hromund wanted. He stared toward the direction of the man's voice, giving no answer. But he'd gladly tear him apart for his arrogant taunt. Kaall shifted his battleaxe into his right hand, balancing the weapon.

'Go back home to your mother, Hromund.'

The snarl from the man alerted him that his enemy had changed positions. Kaall spun, holding his weapon ready.

'I could take her from you now, Kaall, and you couldn't stop me.'

'Is that what you think?' His voice was cold, revealing none of the raw energy coursing through him. It had been half a year since he'd faced an opponent, and it was a struggle to hold steady, revealing none of his fear.

'Kaall, don't fight over me.' He could hear Rhiannon coming closer, as if trying to prevent the fight. But she didn't know the sort of man Hromund was. He was more than a bully; he'd think nothing of forcing himself upon her.

'Do you want him to claim you?' he warned.

'N-no, of course not.'

'Then let me kill him for you.'

From beside him, her footsteps retreated. He wasn't certain how far she'd gone, but at least she wouldn't be in any danger of coming between them.

'You couldn't kill me if you wanted to, Kaall. You don't even know where I am.'

He knew exactly where Hromund stood. The man's voice

pointed to his whereabouts, and the longer he kept his enemy talking, the better his chances of defeating him.

The sound of a blade unsheathing revealed the weapon his cousin intended to use. Kaall held still, pretending as if he didn't know the man had circled behind him. Every ounce of his concentration, every sense he possessed, focused on this fight.

'Come and find me…if you can,' Hromund mocked.

He awaited the first strike. If he allowed the man to believe him weak, he had a better chance of winning the fight.

Like a serpent, Hromund struck, his blade slashing against Kaall's bandaged arm. Though Rhiannon's binding kept the blade from penetrating, he had no opportunity to seize the man before he darted away.

'Your woman is better off with someone stronger. Someone who can defend her.'

Your woman. The words brought a protective edge to his mood, though he'd never considered Rhiannon in that way. He'd saved her life and given her shelter, nothing more. Once she returned home, she would forget about him. The thought cast a shadow over his mood, and he held the axe steady, waiting for the second strike.

'She's already gone to Vigus,' Hromund informed him. 'Because she knows you're incapable of fighting.'

With that, Kaall reached out and caught the man's tunic. He slashed the axe toward his enemy, and from the sudden twist in the man's posture, he was able to locate Hromund's throat.

In one swift motion, he moved behind the man, out of reach. 'A blind man who's good for nothing, isn't that right?' His forearm came across the man's throat, not strangling him, but letting him know he could easily snap his neck.

'Let him go,' came the voice of Vigus. He could hear the

disapproval in his father's voice, but Kaall wasn't about to release a man who had threatened Rhiannon. Instead, he held his position steady.

'Kaall, please,' Rhiannon begged. Her voice held fear, as though she, too, didn't think him capable. He should have known that neither of them would. Frustration tightened his mood, and he exerted pressure against Hromund's throat until the man's knees buckled and he lost consciousness. At least now his enemy would pose no harm to her.

'You shouldn't have fought him,' Vigus chided.

'Because I would lose, is that it?' He didn't bother facing either of them, but turned his back, intending to return to Lína's home.

'Every man faces that danger,' Vigus countered. 'But you lack their abilities. It's too dangerous.'

He'd known his father would say that. Vigus would rather hide him away from the world than allow him to fight. 'Give me back Emla, and I won't fight,' he swore. 'You won't have to lay eyes on me again.'

'I can't do that, and you know it. Besides, she's not—'

'Or I'll stay here among the others.' He cut his father off, not wanting him to finish the sentence. 'You won't be able to hide me then.'

'I've arranged for Emla to be fostered with the MacEgans,' Vigus interjected. 'It is best for her, and you know it.'

He could feel Rhiannon's tension, but she took his hand in hers. 'Your son gave me shelter, during the storm two nights ago. I would ask that he escort me home again.' Not once did she mention her connection with the MacEgans, and he wondered why she'd omitted the information.

'You would be better with a different escort,' Vigus said. 'I could arrange for someone else.'

'No, I would prefer your son.'

'He can't find his way back home again.'

'Then how do you suppose he brought me here?' she countered. When his father gave no answer, she'd made her point.

'I will take her back,' Kaall promised. 'And I won't return here again.'

'You didn't have to leave the first time,' Vigus said. 'This is your home.'

'Is it?' He refused to believe it. They'd taken Emla from him before, and the last thing he wanted was to live among others who viewed him as a blind outcast.

His father said nothing, but told Rhiannon, 'You are welcome to take a horse on your journey home.'

'Thank you.'

Kaall walked with her toward the stables while one of the boys readied a horse for them. He helped her to mount and took the reins. He soothed the animal by touching the mare's head, running his fingers over her mane, until she grew calm.

'Ride with me,' Rhiannon asked, after he'd walked alongside the animal outside the gates. 'And then we'll talk some more.'

He swung up behind her, urging the mare faster. The sooner he brought her back to Laochre, the sooner she could return to her life there. And he, in turn, intended to find out which of the MacEgans was fostering Emla so he could bring her back with him. He couldn't let her believe he'd abandoned her—not after she'd lost her mother. Somehow, he would find a way.

Rhiannon's mind churned with her own rising anger. His claim, that he didn't want to hide behind her skirts, had been like a physical blow to her feelings.

Behind her, she felt the dark tension emanating from Kaall. He'd won the fight against Hromund, but his father had treated him like a child instead of a grown man. It was no wonder he resented his family. But it hadn't been necessary to lash out at her.

When they reached the dolmen where she'd met Alanna and Cavan, she pulled the horse to a stop. Turning slightly, she dismounted and waited for Kaall to do the same.

'We haven't reached your uncle's castle,' he said.

'No. I wanted to talk with you. I didn't like what you said to me during the fight.'

He swung down from the horse. The brooding energy hadn't faded, and his blue eyes had turned angry. 'I don't need you to stand up for me, Rhiannon. I'll fight my own battles.'

'I was only trying to help.'

'I didn't *need* your help,' he shot back. 'And if you'd stayed where you were, you could have been hurt.'

'I don't think he—'

'Oh, yes, he would have.' Kaall strode toward her, his hand moving until he found her shoulders. 'Hromund would have killed me and claimed you for himself. He'd have taken you to his hut and forced you.' His hands moved to her waist, as if the jealousy were eating away at him. 'I wasn't about to let that happen.'

With shock, she realised that…he cared. He'd defended her, refusing to let any harm threaten her.

Kaall's blue eyes held the intensity of a fighter, though his stoic face could have been carved from stone. Only the slight pressure of his hands upon her shoulders revealed any emotions. Her heart trembled inside, wondering if she was misreading him.

His hands came up to touch her hair, the gesture so quiet,

she held her breath. Then his palms moved over her face as if he were trying to remember her. As if he were about to let her go.

'Thank you,' she whispered, leaning in. Against her cheek, she felt the rapid beating of his heart. She wanted to give him something in return, a way of returning the favour.

'I'll try to find out where Emla is,' she offered, 'and I'll talk to her foster parents on your behalf.' She tried to remember if any young children had been brought to Laochre lately, and could not think of any girls. But the child could have been fostered with another family member who lived in the region.

'You can't,' he said. 'They think I'm a murderer, remember?' He drew back and held the reins of the horse, waiting for her to mount again.

Instead of accepting his help, Rhiannon retreated to the dolmen, quelling the frustration inside. Kaall was right. The old wounds of loss hadn't healed, and the MacEgans would never allow him to set foot within the gates.

Still, she wanted to try. He'd saved her twice now, and this was important to him. She closed her eyes, knowing that her feelings were on treacherous ground. Although outwardly, he was rough-mannered and harsh...inside, he possessed an inner strength, an unyielding refusal to give up on his daughter.

No longer did she fear that he would hurt her. But she was terrified of the way her defences crumbled when he was near. She'd tended him over the past two days, and at night, he'd pulled her against him, as if he needed the comfort of her presence. Lying in his arms at night had only awakened more dangerous desires.

The thought of returning home, never to see him again, left her cold in a way that had nothing to do with the winter. When she looked upon him, her mind and heart warred with desire and regret. Kaall Hardrata was a man she could never have. She should shield her heart at this very moment, letting him go.

'Where are you standing?' he asked, taking tentative steps toward the dolmen.

'Here.'

The granite stone was frigid against her fingertips, and she stared into his blue, sightless eyes. Torment brewed behind them, of a man who hated his life.

'I have to go back,' she whispered.

'You must.' He reached out to her, and she placed her hand within his large palm. 'After you enter those gates, you won't see me again.'

A lonely ache caught within her throat. 'If things were different,' she murmured, 'would you still ask me to leave?'

Moving closer, he rested his hands on either side of the stone dolmen. 'You know what I am, Rhiannon.'

'I know.' She stepped forward, resting her hands against his chest. Unknown feelings rose up inside her, along with a longing she didn't understand. She ached for his touch and the way his kiss had transformed her. 'And if I said I wanted to stay?'

His hands moved into her hair, holding her face. 'You could have any man you desired.' In his voice, she heard the warning, but beneath it, lay a hint of hope.

'There's more to you than the others see. I believe that.' She reached out a hand and rested it upon his heart.

He leaned in, his forehead touching hers. 'You don't belong with me, Rhiannon.'

The hunger in his eyes and the way he held her, gave her the courage she needed. Standing on tiptoe, she leaned in as close as she dared, murmuring against his mouth, 'Do you want me to come back tomorrow?' The slow burn of desire ignited between them, and the heat of his body reminded her of sleeping beside him.

'No. I don't want you to come back.'

The words were harsh, weapons meant to wound. She drew back, lowering her hands to her side. Her eyes burned with humiliation, until suddenly, he pressed her against the dolmen. Against her body, she could feel the dark fury of his temper rising. 'I don't want you to go at all.'

She reached up to his face and pulled him down into her kiss. His mouth was starving, of a man who'd been cast out by everyone else. And she knew how badly he needed her. She met his tongue with her own, pouring herself into it, and his hands moved down her body, pulling her close until she could feel his need. He rocked against her core, and she went liquid, her body tantalised by this forbidden man.

'If I could, I'd take you now,' he said against her throat, his hands moving her waist, to just below her breasts. 'I'd learn every inch of you with my hands, until I could see you in my mind.'

She closed her eyes, guiding his hands higher, until he cupped her breasts. The fervid sensation made her breath catch, as his thumbs stroked the erect nipples.

'The choice is yours, Rhiannon. You don't have to return. But if you do…' his mouth bent to her neck, his tongue sliding over her pulse '…I'm going to claim you as mine.'

Chapter Four

Rhiannon trembled, but said nothing. Kaall knew he'd pushed her too far, but it was better if she remained afraid of him and didn't come back. With every moment he spent at her side, she made it harder to turn her away. This last kiss had shaken him, making him wonder why she would embrace a man like him when she could have any other.

But she likely wouldn't return. She was an innocent, highborn, and meant for marriage. The distance between them was too great to be spanned, and no doubt she would regain her senses when she returned to her own people. Slowly, he drew back, holding her hand for a moment before he released her.

In the distance, he heard the sound of men approaching on horseback. Rhiannon inhaled sharply and confessed, 'They're searching for me,' she told him. 'If my father is with them… he can't find us together.'

Kaall didn't like hiding. Not at all.

But Rhiannon seized the horse, guiding it with one hand into the woods while she gripped his palm and led him with her. 'Can you find your way back, with the horse?' she asked.

He gave a nod, though it would take time to regain his

bearings. Rhiannon handed over the reins and squeezed his hand. 'I promise, I'll come back.'

A strange hollowness clenched in his gut as he released her hand and voiced the words that needed to be said. 'It's better if you don't.'

Rhiannon avoided her father's men, making her own return to Laochre. Inside, it felt as if the past two days were nothing but a broken dream. She'd been stranded alone with a handsome, fierce warrior...and Kaall was just like all the others—avoiding her because of who she was. Though her mouth was still swollen from his kiss, it was her heart that held the bruises. As soon as she walked in the gates, her mother descended upon her, embracing her hard.

'Oh, thank God you're safe.' Aileen MacEgan squeezed her tightly, touching her hair and breathing a sigh of relief. 'We've been searching since yesterday. When we couldn't find you—' Her mother's words broke off with fear.

'I'm all right. I found shelter in a cavern.' Piecing together the story, she told what truths she could, leaving out any mention of Kaall. Her mother brought her inside and ordered a meal of hot stew and bread. Though Rhiannon ate and answered more questions, she couldn't stop thinking of Kaall.

In the background, she saw her cousin Brianna with a basket of pine boughs. The young woman was busy hanging them around the Hall, decorating for Christmas.

Guilt sank deeply into her, for she knew Brianna had not forgotten her husband's death. The young woman still grieved for Murtagh. If she learned that Rhiannon had taken shelter with the man who had killed her husband, her cousin would never forgive her.

Worse, Rhiannon had kissed him. And she'd liked it far more than she should.

Kaall wasn't a tame man, nor one who would ever fit into the role of a husband. Blind and carrying the weight of grief, he didn't care about what anyone thought. He only wanted his daughter back. Melancholy sank into her, and she lost all appetite for food. Even if she did find out what had happened to Emla, he'd warned her not to return. Her hands drifted up to her lips with the phantom memory of his last kiss.

'Rhiannon,' her father called out to her. Connor MacEgan strode through the Hall, his face taut with worry. 'Where were you?'

In his voice, she heard a father's greatest fear, of losing her. Without responding to his question, she reached out and hugged his waist. He gripped her so hard, she could feel the tension in his embrace.

'Well?' he repeated. 'Where did you spend these past two nights?'

'I…took shelter in a cave in the woods,' she said.

When he drew back, his blue eyes held wariness. 'Cavan said you were helping a wounded man. Who was he, Rhiannon?'

She averted her gaze. 'A wolf attacked me, but the man who saved me was hurt. Since he saved my life, I felt obligated to save his.'

'You spent two nights alone, with a strange man?' Her father's tone had turned deadly, as if he intended to hunt the man down and murder him. She could only imagine what he would say if he learned Kaall was responsible for Murtagh's death. He'd lock her away for the rest of her life.

'She's tired, Connor,' her mother intervened. 'Let her be, and give thanks that she's home safely.' Aileen stood and kissed her husband lightly, silently drawing his attention away. She was grateful for it, but her mother sent her a warning look that the questioning was not yet over. Even so, Connor took his wife's hand and took her away with him.

There was an unfailing love between them, and she envied that. She'd grown older over the years, but never had any man looked at her the way her father viewed her mother. It was as if Aileen were the missing part of himself and he would never be whole without her.

Had it been that way between Kaall and Lína? Though he'd said the woman hadn't wed him, it was clear that he'd loved her once. They'd even had a child together.

Jealous feelings slid inside her, while she wondered if Kaall pined for the woman still. The memory of his handsome face and the brooding pain in his eyes, made her want to heal the empty spaces in his heart. Even if it came to nothing.

Her cousin Brianna beckoned to her, and as she started to join her, she caught sight of the queen inspecting the decorations. If anyone had seen Kaall's daughter, it was Isabel.

She hurried to her aunt's side and saw the queen's relief that she was unharmed. 'Your father was pacing ever since he learned you were gone,' Isabel admitted. 'I know he was glad you returned.' Her hand moved to her waist, her complexion going pale as if she remembered the worry.

Rhiannon nodded, and then asked, 'Isabel, was there a young girl called Emla who was brought here for fostering?'

The queen frowned and nodded. 'Several months ago, the Hardrata chief brought her to us. She went to England to be fostered with Sir Ademar and Lady Katherine of Dolwyth.'

So far away. Rhiannon's spirits sank, for it was doubtful Kaall would see the girl again. 'Will she return?'

Her aunt shrugged. 'It's possible they might come to

visit at Christmas, but we've received no word of it. Why do you ask?'

'Someone asked me about her and wondered if she was well and happy' was all she could say.

The queen seemed to accept this, and as Rhiannon continued walking through the Hall, she wondered how she could possibly tell Kaall that his daughter now lived across the sea.

'Rhiannon,' her cousin called out to her. 'Come and help me with the garlands.'

It was certain that the young woman would want to know the true story of what had happened while she was gone. She crossed the room and reached into Brianna's basket, handing her a piece of greenery. The vivid scent of pine emanated from the branches, a scent that reminded her of the solstice this night and the forthcoming Christmas celebration in a few days. Her cousin was tucking sprigs of mistletoe into the greenery, and Rhiannon knew that many of her tribesmen and women would steal kisses this night. Her mind drifted to thoughts of Kaall, and though she tried to shut away the futile yearning, she couldn't deny that she wanted to see him again.

'I'm so glad you're all right,' her cousin whispered. 'You met someone, didn't you?'

The pine bough dug into her hand as she pondered what to say—especially since that someone was responsible for killing Brianna's husband. Though she wanted to confide in the young woman, as they had done since they were girls, she could not tell her about Kaall.

'I was lost in the forest, and he rescued me,' she admitted. 'It was too dark to find my way back, so I stayed with him.'

She risked a glance at Brianna and saw the conspiratorial smile. But if her cousin knew the truth, she would be furious.

Rhiannon turned her gaze back to the branches, pretending as though it were nothing.

'Was he handsome?' Brianna prompted.

Handsome, yes. And despite his blindness, she'd been irrevocably drawn to him. Each time he'd kissed her, she'd found herself craving more. His vow, that he wanted to spend a night learning her body by touch, took her breath away.

'He was…like no one I've ever met before.' He'd awakened her to new feelings, and though she was frightened, she was determined to help him. Now that she knew where his daughter was, she intended to share the news with him.

Which meant going back. She swallowed hard, remembering what he'd said: *If you do…I'm going to claim you as mine.*

God help her, she wanted that. He'd granted her freedom, giving her the choice to leave him. But the thought of never seeing him again left behind the bitter taste of regret. She simply couldn't do it.

'I'm going to see him again. I don't care what anyone says.' As soon as she spoke the words, she felt the rightness of them. So many others had turned their backs on Kaall, seeing only his blindness and not his strength. But she saw far more than that. He was a man of honour, a man who made her feel alive.

'I'll give you my help,' Brianna promised, 'if you'll tell me who he is and where you were.'

Rhiannon reached for another pine branch, steadying her nerves. 'I can't tell you. You wouldn't approve of him. Nor would anyone else.'

'Then why risk it? You only just met him.'

'Sometimes a few nights is all it takes.' The words came out without thought, but it was true. Despite the past, she did care about what happened to Kaall. He'd saved her life and had been wounded as a result. And though she couldn't know if they would have a future together, she wanted to return. Even if it could only be for a short time.

'He needs me,' she told her cousin. 'Like no one ever has.' Her cheeks flushed, and she sent her a soft smile before returning outside.

'She wasn't there.'

The voice of Rhiannon cut through the darkness. Kaall didn't move or speak. His body was freezing cold, for it had taken most of the morning and early afternoon to find his way back to the cavern. After he'd arrived, he hadn't bothered to build a fire.

'Kaall?' came Rhiannon's voice, as she pushed the hide aside. 'It's dark and freezing in here. Are you all right?'

He stood up, his hands and feet numb. For a moment, his mind clouded with confusion, and he didn't know if he was dreaming. 'Why did you come back?'

'I have news about Emla.' Her voice was soft, almost tentative as she spoke. 'I thought you might want to know.'

'Did you learn where they took her?' The fervent hope, that his daughter might be near, caught him, and he took a step toward Rhiannon.

'Let me build a fire, and I'll tell you everything.'

Her hesitation didn't mean good news. His spirits descended as she pulled back the hide covering to allow light into the cavern. She gathered peat and tinder, then struck flint, struggling to make a spark. When she muttered words of frustration, he took hesitant steps until he found her. He covered her hands with his own. 'Strike harder, Rhiannon. As if you mean it.'

He took the stone and blade from her, and though he could not see the spark, he smelled the flare of smoke as it caught upon the tinder. He moved closer, giving it breath until he felt the warmth of a tiny flame. Rhiannon fed more tinder, and eventually, he layered the peat on top.

'She's in England,' she said quietly. 'I don't know when they will return with her. My aunt's sister is fostering her.'

England. He closed his eyes, unable to fathom how far away she'd gone. Emla was now living with strangers in a land she'd never seen, and they likely spoke a language she'd never heard.

'I have to bring her back, Rhiannon.'

'I know.' Her hand moved to touch his, and he felt the assurance of her fingers squeezing his palm. 'If I can, I'll send word on your behalf.'

Was she truly so innocent to believe that her family members would simply hand his daughter back to him?

'They won't do it. Not after what happened last winter,' he reminded her.

'I could hide it from them,' she offered. 'They don't have to see your face. And Katherine and Sir Ademar aren't the sort of people who would deny a father his child.'

They would if they knew the truth, he thought. 'It isn't that easy.'

'Don't you want her back?' she fired back.

'Yes, but—'

'Then for God's sake, stop pitying yourself and fight for Emla! *Demand* that they give her back to you. If they deny you because of Murtagh's death, then tell them the truth about what happened!'

Her vehemence surprised him. 'Why do you care so much, *kjære*?'

'Because she's a little girl, being kept from her father,'

she said softly. 'For so many years, I didn't know my father, either.'

The regret in her voice touched him, and he sensed that Rhiannon was as lonely as he was.

The cool winter air swept inside the cavern, though the fire was beginning to warm the interior. 'Your hands are cold,' Rhiannon said, rubbing his palms between hers.

The motion, though innocent, was stirring up his own thoughts, and he caught her fingers in his. 'Thank you for telling me what happened to Emla.'

'You're welcome.' She moved to sit beside him, her knee resting against his thigh. 'I wish I could have brought her to you today.'

Rhiannon had a soft heart, and though she'd risked a great deal by coming here, he was grateful she had. At least now he knew where Emla was.

The warning voice inside his head reminded him that it wasn't at all wise to keep Rhiannon here. The touch of her fingers upon his, the nearness of her body, was already making him want more.

'You should go,' he said. 'Your family will want to know where you are.'

'Tonight is the solstice,' she said. 'There will be feasting and…' Her voice drifted off, holding a slight note of embarrassment.

'And what?'

She gave a rueful laugh. 'Let us just say that there will be more MacEgans born next autumn. No one will even notice I'm gone.'

A flare of interest rose within him, for he wouldn't mind sharing this night with her. Exploring her soft skin, learning the curves of her body.

'Will you walk with me before the sun sets?'

'Where?' He took her hand, guessing that she likely intended to return home.

'Just outside, through the woods.'

The fire had warmed the space, and right now Kaall welcomed the crisp air to clear his mind. In answer, he led her outside the cavern.

Rhiannon guided him through the forest, her warm palm in his. 'It's beautiful outside,' she said. 'The tree branches froze last night with ice, and it looks enchanted.' His fingers laced tighter with hers, and as they walked, she described the colours and shapes to him. Once, she brought his hand to a frozen branch, letting him touch the cool feathered shape. 'It's like silver.'

When they reached the centre of the woods, she stopped and took his knife from his belt. 'I spent time this morning, helping my cousin decorate the Great Chamber for Christmas. We hung pine branches everywhere, and there will be candles.' She handed him pieces of greenery, and the sharp scent brought back memories of his own childhood.

'Why are you giving these to me?' No woman had ever done anything like this for him, and he grew wary of her intentions.

'Because we'll decorate your home for the solstice tonight. You might not see it, but you'll be able to smell the evergreen branches. It might brighten up the space.'

He wanted to argue with her that she didn't need to bother with it. But from the joy and anticipation in her voice, he found he couldn't deny her the pleasure. If it made her happy, it didn't matter.

But the longer she worked, the more he came to understand that she wasn't planning to leave him tonight. And though he ought to protest and force her to go back, he held back the words. Instead, he kept the branches for her while she continued talking and leading him through the woods.

After an hour, she said, 'I think that's enough. Come with me, and we'll hang them within the cave.'

Her hand rested upon his arm, guiding him through the trees until he smelled the scent of smoke from his hearth fire. Kaall stopped at the entrance, setting the branches down in the snow. 'Why are you doing this, Rhiannon?'

'I thought you could use something beautiful in your life.'

Disbelief tightened within him. When he reached her side, he moved his hand up to her face, his thumb stroking her cheek. 'I don't deserve beauty, after all that I've done, *kjære.*'

'Don't you?'

He rested his face against the softness of hers. 'No.'

Rhiannon didn't move, and for a moment, they shared the same breath, standing so near to each other. 'It's growing darker outside.'

He knew it. With each day of winter, the warmth of the sun had departed a little more, until now he could feel the coming of night upon the air. 'I suppose you'll want to celebrate the solstice with your family.'

But she said nothing, reaching down to retrieve the branches. 'Will you help me hang the greenery? I could find some vines to tie it up, and we'll use rocks to secure it.'

Before he could speak a word, she pulled him inside, guiding him near the fire to get warm. 'I'll go and get some vines now. Wait for me.'

In her absence, Kaall gathered up more peat and rebuilt the fire. She'd chosen to stay, once again. He'd given her every opportunity to go, to be with her family instead of him.

But she hadn't left. And both of them knew what would

happen in the hours ahead. Anticipation coursed through him, mingled with a fierce desire. For this night, he wanted to be with her, to learn her body so well, he might touch her heart.

Rhiannon returned a few moments later, and said, 'I found them. Hand the branches to me, one by one, and I'll tie them into garlands.'

Over the next hour, she talked steadily, filling the empty space with her voice. It didn't bother him; in fact, it alleviated the emptiness of his dwelling. Before long, she'd finished, and brought him over to help hold the garland in place.

'I'll secure it with stones, and you keep it there until I tell you to let go.'

He obeyed, and the pine scent emanated a sharp fragrance. Rhiannon laid stone after stone upon the branches, every arm length, and when she'd set down the last one, he trapped her in his arms, against the cool stone. From behind her, the scent of pine intertwined with her own unique scent.

'What is it?' she whispered.

He framed her face, threading his fingers into her hair. 'Why didn't you go when I asked you to?'

She leaned her forehead against his. 'Because I didn't want to leave.'

Kaall stood motionless while her arms came around his waist. At her touch, he voiced the warning she needed to hear. 'You deserve better than this.'

She raised her fingertips to his mouth, silencing him. 'No man ever defended me, the way you did against Hromund. It was my choice to return.' She raised her hand to rest upon his chest. 'Tell me now if you don't want me to stay.'

He covered her hand, though he could never understand why this beautiful woman would want to be with him. 'What

I want has nothing to do with what is right.' He couldn't ask this of her, no matter what he'd said before.

'You still love Lína, don't you?' she whispered.

He was about to say yes, but the words were untrue. Lína had not been like the others, for she'd treated him as a man instead of an outcast. And because of it, he'd idolised her.

But he'd known she hadn't loved him. Nor had she ever wanted him or sought his company. He'd simply been there in the background, dreaming of the day when she might change her mind. She never had.

'I did once,' he admitted. He held her hand and drew it down to her side so she wouldn't see the effect she was having upon him. For so long, women had turned away from him. And now that Rhiannon was here, offering herself, he couldn't accept a gift that would damage her in the eyes of the man she would one day wed.

'But—'

He cut her off by touching his fingers to her lips. Rhiannon deserved to know the truth. 'Lína was a good woman, but we were never more than friends. She wed another man.' He let his fingers fall from her lips, and she remained silent.

'Emla is not my daughter by blood. When Lína died last year, I took her child into my home and cared for her. I held Emla when she cried and did the best I could. But after the raid, they believed I would hurt her without meaning to. I couldn't stop them, because I had no right to. I'm not her real father.'

'What happened to him?'

'He died in a small battle, northeast of here. The last time Emla saw him, she was hardly more than a year old.'

Rhiannon moved into his arms, holding him tight. Against

his heart, he felt the wetness of her tears. 'You were her father when it mattered most. When she needed you.'

He nodded, lowering his mouth to her hair. Although he'd only lived with Emla for a year, the young girl had become such a part of his life, the loss of her had carved a hole inside of him. 'Now you know why the MacEgans will never give her back to me. Because she's not mine.'

'Even so, we'll try,' she whispered.

He brushed his hands over her cheeks and felt the wetness of her tears. 'Why do you weep for me?'

'You're a good man. And you should have had your own wife and children, long before now.'

'It wasn't meant to be, *kjære.*'

Her cool hands covered his. 'If you'd lived among my tribe, would you have ever courted me? Or asked my father's permission?'

'If I'd had my sight like most men, I would already have claimed you as mine. No matter what your father thought.' Her body was growing warmer, and he drew her hips against his, letting her feel his desire. 'I'd have stolen you from them.'

'And if I were your captive,' she breathed, 'what would you do with me?'

Her words held the innocence of a woman untouched and the promise of sensuality. 'I wouldn't stop with a kiss, Rhiannon.'

His hand wound into her hair, drawing her closer. Softly, he nipped at her lips, tasting her sweet skin. 'I'd torment you, touching you everywhere.'

'Show me.' In her voice, he heard the breathless excitement, and it only heightened his own arousal. Though he'd lain with a few women whom he'd paid for the privilege, no one had ever chosen him. Not like this.

He led her through the space until his foot brushed the

edge of the fur pallet he used for sleeping. 'If you were my prisoner, I would order you to take off your gown.'

There was a moment of hesitation, but he heard the sound of Rhiannon removing her shoes and stepping on to the furs. Then the soft shush of fabric as her clothing slid to the ground.

His imagination raged with visions of what Rhiannon looked like with bared skin. He ached to touch her, and no longer did he care that this was dishonourable, to accept her innocence. He didn't deserve such a gift but he was going to accept it with both hands.

'It's cold,' she murmured, her teeth chattering.

'You won't be cold for long.' He removed his own tunic and guided her down to lie upon the fur. 'Not after I've finished with you.'

'What about your arm?' she asked, reaching out to touch it.

'It doesn't hurt any more.' He reached out and lifted her fingers to his eyes. 'But I wish, for a moment, that I could look upon you and see how beautiful you are.'

'See me with your hands,' she offered.

He knelt beside her and started at the top of her head. With his fingers, he drew a picture in his mind of a beautiful woman with dark hair and slender features. He captured her mouth, and in her kiss, he glimpsed hope.

For so long, the loneliness had stretched out before him, endless moments of darkness. But she had come to him now, and he wasn't about to turn her away. He wanted to give Rhiannon pleasure, to have her come apart in his arms, knowing that *he* had given her this. He wanted her to cry out *his* name.

With his hands, he touched the curve of her cheek, moving down to her throat.

Rhiannon held herself motionless, and as Kaall's hands slid to her shoulders, it drew a path of heat over her bare skin.

'You're the most beautiful woman I've ever touched,' he said, lowering his mouth to her shoulders while his hands explored her arms, moving to her wrists. She couldn't catch her breath, nor would he let her touch him in turn.

The firelight cast a glow over his bronzed skin, and when his palms cupped her breasts, she let out a shuddering breath. It was as if she'd flung herself off an ocean cliff and was falling fast. The heady sensations prickled through her, conjuring up a fierce need.

'Shall I warm you?' he murmured.

She tried to reach up to pull him down to cover her bare skin, but instead, his mouth covered one breast. Shocked, her hands moved into his hair, uncertain of whether to push him away or pull him closer. His mouth suckled against her, drawing out sensations of desire that echoed between her thighs.

With every lick of his tongue, the building ache intensified. He moved to the other breast and did the same, covering the first with his palm. 'Are you growing warmer?'

'Yes,' she sighed, reaching up to his shoulders. She'd never touched a man before, and it fascinated her to trace the outline of his muscled skin. Her fingers moved down his broad shoulders, back to his chest, and finally over his ridged abdomen.

Kaall did the same, his fingers spanning her waist.

'If you were my captive, I'd feed you more,' he teased, kissing her flat stomach. But when his mouth moved lower, she grew more fearful. Though Kaall couldn't see her, his face was dangerously close to her womanhood. And though she understood what would happen between them, it unnerved her to feel the warmth of his breath so near.

As if he sensed her fear, he moved to her hip, kissing it gently while he moved down her legs.

'Such long, beautiful legs,' he said, his mouth moving

down the outside of her thigh. When he reached her calf, she fought to hold still, for he'd found a sensitive place. Her fingers dug into the furs, her skin fiery from the blood coursing through her. As he explored her other leg, his mouth moved up the inside of her thigh, gently nudging them apart.

She couldn't bear it. Not if he were to kiss her there. Reaching to him, she fought to bring his face back toward hers.

'Frightened, are you, *søtnos*?'

He wouldn't obey, and his strength far overpowered hers. If he wanted to kiss her intimately, he would, and the tension nearly broke her apart. Instead, he balanced his weight on either side of her, his mouth coming on top of hers. He kissed her hard, and she nearly melted with relief when his tongue entered her mouth.

Her body trembled, her skin growing hotter. The kiss had already crossed over into another boundary, imitating the sexual act she wanted. Against her swollen mouth he demanded, 'I can feel your need, Rhiannon. You want me, don't you?'

'Yes.'

And God help her, she no longer cared that they were virtually strangers. That he would never share her life the way she wanted him to. But for this night, she could love him.

'You can feel it, can't you?' he coaxed against her lips. 'When I touch you, you're imagining what it would be like if I were inside you. You're wet, and you don't understand why.'

His words were another weapon against her, and she felt another rush of desire.

'Yes.'

At that moment, his hand reached between her legs, and she felt the blunt invasion of two fingers slipping inside her damp opening.

'Kaall,' she whispered, and her gasp was all the encouragement he needed. He seized her mouth again, silencing her moan while his fingers entered and withdrew.

'I can't stop shaking,' she whispered, her hips arching as he thrust against her. His thumb brushed against her, and at the unexpected pressure, a cry escaped her mouth. She leaned into him, needing him to touch her there again. But instead, he kept up the rhythmic pressure.

'Feel me inside you,' he ordered. 'And let yourself go.'

'I can't.' Though the pressure was building, it was the sensation of touch upon another part of her that she needed. She reached down to guide his hand higher, and when he found the point of pleasure, she nearly sobbed with relief. 'There,' she pleaded.

'Like this?' He experimented with his touch, rubbing her until prickles of rising pleasure gripped her. With his hand, he played with her, dipping his hand into her wetness and using it to drive her into a place where there were no thoughts, no regrets…only mindless ecstasy.

She lost herself in him, letting go as he tormented her the way he'd promised to. And abruptly, her body tightened against him, her body shaking hard until she spasmed against him, her body climaxing as the pleasure took her over the edge.

He spoke words in a language she didn't know, and it was then that she realised his intent. He'd planned to touch her, to give her pleasure, without taking anything for himself. He would leave her a virgin, and it bothered her.

'My turn,' she ordered. With her hands, she unfastened the ties of his trews, guiding them lower.

'Rhiannon—'

'You're my captive now,' she said. 'Unless you don't want

me to touch you.' Her hands moved over his bare hips, and
he let out a slow breath as she helped him out of the clothing.

'Lie down,' she commanded, straddling him. His arousal
pressed against her wetness, and in the dim light, she saw the
strain upon him as he fought for control.

Just as he'd touched her, running his hands and mouth over
her body, she did the same. She kissed his broad shoulders,
exploring his chest muscles, while against her fingertips she
felt his heart beating faster.

Between her legs, he was rigid, and when she pressed
lightly against him, he let out a dark groan. 'Show me,' she
pleaded, guiding his hand below his waist. He curled her
fingers around his shaft, showing her how to stroke him up
and down.

And as she did, it intrigued her to see the play of expres-
sions upon his face. A desperate need, a savage man who
hissed when she squeezed lightly. His eyes were closed, and
she rose up on her knees, wondering if she dared to take matters into her own hands.

She'd never been with any man before, but there was no
one she wanted more than Kaall. Beneath his fierce exte-
rior lay a lonely man, one who had been turned away from
women. She wanted him to know that *she* cared about him.
And just as he'd awakened her to sensual pleasure, she wanted
him to know the same.

With a gentle rhythm, she continued her stroking, as she
moved herself into position. His eyes were still shut, and she
didn't know if her actions would anger him.

Slowly, she guided him to her wetness, and used her body
weight to sit upon his length. Kaall's eyes flew open. 'What
have you done, Rhiannon?'

'Claimed you.' His thickness stretched against her, so tight, she felt the loss of her innocence. It was painful, but when he was fully inside her, she felt the resurgence of the quaking desire he'd given her before.

She rose up, withdrawing slightly, before sinking against him once more. His hands moved to her hips, and he guided her again, the slow rise and fall beginning to take her back into the deepening pleasure.

Then he held her firmly while he quickened the penetrations, forcing her to bounce upon him. The shallow thrusts were angled, sliding against her wetness, until she was panting and countering his motion with her own force. When she let out a cry and came apart, his hands moved up to squeeze her nipples making her surrender to him.

He rolled her beneath him, and she was breathless with relief as he ignored caution and gave in to instinct. He drove within her, over and over, while her hands dug into his hair and she met him with every grinding thrust.

She was drowning in him, in the feelings she had no name for, but when he gave a shuddering groan and emptied within her, she could do nothing but hold him close. His body was inside hers, and whether or not he'd given her a child in this act of love, she held no regrets.

He lay atop her for an endless eternity, and she never wanted him to leave. Joined together like this, she could almost believe there was hope for them.

At last, he withdrew from her body. Without a word, he moved behind her, wrapping both of them in the furs until she was cocooned in his arms.

Chapter Five

Kaall's hands drifted over Rhiannon's bare skin, and for the first time in his life, there were no words for the feeling of contentment that had taken root inside him. Never before had any woman chosen to be with him. They had seen only his lack of vision instead of the man he was.

But Rhiannon had come to him of her own free will. She'd kept her promise and discovered the whereabouts of his daughter.

'It's nearly morning,' he heard her whisper, as she pulled him down for a kiss. At the soft touch of her lips, he felt the urge to spend every morning with her. To awaken with this woman in his arms, even if he had to fight hard to prove that he deserved to have her.

A rush of need slipped within his veins, with the desire to bind her to him. He explored her body with his hands, touching her with the intent to arouse. She caught her breath and as he moved his hands over her, she guided him inside her until their bodies were joined.

'Will you go back with me to Laochre?' she asked.

The urge to refuse crept to his lips, but he silenced it. This day, his future hung in the balance. It was no longer just about

Emla, but Rhiannon as well. She'd already admitted that her
father had refused to let her marry any man. He didn't expect
Connor MacEgan to approve of a match between them, but
he was willing to fight for her. Even so, the greater question
was whether Rhiannon would consider staying with him.

'We'll go together,' he swore, and he made love to her
until she trembled in his arms, holding him tight and crying out his name.

When they rode out together an hour later, Rhiannon
slowed the mare. 'Your father is approaching with other members of your tribe.'

A familiar tension gripped him as he wondered why Vigus
would bother. Possibly because of Rhiannon.

She reached down to grasp his hands. 'We should join
them.'

He didn't want to, but he doubted if there was a choice.
If Vigus had spied them together, his father would not allow
them to pass without confronting them first.

She nudged the mare around, moving toward the others. The crisp winter wind was cool against his cheeks, and
when he leaned into Rhiannon's hair, he scented pine, like
the branches she'd hung everywhere.

It had been a gift, but her acceptance of him was the
greater prize.

When they reached the others, Rhiannon called out a greeting to Vigus. Kaall couldn't sense how many men there were,
but he listened hard for the sounds of other horses.

'I am glad to see you once more,' Rhiannon said to his
father. 'If you are travelling to Laochre Castle, might we
join you?'

'You may. The king's brother Trahern MacEgan sent word,

inviting us to join in your festivities. He believed it would be wise to make peace after what happened last year.' Vigus glanced over at the castle. 'He has been a good friend to us, especially with the kinship and relations between our two tribes.'

Rhiannon drew their horse beside the chief's. 'Why did your men attack last winter, when there was never any cause?'

'Hromund and several others took it upon themselves to act. We followed to try and stop them. Kaall was with me.'

Against his palm, Kaall felt Rhiannon's fingers squeezing his. Though his efforts had failed, resulting in the death of a MacEgan, there was nothing he could do to change it. Except try to make amends as best he could.

'I am glad to hear that there will be friendship among our people,' she said to the chief. 'And you should consider making peace with your son, after what you did to him.' With that, she drew their horse to the back of the others. 'Kaall, when we get closer, I'll have to go in alone. I can't be seen with the rest of you, or my father will know I wasn't there last night.'

'I thought you wanted to face him together,' he countered. Frustration tightened inside him, though he should have expected this. 'Or would you rather we ended what was between us?'

'I don't want it to end,' she protested, leaning her head back against him. 'But you don't understand the kind of man he is. I'd prefer it if you meet him when he isn't trying to kill you.'

'I'm not afraid of him, Rhiannon.'

'It's not that. It's just that—'

'You don't want to be seen with me,' he finished. She pulled on the reins until the horse stopped.

'Give me a chance to speak with him,' she pleaded. 'I might be able to convince him.'

He drew his hand up her arm until he found her cheek. 'It's not about him, Rhiannon. It's about you.'

Her hand covered his, but she could give no reply to his words. He didn't ask if she wanted to be with him. Her actions would give the answer.

In the end, she dismounted, retreating to go in alone.

Rhiannon hung behind the rest of the men, knowing that she'd cut a bitter blow into his pride. But if she rode in with him, her father wouldn't ask questions. He'd sooner drag Kaall from the horse and slit his throat.

As she slipped inside, she saw Arturo de Manzano staring at her. She prayed the Spaniard wouldn't speak a word, or reveal where she'd spent last night. Though he'd come to witness his sister's marriage, he'd also grown closer to Brianna.

Which meant he could reveal everything to her cousin.

She touched her finger to her lips, praying he wouldn't betray her. But it wasn't long before Brianna emerged from her home and saw the others.

As soon as the young woman spied Kaall, her face transformed into fury. She strode across the grounds with hatred in her eyes. Rhiannon had no doubt her cousin wanted vengeance for the death of her husband.

'Don't,' she pleaded, stepping into Brianna's path.

'Don't what?' the woman countered. 'Don't face the *Lochlannach* who murdered my husband?' Her words were bitter, laced with the grief of a woman who had lost the man she'd adored.

'It's not what you think.' She struggled for an explanation that would calm Brianna's fury, but could only offer, 'He came to make amends.' It wasn't exactly true, but it was the best she could come up with.

'There's nothing he could ever say or do to make amends. He killed my husband, and that, I'll never forgive.'

Despite her cousin's harsh words, Rhiannon saw the glint of tears in her eyes. Brianna wasn't thinking clearly, and the longer she could keep them apart, the more likely it was that she could help the woman understand what had truly happened.

'They didn't come here to fight.'

'Do you think I care why they came?'

Rhiannon stared at her, seeking the right words, but there was nothing that would console her. Brianna had lost her husband, and grief was dictating her actions now.

With a glance behind her, she saw that the men had gone inside, Kaall with them. For now, he would be safe enough. She squeezed her cousin's hand and left, knowing there was only one person who might change Brianna's mind.

She had disappeared among her people. Kaall remained with Vigus and the others, but Rhiannon's abrupt departure left him cold. She'd asked him to come to Laochre, but not at her side. And the longer he stayed here, the more he understood that she wasn't ready to accept him as her lover. He never should have let himself dare to hope for more.

He'd encountered a weeping lady, moments ago. After following the sound, he'd spoken to Adriana de Manzano, the bride of Liam MacEgan. Though the young woman had been embarrassed by her tears, her words had stayed with him: *Sometimes I feel I don't deserve to be with him.*

Kaall knew what that was like. Just as he knew what it was to love someone and not be loved in return. First with Lína. And now, surrounded by her people and loved ones, he fully expected that Rhiannon would turn from him, too.

He remained in place a few moments longer, and within the Great Chamber, he could smell the pine boughs Rhiannon had described. In another few days it would be Christmas, and he could imagine this place filled with people. There would be music and feasting, the aromas of food mingling with pine and beeswax. Already there was anticipation in the air, with the children running around, talking excitedly about the celebration that would come.

Kaall reached up the edge of the wall and his hand brushed against the pine needles. It reminded him of Rhiannon's decorations and the night they'd spent together. He hated feeling so damned helpless—waiting for her, instead of taking action.

A group of men passed by, talking of competitions, and Kaall joined their crowd, following their voices and footsteps outside. Though he doubted he could find Rhiannon, he wanted an escape from the closed-in walls.

It took the greatest concentration to gain a sense of where he was. The large castle was immense, with open training grounds and he scented peat fires burning from homes nearby. He found a space against one wall of the inner bailey and edged his way along the perimeter, stopping every so often to gauge where he was.

But as he neared the competitions, the noise grew so loud, it was impossible to move. He would undoubtedly stumble into people, or worse, the wall itself. Better to stay in one place, pretending to be a bystander, than to get even more disoriented than he already was.

For a time, he was able to feign indifference, in order to calm the disorder rising inside of him. He didn't want to make a fool of himself, walking around in an unfamiliar setting, but neither could he stay here for the rest of the afternoon.

Strangely, the voices around him quieted. He sensed a

shifting in the crowd, and footsteps drew closer to him. Who it was, he couldn't say. But he sensed danger.

'What do you want?' he demanded. He kept his voice steady, revealing no fear. A dagger hung at his waist, but he didn't grasp the weapon yet.

'You killed my husband a year ago,' a woman's voice accused.

He knew immediately who she was, and made no denial. Though he'd never intended to kill anyone, he wouldn't apologise for defending himself. 'I've killed many men. Especially those who attack me first.'

'You were among those who raided Laochre. When my husband attacked you, he was trying to protect me.'

Kaall didn't argue with her, nor admit the truth about what had happened. This woman was hurting, wanting answers he couldn't give. Nothing he said or did would bring back her husband.

'And you've come here to kill me now. Is that it?' He took a step closer and unsheathed his blade, offering it to her hilt-first. He chose his words as weapons, hoping his instincts were correct—that it was pain guiding her actions, not blood lust. 'Take your vengeance, if that is your will. But know this—'

Instead of a warning, words of truth came out. Words he hadn't known were at the tip of his tongue, revealing thoughts he'd believed were buried inside.

'I am already cursed and have been, since I was a child. If you kill me, it will end my suffering, granting me what I deserve.'

'Where were you last night?' Connor MacEgan demanded.

Rhiannon walked alongside her father, feeling the familiar resentment rise up. 'Why do you ask?'

'Because you keep disappearing from Laochre. A few nights ago during the storm, and last night as well. No one saw you at the solstice celebration.'

Her face warmed, but she recognised the concern in his voice. He reached for her hand, and his twisted, misshapen fingers laced with hers. Years ago, an enemy had crushed his hands, and her mother had saved Connor's life. Rhiannon had been there when the others had brought his broken body to Aileen, not knowing that the man they'd saved was her father.

Aside from his overprotective nature, she'd grown to love the fierce man with only one good hand. Never had he been less of a person, despite his loss.

It struck her that she saw Kaall with the same eyes. Aye, he lacked the ability to see. But there was so much more to him.

'I spent the night with the man I healed,' she admitted to her father. 'The one who saved me from the storm.'

His hand tightened upon hers, his expression darkening. 'Rhiannon…'

'I care about him very deeply,' she continued. 'He's one of the Hardrata *Lochlannach.*'

'Is he here now?'

She gave a nod, and her father quickened his stride, guiding her toward the centre of the castle grounds. Though he said nothing at all, he wasn't pleased by her confession. Murder brewed in his grey eyes.

Ahead, a large crowd had gathered near the competitions. Connor continued bringing her closer, and at first, she couldn't make sense of the noise.

Then she spied Arturo de Manzano running toward her cousin Brianna.

Her heart nearly stopped, when she saw the blade in the young woman's hands.

A cry tore from her mouth when Arturo unsheathed his sword and ran. Rhiannon broke free of her father, praying to God the Spaniard wouldn't strike Kaall down.

In a swift motion, Kaall seized Brianna, shielding himself with her, just as Arturo reached for them. He couldn't stop his momentum, and Rhiannon stared in horror as he stumbled into her cousin, the blade sliding within his ribs. 'Brianna, no!'

Her gaze flew to Kaall, seeing the shock and guilt upon his face. As a blind man, he'd only tried to guard himself against the attack, but the others wouldn't understand that. He would bear the blame, if Arturo died. There was nothing she could do to save him.

Her cousin stared down at Arturo, her face pale at the sight of blood. The bloody knife fell from her fingertips to the ground. To Rhiannon, she ordered, 'Find your mother. We need a healer quickly!'

Rhiannon didn't remind Brianna that *she* was a healer, too, understanding that it was her cousin's fear speaking. She reached out to try and stop the bleeding, insisting, 'It wasn't his fault. Kaall didn't do this.'

The stricken expression upon her cousin's face transformed into fury—as if she'd suddenly guessed why Rhiannon had defended him. 'How could you?'

She didn't have to say anything else for Rhiannon to understand her unspoken words. *How could you love a man who took my husband from me?* And now, Arturo had been hurt.

Whether or not anyone else knew it, Rhiannon hadn't missed the helpless pain upon Kaall's face. He hadn't meant for anyone to be harmed. And once again, by defending himself, the worst had happened.

Rhiannon straightened and revealed the truth as she helped

stop the blood flow. 'He's blind, Brianna. I promise you, he had no intention of killing Murtagh. It was an accident. A terrible one, but I can't hold him to blame for it. Kaall defended himself from a man he couldn't see.'

Rhiannon held pressure upon Arturo's wound, praying her cousin would somehow understand. 'Forgive him, I beg of you. And me.'

Brianna didn't answer her for a long time. It seemed that a year's worth of pain and resentment stretched between them as she reached out to touch Arturo's cheek. The man's dark eyes centred upon her as she whispered, 'I never meant for this to happen.'

While the woman tended to him, Rhiannon sent a runner to find her mother. Though she was a skilled healer, Aileen was better. And though this wound appeared shallow, it was perilously close to his lungs.

Whether or not he lived was out of her hands. She could only pray that Kaall would not suffer for it.

The chaos of sound blurred around him, until Kaall couldn't tell if the man had died. A coldness seized within him, knowing that he'd inadvertently harmed someone else. Rhiannon's voice had grown more distant, and the widow Brianna was pleading with the warrior to stay with her.

Around him, he heard the sound of men gathering closer. If the Spaniard died, he had no doubt that the MacEgans would hold him responsible. There was no hope of ever getting Emla back now, not if he'd caused two deaths.

And then there was Rhiannon. He'd heard her defending him, something he'd never expected. No one had ever stood up on his behalf—not even his family. They'd never seen anything beyond what their eyes revealed. Only Rhiannon had glimpsed the man beneath the surface.

He'd expected her to turn away from him. Instead, she'd dared to fight for him. And although another man had been hurt, he needed to somehow mend the breach. To give them a chance to be together.

It was a risk, but he took a step toward the women, asking, 'Will he live?'

There came no reply at first, and he feared the worst had already happened. But then the widow spoke. 'I hope so.'

Fear lined her voice, but there was still anger toward him. There was no way of knowing if he could gain forgiveness, but he dropped to one knee, in the hopes that Brianna MacEgan might come to understand.

'Rhiannon didn't mean to betray anyone. I know what I am and what I've done over the years. I deserved to lose my sight.'

'Kaall, no.' Rhiannon reached out to him, but he continued on.

'She needs to know.' If the MacEgans believed he was nothing but a murderer, there was nothing left for him. Not his daughter. Not Rhiannon.

'There was a time when I could see blurred shapes,' he admitted. 'But when I raised my spear to defend myself that day, I never saw your husband.' He bared the truth to her, even knowing that the words might not be enough. 'I can see nothing. Not even her face.'

All around him, the silence spread through the crowd. He remained on one knee, unable to know what was happening. But when Rhiannon reached out to him, he gripped her hand hard. Her quiet support meant everything.

'I believe your words,' Brianna said at last. 'Perhaps we might…talk later. I need to tend Arturo now.'

It wasn't forgiveness, but neither did she condemn him. Rhiannon guided him to stand up, and she whispered, 'Come with me. My mother will help to heal his wounds.'

'I thought you would want to go with them.'

Her hand tightened upon his. 'My father is standing there, watching. And the soldiers of Laochre are all around us. I can't leave your side.'

'I'm not afraid to face him, Rhiannon.'

'I don't want you blamed for any of this. It wasn't your fault. He needs to know that—'

Kaall cut off her words, taking her mouth in a kiss. She was afraid for him, but this was one battle he needed to fight on his own. He claimed her lips, silencing her arguments. Against them, he murmured, 'If you want me to leave you and never return, say the word, Rhiannon.'

He tasted the salt of her tears against his mouth, taking her face between his hands. It might be that this was the last moment he'd ever hold her in his arms. Her bravery was unlike anything he'd ever known. And if there was any hope at all that he might spend his life with her, he'd give up everything.

'I don't want anything to happen to you,' she whispered. 'I couldn't bear it.'

He broke away from her, and took her hand in his. 'You're worth fighting for, Rhiannon.'

When the men closed in, she was pulled away from him. The soldiers took his wrists and forced them behind his back, while he heard her cry out, 'Kaall!'

A motion in the air caught his attention, but the soldiers prevented him from dodging the blow that caught him upon the jaw.

'Tell me why I shouldn't kill you right now for touching my daughter,' came a deep voice.

He had no doubt it was Connor MacEgan speaking. Kaall turned toward the sound, meeting the man squarely. 'Because I intend to marry her, if she'll have me.'

'If you think I'll let a murderer anywhere near Rhiannon, you're mistaken.'

'I murdered no one. I defended myself, just as I would defend her if she were mine to protect.' With all of his strength, he broke free of the soldiers and faced down the MacEgan. 'I would fight for her until the last breath left my body.'

'And you think you're able to guard her? A man who cannot see?'

Every sense went on alert, and the air shifted as another blow came. He threw himself to the ground and the man's fist caught him on the shoulder instead of the face.

Rhiannon cried out, 'Da, no, please!'

But Kaall rolled away, dodging another blow. He understood that this was a test, that Connor MacEgan would never let him near his daughter if he couldn't defend himself. A hand caught his wrist, but he twisted, bending the man's arm with all his strength. Perspiration beaded upon his forehead as he held the man at bay, until MacEgan was forced to release him.

'I don't need eyes to know that you want a better man for her than me,' Kaall said, raising up his hands as he judged where the MacEgan warrior stood. 'But I'm not like the others who will cower before you.'

'She deserves better than you.'

'I won't argue that. But it's her choice to make.'

'Cease the fighting,' came another man's voice. Kaall recognised it as another of the MacEgans, their brother Trahern, who had often visited among the *Lochlannach* of Gall Tír. 'Connor, the Hardrata chief has something to say that may be of interest to you.'

Kaall halted at the mention of his father. He had no doubt that Vigus had come to intervene once more. His father had never believed him capable and could not see past his blindness. Bitterness rose up within him, but he held his silence.

'I came to speak with the king,' Vigus said, moving forward until he stood at his side. Whatever his father's intentions were, Kaall held no faith in the man. Not after all he'd done.

'For what purpose?' Connor interjected.

'Several months ago, I brought a young girl here to be fostered. I believed it was best that Emla be raised by others who could take care of her. And I had her taken away from Kaall.' His father rested his hand upon his shoulder. 'It was wrong of me, and I ask that she be given back to him.'

He'd never expected this from Vigus. Not after all the years of distrust. Though he couldn't see his father's face, the man's grip tightened upon his shoulder.

'I know the girl you speak of,' Connor said. 'And she is expected to arrive soon with Sir Ademar and Lady Katherine. All of the MacEgans and their families will be here for the Christmas celebration and for Liam's wedding afterward.'

The tightness of hope seized up within Kaall at the possibility of seeing Emla again. He wanted so badly to be with her again, to know that she was happy.

But Connor's next words stopped him cold.

'I offer you this, *Lochlannach*. If I arrange for the child to be returned to you, you will leave Rhiannon and never see her again. Your daughter…in exchange for mine.'

Chapter Six

Fury tore through Rhiannon at the thought of her father manipulating her like this. She couldn't speak, she was so angry with Connor for forcing Kaall to make such a choice. It was wrong, and she intended to stand up to him.

But then she saw Kaall's face. His emotions were cool, shielded as if he'd expected such a bargain. Rhiannon felt her own breath catch in her lungs.

Her heart was breaking apart, for she knew that no matter the hours they'd spent in each other's arms, her father had offered Kaall a bargain he couldn't refuse. How could she imagine that he would choose her over the daughter that could have been his own flesh and blood? It would never happen.

Even so, she crossed through the people until she stood before him. 'Is this what you want, Kaall?' Her voice came out in the barest whisper, even though she saw the resolve in his eyes.

'What would you have me answer, Rhiannon?'

And she knew. God help her, she knew what he would choose. But she admitted the truth.

'I want to stay with you. I would have married you,' she confessed. 'But I know the choice you have to make.' Standing on tiptoe, she pressed her mouth to his in a last kiss. Against his ear, she finished, 'I hope she brings you happiness.'

But his hand caught her wrist. 'Do you think so little of yourself?'

Startled, she gazed at him, not knowing what to say.

His hand moved to her waist, and he pulled her so close, she was in his arms. Rhiannon held him tightly, burying her face against his chest. 'If you want me, there's no man who will take you from my side. Not even him.'

She was openly weeping, unable to believe what she was hearing. Her father was staring at them, a hardened expression on his face.

Kaall bent low to her face. 'You gave me light. And taught me how to see beyond my eyes.'

Rhiannon kissed him lightly, her heart filling up with love. 'I will stay with you. No matter what anyone else says.'

She turned back to Connor and saw the resignation in his eyes. Pulling free of Kaall, she went to his side and reached for his hands. 'You were hurt, years ago.' She held his gnarled hand that had once been crushed by an enemy. 'And my mother loved you, despite what happened. She saw the warrior of strength beneath these scars.' Lifting his hand to her cheek, she held it there a moment before he embraced her.

'Could you ask any less of me?'

On the morning of their wedding, snow fell from the sky. It was just past dawn, and Rhiannon slipped from the castle, to one of the smaller dwellings where Kaall was staying with his father and the other *Lochlannach* men.

She didn't have to knock on the door, for he was already walking outside. When she approached and greeted him, his face brightened.

'I couldn't sleep,' he admitted. 'I was thinking of you and wondering if you would change your mind.'

'No. But I did come to bring you a gift.' Taking his hand, she guided it low, until he felt the grasp of a small child. Shock and joy spread over his face as he pulled Emla into a hug. The girl's small arms locked around his neck, and she chattered at him in the *Lochlannach* language, beaming with delight.

Kaall's large palm smoothed back Emla's hair, and he smiled. 'I am glad you're here, *minn skatt*.' When his fingers caught upon the crown of holly she wore, he pretended to prick his fingers and groan at the pain. Emla laughed, kissing at his fingers until he swept her up in his arms.

With his other arm, he pulled Rhiannon close. 'Thank you for bringing her to me.'

'She'll be fostered with us during the winter, and she'll return to England in the spring,' Rhiannon admitted. 'Sir Ademar and Lady Katherine agreed to share the fostering, though they didn't want to give her up.'

'I can understand that.' He lowered Emla down and kept her hand in his while he bent in to Rhiannon. 'But she can stay with them this night.'

'Were you wanting to wager with stones again?' she teased. 'Rough side or smooth?'

He brought his bristled cheek against hers and whispered, 'Rough upon smooth, *kjære*. Or both ways, if you'd rather.'

Her face burned at his wickedness, but she accepted his kiss and the promise of a night filled with love.

And when she walked at his side to celebrate their wedding day, she caught sight of Alanna. The young girl was smiling and nodding with pride.

For the love charm had worked.

* * * * *

A SEASON TO FORGIVE

Chapter One

Ireland—1192

'*L*iam MacEgan disobeyed my orders. And he deserves to die.'

King Richard spoke the words in a cold voice that revealed no mercy. He had ordered the deaths of over a thousand women and children hostages, and Liam's refusal to lift his sword against them had resulted in his captivity and torture.

'Please,' Adriana whispered. 'Spare him.' She couldn't bear to think of what her betrothed husband was suffering at this moment.

But the king's smile held the promise of death. He reached out and cupped her cheek, and his touch made her stomach twist with fear. Richard had been faithful to his queen for a time, but his attentions had already wandered. When the king's hand drifted down her throat in a caress, Adriana suppressed the shudder of revulsion.

'Then what would you do to save him?'

Adriana de Manzano awakened in the darkness, her body shaking with remembered fear. God help her, the horrifying vision never ceased to plague her. She closed her eyes, trying hard to silence it.

She slid out from her bed, the stones freezing against her feet as she tiptoed to the hallway outside. It was still the middle of the night, but she needed a moment to collect her thoughts and calm herself. The other women in her chamber continued to sleep, undisturbed by her departure.

The door to Liam's chamber swung open, and in the dim light, she saw him approach. His handsome face was stoic, his grey eyes furrowed with concern. 'The same dream?'

She nodded, feeling guilty that she'd awakened him. Or perhaps it was his own dreams that had bothered him. Ever since they'd fled the Holy Land, they'd made an unspoken vow not to speak of that time. His scars were visible upon his skin, the physical manifestation of the tortures he'd suffered.

Hers lay within, buried so deep, she didn't want him to ever know them.

Liam reached out to take her in his arms. 'You've been having these dreams more and more often.'

'They're just dreams.' But she held him so tightly, she wanted him to silence the nightmares, to help her forget them. Her hands moved up to touch his dark gold hair, that had been cut short to better fit within an iron helm on the battlefield.

'I wish your parents would arrive soon,' he said, leading her down the hallway toward the stairs. 'Then you'd be my bride and I'd sleep beside you. If the dreams returned, I would give you comfort.'

She managed a half-smile, and when Liam reached the stone steps, he sat and pulled her on to his lap. With his hands, he massaged the coldness from her feet.

While he touched her, she buried her face against his chest. He was alive and strong, and never would she reveal to him what had happened in the Holy Land. It was best forgotten, and she would find a way to leave the past where it belonged.

Liam need never know the terrible price she'd paid for his life.

Ever since he'd returned to Laochre, Liam couldn't dismiss the feeling of being out of place. Though he ought to be relieved to be back in Éireann, it was impossible to release the tension he'd carried over the past year. He'd grown accustomed to sleeping with a weapon in his hands, slaughtering the enemy, and fighting to take command of Acre. There'd been so much blood and death, it seemed impossible to return to a peaceful life.

Last night, his own nightmares had plagued him, just as Adriana had been unable to sleep. Like him, she had witnessed the bloodshed during this Crusade—though she wouldn't speak of it. But the shadow of pain was there, and they understood one another.

She'd comforted him on their long journey from Acre and was always there when he'd needed her. But he had not yet shared her bed. On the few times he'd touched her, she'd shied away from him, and he hadn't wanted to pressure her. There would be time enough for that, after they wed.

Liam walked outside in the frigid winter air, his footsteps crunching in the early morning snow. He found Adriana on the training field with her brother and his cousin Brianna. Her long dark hair was bound back from her face, her cheeks flushed from the cold. Her olive skin contrasted against the blue *brat* she'd lifted to cover her head in the winter chill. Her features were exotic, like a rare blossom amid the paler skin of the women he'd known.

Any man who saw her would believe her to be innocent

and fragile…until she lifted a dagger to his throat. As the queen's former lady-in-waiting and personal guard, Adriana could defend herself from nearly any threat.

And she'd just stolen her brother's blade. When she saw Liam watching her, she smiled and returned the dagger to Arturo, before she came over to join him.

'I thought you might like to walk with me this morn,' Liam offered. 'Or we could ride together down to the coast.'

She nodded and bade them farewell, taking Liam's hand. They walked toward the gates, and he asked, 'Were you teaching Brianna how to fight?'

'She wanted to learn how to defend herself. But I suspect my brother was using it as a means of getting to know her better.' A wry smile came over her face. 'It wouldn't surprise me if he found someone to marry while we're here. He's been lonely for many years.' She cast a glance behind her. 'Once he's set his sights upon something, he'll never stop until he's won it.'

'As long as he treats our women well, no one would mind. But if he hurts anyone, he'll return to Navarre missing a few limbs.'

'Arturo loves women,' she countered. 'It's more likely they would pursue him.'

Liam shrugged. 'Even so, he'd best keep a respectful distance.' Though he spoke the words in teasing, they were the truth. If Arturo wanted to court Brianna, Liam saw no harm in it. But if he broke her heart, there were many who would rise up to defend the young woman's honour.

They had nearly reached the gates, when he saw his father approaching. Liam stopped to wait, and from the grim look on King Patrick's face, something was amiss.

'What is it?'

His father pointed outside the gates. 'Early this morning, my men reported the presence of a ship off the coast. It's too soon for it to be Adriana's family, and it wasn't a fishing vessel. It had the look of a Venetian ship.'

Liam exchanged a look with Adriana. King Richard had granted them leave to return home, months ago. They had travelled inland for several months until they'd met with Arturo off the coast of Navarre and sailed the remaining distance. There was no reason for a ship to follow them—not all the way to Éireann. Unless he'd somehow offended King Richard. 'Could it be merchants, come to trade with us?'

Patrick's expression held wariness. 'I doubt it. We haven't faced invaders in many years, but it's possible. The ship was too large to go unnoticed.'

'Adriana and I could ride out to the coast and look,' he offered.

'Not alone. Take a group of my men with you.' His father's expression turned grim. 'I wasn't much older than you are now when invaders killed my oldest brother.'

His implication, that the same fate could happen again, wasn't lost on Liam. But his father had left out the words that had divided them: *And I became king because of it.*

For the past three years, his father had insisted that he attend every gathering of soldiers, every discussion that involved Laochre Castle. Liam had trained among the best fighters, and all eyes looked to him to become the future king when Patrick stepped down.

It weighed deeply upon his father, for there were no other sons or daughters to assume that role. Though Liam knew it was expected of him, his father had earned the love of the people. During the first invasion, Patrick had united the Norman forces with the Irish, until now the two were blended and intermarried as one people. Taking his father's place would be an impossible feat.

'One ship is hardly an invasion,' he said, dismissing his father's fears. 'There's no reason to make that assumption.'

Doubts clouded his father's face. 'Making assumptions is why we're still alive instead of driven out by the Normans. I'd rather anticipate the worst than presume it's not a threat. When you become king, you'll understand.'

And there it was. The argument that continued to rise between them, year after year.

'I've no wish to become king.'

'All your life you were trained for this,' Patrick countered. 'You have the strength and the intelligence for the role.'

'But not the desire.' Liam met his father's gaze, standing firm in his resolution. 'It's why I left on Crusade. You never listened to what I wanted. Only what you believed was right.'

'That isn't true.'

'Isn't it?' He could tell the conversation was making Adriana uncomfortable, and he threaded his fingers with hers in silent reassurance.

His father expelled a sigh. 'One day I won't be strong enough to lead them any more. I want to pass the throne to you before I die, so that I can advise you when necessary.'

'They will never accept me as king, so long as you're alive,' he pointed out. And whether or not his father would admit it, it was true.

'There is time to discuss this later,' Adriana interrupted. 'Why don't we go and see if the ship is still there?'

Her soft tone was enough to temper his father's anger. 'You are right, Lady Adriana. Perhaps you'll talk some wisdom into my son. If you'll wait here, I'll send soldiers to follow.'

Liam said nothing while the king returned to the inner

bailey. There was nothing he could say that would ever convince Patrick of the truth. While he considered himself to be an adequate fighter, he wasn't among the best. And how could he hope to lead men against their enemies if his skills weren't the strongest?

As if sensing his unrest, Adriana suggested, 'Why don't we go on ahead and ride slowly until they catch up to us?'

He agreed, and when their horses were ready, he lifted her on to her mount before he swung up to his own stallion. Frustration and discontent darkened his mood, and he walked the horses down the hillside.

'He loves you, Liam,' Adriana said, when they were alone, 'and only wants what is best for you.'

'I'd rather live among the others as an ordinary man,' he said, drawing his horse alongside hers. 'It doesn't matter what my birthright is. And if you were wanting to be a queen—'

'I want to be your wife, not a queen,' she corrected. Her mouth tightened at his remark, a sudden coolness surrounding her demeanour.

'I wasn't implying that you agreed to marry me only for my rank.' He reached up to her cheek and drew his hands down in a soft caress by way of apology. Though Adriana remained motionless, her expression shifted as if she'd wanted to turn away from him. 'I'm sorry.'

She took his hand, pulling it away from her face. Though she held it a moment, he could see the apprehension shadowing her.

Liam studied her more carefully. 'Were you able to go back to sleep after your bad dreams last night?'

'Not really. I'm sorry for my mood, *mi corazon*. I'm just tired.' Her dark eyes held warm affection as she squeezed his fingers.

Her nightmares had grown more frequent, and she'd refused to talk of them. But then, Adriana wasn't the sort of woman to weep or reveal her emotions. He admired her strength, but at times, it was difficult to know what she was feeling inside.

Without letting him press the issue, she urged her horse forward, leaving him to follow. When they reached the open field, she broke free and took the animal into a hard gallop. Her *brat* broke free and fell to her shoulders, leaving her dark hair to blow in the wind.

Liam increased the tempo of his own mount, riding hard while the bitter wind cut into his clothes. It wasn't safe to ride so fast, but Adriana didn't seem to care. She continued on for several minutes until finally she pulled the mare back to a canter and finally into a walk.

He caught up to her and drew her mount to stop. 'That was dangerous. Your horse could have slipped in the snow.'

Her breathing had quickened, and her cheeks were crimson from the cool air. Running her hands over her horse's neck, there was a flicker of remorse in her expression. 'You're right, I know. I just wanted a moment to escape.'

Escape from what? Liam frowned at that and dismounted from his own horse before helping her down. When Adriana tried to move away from him, he held her trapped for a moment. Her dark brown eyes held an echo of his own haunted feelings. 'Tell me.'

She shook her head, staring at the field behind him. This time, he refused to let it go. He held her waist, leaning in. 'Should I have taken you back to Navarre instead of bringing you here?'

'No. We're going to live here, so it was the better choice. But I was glad my brother joined us on the journey.'

He took her lips in a soft kiss, trying to give her comfort. She returned it, pressing herself close to him. But even as she welcomed his embrace, he couldn't let go of the unease. She refused to trust in him, and he didn't know what that meant. Or what it boded for their future.

The ship wasn't there. Although they rode along the coast, there was no longer any sign of the vessel. Though it meant nothing, Adriana breathed a sigh of relief to know that no one had pursued them. She wouldn't put it past Richard to demand Irish reinforcements to join the Crusade. The thought of returning to Acre made her shudder. Never again.

When they were certain that there was no threat to Laochre, the soldiers returned, while Liam stayed behind with her. The morning sun gleamed across the snow, glittering like diamonds.

She lifted a handful of the snow, but it fell from her fingers like grains of sand.

'It wouldn't be good for balls of snow, if that's what you were thinking,' Liam teased. Even so, he picked up a handful and moved in closer. 'But I know another use for it.'

She saw the wickedness in his eyes and scooped her own handful as a precaution. 'What do you mean?'

'If I drop it down your back, the warmth of your skin will melt it,' he murmured. 'Then you'd have to take off your wet clothes.'

'You're coming nowhere near me with that,' she warned, backing away. But Liam paid her no heed, and she was forced to run through the snow, picking up her heavy skirts.

'You've been too melancholy, Adriana,' he said, advancing closer. The predatory gleam in his eyes was that of a man who wanted to play.

'And you think dropping snow down my gown will put me in a friendlier mood?' she demanded, holding back her smile.

'It would be fun. Or if you get cold, I'll have a reason to warm you.'

From the devilish look on his face, she knew he could easily outrun her. They were too far away from the horses, leaving her with only one strategy.

Without warning, she ran toward him, throwing her body weight against him. Her surprise attack worked and he lost his balance, tumbling back into the snow.

'And now you're the one who's wet,' she teased.

The white wetness stuck to his hair and neck, and his expression turned fierce. 'Not for long, *a stór.*' He pinioned her wrists and rolled over until the freezing snow lay beneath her. Adriana gasped against the cold, but Liam held her fast, his warm body atop hers.

His mouth hovered upon her lips, withholding the kiss she was anticipating. Against the juncture of her thighs, she felt the ridge of his arousal. It was a natural response, but one that frightened her. She tried to force the irrational fears away, for never would he do anything to harm her. He loved her and wanted her as a future husband would.

The snow dampened the wool of her cloak, but she held herself steady. For so long she'd avoided Liam, terrified of him touching her more intimately. But perhaps…if she let him closer, he might drive away the nightmares. Perhaps she needed to face the fear in order to overcome it.

She reached up to him, guiding his mouth to hers. His kiss was familiar, and it evoked restlessness within her. She gave in to the heat and longing, opening to him.

But as his tongue slid against her, the old panicked feelings began to surface, of being held down against her will.

Liam lowered his mouth to her chin, kissing a path down her throat. 'Adriana,' he whispered, 'I love you.' He freed her wrists, guiding them up around his neck. 'Will you let me show you?'

She didn't know what he meant by that, but his hands moved to the laces of her gown. She remained motionless, not saying yes…but not refusing him, either.

They were alone, far away from the castle, but out in the open, anyone could come and see them. It added an edge of danger, and she saw the intensity in his eyes as he loosened her gown, drawing it over one shoulder. He kissed the bared skin, and she shivered at the cold of the snow contrasting against the warmth of his mouth. 'What are you doing, Liam?'

He cradled her with one arm, reaching the other hand across her throat, lower, beneath the neckline of her gown. 'I want to touch you, Adriana,' he murmured in a low voice, 'there, if you'll allow it.'

To show her what he meant, he slid his hand beneath the wool, finding the silk of her shift. Warm hands covered the curve of her breast, and she closed her eyes against the dark fears returning. As his hand caressed her, she felt the answering ache between her legs.

The urge to tell him no, to push him back, was at her lips. All she had to do was speak her desire, and he would stop. He would, without question.

But she hated to deny him this, when he'd kept the boundaries between them for so long. As her intended husband, he had the right to worship her body, and she knew he was trying to kindle her desire.

He bared her breast, and the nipple tightened in the frigid air before his mouth came down upon it. His tongue swirled across the tight bud, and she couldn't stop the cry of shock that came from her mouth.

'Am I hurting you?' he whispered upon her skin.

'No.' She gripped his head with both hands, torn between the burgeoning sensations and the dark memories that ripped through her. Of being trapped, forced to endure a man's touch that she didn't want. Knowing that she'd betrayed the man she loved with all her soul.

She didn't deserve to be Liam's wife. Though she'd tried to justify her actions, he would never understand if he learned the truth. Emotions swelled up inside her, but she pushed them back. She'd earned every nightmare, and no matter how this man might love her, her guilty sins were an acid eating away at her conscience.

'I want to be inside you, Adriana,' he said, moving his hips against hers so that she felt his arousal intimately. 'But only when you're ready.' His hands moved lower, toward the hem of her skirt, and this time, she stopped him.

'Not here,' she murmured.

His expression was torturous, but he drew her bodice higher. 'I know you're right.' He kissed her again as he helped her up. 'It wasn't wise of me to start this.'

She took a breath, brushing off the powdery snow. 'I do love you, *mi vida*,' she said.

Deep inside, she pushed away the darkness, refusing to let it haunt her. Liam was her future now, and she wanted to be his wife in every way. Even if it meant facing her worst fear of all.

'Tomorrow night, upon the solstice,' she promised. 'Find a way for us to be alone.' The gauntlet was dropped, and she would somehow drive away the demons with the man she loved.

She had to.

One day later

The night of *Meán Geimhridh* was crisp and cool. Although many had risen at dawn to mark the beginning of the winter solstice, most of the MacEgans preferred to use the long night for their own celebration.

Liam walked amid friendly faces, accepting the greetings with his own smile. But inwardly, he was eager to be with Adriana. After all the months they'd spent together, he'd already begun to think of her as his wife. Though her parents would come to negotiate the terms of the betrothal, it was inevitable that they would marry. She would live with him and in time, they would have children of their own.

He craved a normal life, one without the responsibilities of being a king. When he glanced up at his father's castle, in so many ways the stone walls felt like a prison awaiting him. Upon his skin, the ridged scars prickled at the memory of the last time he'd led a dozen men into battle.

Every last one of them had died, and he'd been the only survivor. He couldn't help but wonder, if he'd made different decisions, would they have lived?

If he led MacEgans into a raid here, the same might happen. Only this time, he'd have to live with the grief of their widows, knowing that he was to blame for their deaths.

No, he wanted no part of the kingship.

As he entered the Great Chamber, the noise of music, storytelling, and conversation wove around him. Adriana stood near the dais with her brother, while many of his uncles and aunts gathered around. Platters of fish and roasted fowl filled the air with mouthwatering scents, but every thought fled when he caught a glimpse of his bride.

She wore a gown of blue silk, a colour that contrasted

against her dark hair and olive skin. A sapphire pendant nestled in the hollow of her throat, hanging from a string of pearls. She stood beside her brother, and though she held herself with confidence, he could see beneath her façade to the nervousness beneath it.

He hoped it was only her uncertainty around strangers and not her fear of the coming night. Now that they were home, he longed to hold her in his arms at night, to soothe her nightmares until she finally felt safe again.

Liam crossed through the crowd of people, plucking a sprig of white berries from a garland of greenery. 'You look beautiful,' he greeted Adriana, leaning in to kiss her cheek. Her brother nodded a greeting and wisely departed to leave them alone. 'Are you enjoying yourself?'

'I've never seen so many people in one place,' she admitted. 'It's overwhelming.'

'I've a gift for you.' He pressed the berries into her palm.

'Mistletoe?' she queried.

'In case you need a reason to kiss me.'

He almost got a laugh from her at that, but her brown eyes held merriment. 'Do you think I'll need a reason?'

'It's possible. It's always a good idea to be prepared.'

She took the mistletoe and tucked it into her hair, leaning forward to kiss him. Liam then led her up the stairs to sit beside his mother, Isabel. Although she gave them both a warm smile, he noticed that the queen was picking at her food, and her face held a wan quality he hadn't seen before.

'Are you feeling all right?' he asked.

'You needn't worry,' Isabel answered. 'I've been tired over the past few weeks, that's all.'

But when Liam glanced across at his father, there was a

new worry lurking behind the king's eyes. Something else was wrong, though Patrick hadn't spoken of it.

The festivities continued and after they ate, Liam led Adriana over to listen to Trahern telling stories. His uncle was taller than his other brothers, nearly a giant among them. But he was a gifted bard, and he lifted his youngest son upon his knee as he wove a tale about a brave knight.

'The evil spirits clouded his judgement,' Trahern said, 'and he could not see that those he loved were trying to protect him. He picked up an enchanted sword and raised it against his own blood.'

'Did he kill them?' the young boy asked, his eyes wide.

'He nearly slew his own beloved wife. But with her voice, she spoke to him, reminding him of her love. She wove her own spell and broke through his darkness. The sword fell from his hands and disappeared into a wisp of smoke.' Trahern reached down to take his wife's hand, smiling at her. 'The enchantment was broken, and they lived and grew old together.'

'Just as we will,' Liam whispered, squeezing Adriana's hand. But instead of returning his smile, her expression held uncertainty. He dismissed it, telling himself that it was only the exhaustion haunting her and not a fear of their life together.

As the celebration continued, it was time for the women's competition. His aunts took Adriana among them, but Liam noticed the absence of his mother. Isabel sat beside Patrick, and though she normally would have participated with the others, it was the first time he'd seen her refuse.

He was so distracted by it, he didn't notice the women pairing off. Each would fight an opponent for the right to choose

one of the men. And before long, he saw Adriana in front of
a fair-haired woman. She glanced at her adversary, as if uncertain of what to do.

Liam hid his smile. He knew, full well, what she was up
to. Adriana would hide her skill in an effort to find the other
woman's weakness. And just as he'd predicted, when the
woman tried to grab Adriana, she avoided her, lifting her
skirts slightly. The young woman grinned, winking at Adriana's brother. No doubt she believed the win would come
easily.

But when she dived at Adriana, his bride seized the woman's hair and jerked it back, taking command of the fight. She
stood there, her expression calm as she used her strength to
hold her opponent helpless.

'She's good,' Ewan remarked, moving closer. 'I like her.'

'So do I. And it's good that you're already married, Uncle.'

The older man grinned, crossing his arms. 'Honora would
kill any woman who dared to look my way. I suspect your
bride would do the same.'

Liam didn't answer, for he was concentrating on the fight.
The fair-haired woman was struggling hard to free herself, but
Adriana pinned her to the ground while the others cheered.
At last she was declared the winner, and she rose with the
calmness of a lady instead of a fighter.

Although another fight began, Liam only had eyes for his
bride. He'd promised to find a way for them to be alone…
and tonight, he wanted no one but Adriana.

She sent him a tentative smile, raising her arms around his
neck to mark him as her choice. Liam claimed her mouth in
a kiss while around them, the others shouted their approval.

He took her hand in his, while inwardly, he was nervous
about the approaching night. He'd touched women before, but

never had he made love to one. Adriana's decision to be with him tonight was one that had surprised him. But he wasn't about to turn her away, not as badly as he wanted her. There were still ways to make it appear that she was a virgin upon their wedding night.

He led her up the winding stone staircase to the chamber he'd shared with the other men. When he closed the door behind them, Adriana eyed the space. 'Will they return?'

'I bribed them to find beds elsewhere.' And the men hadn't minded, for they had hoped to be with their own women this night. His bride sent him a faltering smile, but there was nothing but fear upon her face.

'Are you certain you want to do this?' he asked her with concern.

No. No, she wasn't at all ready to lie with him. But it was the only way Adriana could think of to permanently seal away the past. She didn't at all want to ruin their wedding night by panicking. If there was any way at all to overcome her fears, she would do it.

'*Sí,*' she whispered, offering an assent she didn't truly feel. Inside, her heart was bruised and burdened with guilt over what she'd done in the past. But he need never know it.

Without a hearth in this room, it was cold. There was a stone oil lamp in one corner offering a little light, but most of the room was darkened in shadows. The wind rattled against the shutters, and Adriana moved forward to adjust them. Outside, she glimpsed the softly falling snow. Liam came up behind her, wrapping his arms around her shoulders. Against her ear lobe, he murmured, 'I'll make you happy, Adriana. I promise you that.'

'You already do.'

His hands moved down to her waist, while he kissed the side of her throat. Adriana closed the shutters and then leaned back against Liam, allowing him to touch her as he wanted to.

He turned her to kiss him, and she surrendered to the familiar embrace, trying to still the rapid beating of her heart. But when his kiss deepened, his tongue sliding inside her mouth, she felt herself freezing up. It was as if she were standing outside herself, a shell of a woman with no ability to feel anything.

Liam led her to the single bed within the room. He removed his tunic, and in the dim light of the oil lamp, she saw the scars lining his back. Though she'd seen them before, it still hurt to look at them.

'I want you to lie down first,' she bade him, rising to her feet. 'Let me touch you.'

It was easier this way, for she was not at all afraid of showing him her love. Adriana guided him to rest on his stomach, and she sat beside him on the narrow bed, her hands moving to his neck. She massaged the tension, moving down to his shoulders. Though it had been over a year since his torture, the scars were still red, angry ridges that covered his back.

'Am I hurting you?'

'No.' He lay motionless as she touched the healed wounds, replacing her fingers with her mouth to kiss him. With each touch of her lips, it was a plea for forgiveness, to somehow let go of the guilt and find her own redemption.

'Te amo,' she whispered. For she did love him, no matter what had happened.

Liam turned at that, and sat up. In his grey eyes, she saw the primal need. 'Your turn.'

He stood and she acquiesced, allowing him to unlace her gown. Adriana's breath caught as he lowered it down her shoulders, then her shift, until she lay bared from the waist up. She lay upon the coverlet, hiding her breasts from view, but when his hands moved to her back, she bit her lip against his sensual touch.

Gather your wits, she ordered herself. Liam was only trying to do the same for her that she'd done for him. As his hands caressed her skin, he kissed her shoulders, his mouth travelling down her spine.

'I want you like nothing I've ever wanted this badly in my life,' he admitted. He turned her to the side, his body pressed against her back. When his palm covered her bare breast, she inhaled a gasp. Immediately, her mind filled up with the horrors of that night. Of being forced against her will, of a man touching her in a way she didn't want him to. All to save Liam's life.

You had no choice, her conscience reminded her. She prayed that was true. Every memory of that terrible night burned within her.

When his fingers plucked her nipple, drawing out sensations of arousal, her body tightened with fear. Her eyes filled up with tears, but she tried to steady her feelings.

It had been so dark that night, so many months ago. She hadn't seen the king's face, for he'd come to her in the shadowed tent. There had been another man there, possibly a guard or a witness.

The shame broke through her, and oh, God, she didn't want to remember this. Her eyes blurred, and the more Liam touched her with love, the more she hated herself. Inside, she was suffocating, not gaining any pleasure at all from the man she cared about.

She needed him to finish it, and she would simply endure it. Holding back the tears, she rolled to her back. 'Come inside me,' she whispered.

Instead, he stopped and demanded, 'Adriana, look into my eyes.'

She took long, slow breaths until she was able to do so without crying. Though she was exposed to him, he no longer touched her. Instead, there was an expression she'd never seen before in his eyes.

Suspicion.

'That's not the sort of man I am, Adriana. You know this.'

Through glassy eyes, she took another breath and tried to smile. He bent down, taking her into his arms until her breasts were pressed against his chest. 'Do you think I don't see your fear?'

His hands came to her face, and at his kindness, she couldn't stop the tears from escaping. A sob broke forth, and she drew her knees in, unable to face him.

Though he tried to comfort her, she broke free of his arms and stood up. Unable to speak, she fumbled with her clothes, trying to dress herself again. 'I'm sorry. I thought I could, but—'

He grew quiet as he helped her draw the laces tight. 'It's all right. We'll wait.'

She reached out to him, burying her face against his chest while he held her. For a long time, he said nothing at all, merely stroking her hair back.

But she could feel his qualms rising. And there were no words to dispel them.

Chapter Two

Early the next morning, Liam walked alone in the castle grounds. The faintness of smoke clung to the air, while men and women slept within their homes. He didn't doubt that for many of the couples, new children would be born next autumn.

But not for himself or Adriana. He'd thought about it all last night, unable to sleep. She'd asked him to arrange the time alone, only to start crying when he'd touched her as a lover would. It had startled him when she'd asked him to take her, as if he were nothing but an animal with no concern at all for her pleasure.

As if she'd not wanted to feel any sort of desire.

It made little sense at all. He paced across the training ground, needing the physical exertion to take his mind off the sense that something was wrong. Had he done something to hurt her without meaning to?

At the far end of the inner bailey, he spied his Uncle Trahern and his wife, Morren, approaching. The pair of them were smiling at one another, while Morren held their sleeping four-year-old son in her arms.

The fist of longing gripped him in the heart, for this was

the way he wanted it to be with Adriana. The two of them, sharing the joy of being together as a family.

Trahern greeted him with a warm smile. 'It's early, Liam. Shouldn't you be with your bride?'

He didn't know how to respond to that, but gave a shrug. Trahern kissed his wife and whispered to her a moment before Morren departed with their son. 'Come and walk with me, lad.'

Though he hadn't been a lad in many years, Liam followed his uncle. 'You're looking restless, as if you want to spar. Am I right?'

'I wouldn't mind it.' He faced off against the older man and drew his sword. Though Trahern's height towered over him by a full head, the man's Viking heritage was to blame for it. His uncle circled him slowly, eyeing him with interest.

'Did you learn anything in the Holy Land? I've heard the Saracens are strong fighters.'

'So they are. I was lucky to come home alive.'

'And we were glad of it as well. Your mother especially.' Trahern thrust the weapon toward him, and Liam parried it with a strong block. 'But war changes you, doesn't it?'

He could only nod, swinging his sword as Trahern raised his own weapon in defence. The months he'd spent in the Holy Land had not been like anything he'd expected. 'It was like fighting within fire,' he admitted. 'The sand would sting my eyes, and the heat burned my armour. Even with the padding, the metal burned all of us.'

'And what of your lady? What brought her on Crusade?'

'Adriana was Queen Berengaria's lady-in-waiting, as well as her guard. She followed where the queen went.'

'And the queen is still there?'

Liam shook his head, his sword striking hard against

Trahern's. 'She journeyed home by way of Rome. Richard planned to join her later, but Adriana stayed behind for me.'

This time when Trahern counter-attacked, Liam struggled against the blows that rained against his shield and sword. 'That must have been hard on her.'

'It was.' Without meaning to, his worries spilled out. 'She's been behaving strangely since we left. Whenever I touch her, she flinches.'

Trahern lowered his sword and sheathed it. He cast a glance toward his wife, Morren, who was now on the far side of the castle grounds, near the stairs leading to the Great Chamber. 'Does she seem afraid of your touch?'

Liam returned his own weapon to his scabbard and nodded. 'She tries to hide it, but aye. It's as if she can't bear it.'

Trahern's gaze turned troubled. 'If it would be of help, I could have Morren speak with her. Sometimes one woman can help another.'

'Morren has never faced battles like those we saw in the Crusades,' Liam admitted. 'Even the children were slaughtered.' His mouth tightened at the memory. 'What sort of king would kill innocents?' Liam's gaze settled upon the young boy Morren was holding on her hip. 'Could you raise your sword against another man's son?'

'No.'

He let out a breath. 'And neither could I. Richard had me imprisoned for disobeying orders.' He continued along his uncle's side, and Trahern rested a hand on his shoulder. 'After I was released from chains, we were allowed to go. I never understood why.'

'You're home now, Liam. And your father needs you more than ever. Especially, now that Isabel—'

Trahern's words broke off as if he realised what he'd been

about to reveal. Liam stopped walking. 'Now that my mother is what?'

'Nothing. Patrick will tell you, when the time is right.'

He didn't like the sound of that. His mother, though younger than their father, hadn't looked well recently. Was she sick or suffering in some way?

'In the meantime, I'll have Morren speak with Adriana. It may help.' The expression on Trahern's face held sympathy, and though Liam doubted it would do any good, he supposed there was no harm in it.

'All right.' He followed his uncle back toward the Great Chamber, but his uncle spied a group of visiting *Lochlannach* from Gall Tír. Trahern apologised and went to greet them, stopping first to voice a few words to his wife. Liam thought about following his uncle but decided to go in search of Adriana instead.

Last night, she had returned to her own chamber after their disastrous time together. She'd been so miserable, and he couldn't help but think he'd caused it by daring to push too hard. He wished he'd never laid a hand upon her, for it had created an invisible rift between them.

Trahern's question, about whether she was afraid of his touch, weighed upon him. For it was true. Somehow, in the past few months, Adriana had come to fear being touched. That, coupled with her nightmares, began to dig into his consciousness. Had she been hurt somehow? He couldn't think of any moment when she'd been left alone to fend for herself. She'd always been surrounded by the queen's guards.

But the possibility was there. And the more he thought of it, the more he realised how little she trusted him.

Adriana sat upon the stairs, leaning against the cold stone wall. It was early, but she'd been unable to sleep at all after she'd retreated to her own room. She'd mistakenly believed that last night she could end her fears by giving herself to the man she loved.

The fears had conquered her after all. Liam's sympathy and promise to wait only made her feel worse. For she'd realised, last night, that she could not hide the truth from him—she was no longer a virgin. He would learn of it, and once he did, he could refuse to wed her. This betrothal was one of their own making—not one negotiated by her parents. It could still be broken before the documents were formally signed.

The thought of returning to Navarre without him broke her heart. It was something she could never endure, and if it meant fighting past her fear to keep him, she'd do anything.

She wept, releasing the terror of losing Liam, along with the pain she'd hidden from him. Though she tried to keep her sobs quiet, footsteps approached and she saw a tall man standing before her. She hadn't seen him before, but despite his blond hair and blue eyes, his facial features didn't resemble Liam or any of the others.

'I'm sorry.' She wiped her eyes and stood. 'I'll move out of your way.'

'I wasn't intending to go above stairs,' he said. 'I heard you crying.'

Her face grew crimson as she wondered who else had heard her self-indulgent weeping. 'Forgive me,' she apologised as she took a step down. 'It's nothing.'

She wanted to move past him, but the man refused to move. Even more disconcerting, his gaze centred above her, as if he weren't looking at her face.

'You're not one of the MacEgans,' he guessed.

Neither was he, from the faint accent within his voice. She couldn't quite place its origin. 'Not yet,' she answered.

'But I hope to marry Liam MacEgan. My name is Adriana de Manzano.'

She continued down the stairs until she stood before him. This time, he shifted his gaze to her face. 'I am Kaall Hardrata.'

A Norseman, then. She'd heard that many of them dwelled nearby, after their ancestors had traded and settled here.

She started to move past him, and he added, 'Is he that terrible, the man you intend to marry?'

'No. He's wonderful. And far too good for me.' She didn't know why she'd told him that, but it was the truth she held deep inside.

'I know what that feels like.'

In his words, she heard the echo of her own heartbreak. She couldn't say what drew her back to him, but she returned to stand before Kaall. 'What happened?'

'The woman I wanted refused to wed me.'

In him, she saw a glimpse of herself. Wasn't that what she feared most? That Liam wouldn't love her any more, if the truth ever came out?

But if he turned her away, knowing the price she'd paid, it meant that his love for her was hollow, held by boundaries of pride. And that wasn't love at all, was it?

'I'm sorry for it.' Without knowing why, she touched his arm for a brief moment, offering her own sympathy. 'If she didn't love you enough, then you're better off without her.'

Kaall crossed his arms and leaned back against the wall. 'Does Liam love you?'

'Yes.' Her voice came out in a whisper, and she added, 'Sometimes I feel I don't deserve to be with him.'

'If he loves you, it doesn't matter.'

She wanted to believe that. Even so, she didn't know if she had the courage to shatter whatever love he felt for her.

'I hope you're right.'

Liam found Adriana standing near the hearth at the far side of the Great Chamber. She still wore the gown from last night, but her dark hair was tangled down her back. From her profile, he could see swollen eyes, as if she'd been weeping.

The urge to avoid her came over him. She would be embarrassed by what had happened, and he didn't want to see her unhappiness. But it wasn't right to turn from the woman he wanted to marry. He needed to talk with her and understand her fear.

Taking a deep breath, Liam crossed the room. Adriana glanced behind her, and he knew she was aware of his presence. He stood at her back while the fire sent up sparks into the cool morning air. 'We need to talk.'

She remained silent, her arms crossed over her chest as she continued to stare at the fire. 'I can only say that I'm sorry.'

He moved beside her, hoping she would say more, but she held in the words, giving him nothing. The terrible question hung between them, and though he didn't want to voice it, he needed the truth. 'Did someone hurt you in Acre?'

'No.' Her response came too quickly, and she tightened her arms around her shoulders. 'Not that.'

'Come with me, away from here,' he commanded. 'We don't need to have this conversation around others.'

He didn't wait for her to protest, but took her hand and led her away. She was clearly reluctant, but eventually she relented to his bidding. He ordered horses for them, and guided Adriana outside the gate.

They rode away from Laochre, through the snowy meadow

and toward the coast line. His breath formed clouds in the chilled air, and when they were far away from everyone else, he turned to face her.

'I know something happened in Acre. You're not the same as you were in Cyprus.'

'None of us is.' She wouldn't meet his gaze, but stared off into the distance. 'I hated the Crusade. So much death…and all for a king's glory.'

'He let us go,' Liam reminded her. At the sudden flicker of unrest upon her face, he prompted, 'You know why, don't you?'

'I asked it of him,' she whispered. 'He granted my request.'

'After I was imprisoned and tortured?' Liam countered. 'Why would the king let us go when I disobeyed his commands?'

Her face went white, and he suspected he was finally getting closer to the truth. 'Look at me,' he demanded. 'I know there's more you haven't told me.'

The anguish upon her face only confirmed it, but her dark eyes stared into his. 'I don't want to speak of that time again. It's in the past, and we're here now.'

'But it burdens you,' he pressed.

'It haunts my sleep,' she shot back. 'I close my eyes and I see those women dead. I see their babies, slaughtered like animals.'

'What happened that made you fear being touched?'

'Nothing. It was a terrible time for both of us, and it's best forgotten.'

Was it the truth? Or a lie of omission? She'd cast her gaze downward, and he tilted her chin to face him. Her eyes were brimming with tears, and God help him, he didn't know what to think now. He'd brought her here, thousands of miles away, to a place where she knew no one, save her brother.

Then he voiced the question preying upon his conscience. 'Do you still want to marry me?'

Her answer was to embrace him hard. 'Yes. Yes, I do. You shouldn't even ask such a thing.'

Though he brought his arms around her to return the embrace, he sensed the silent barrier between them growing stronger. He knew her too well, and she was clearly withholding secrets from him.

His gaze moved toward the water, and as the mist lifted, Liam saw the faint outline of a ship like the one his father had spoken of. It was indeed a Mediterranean vessel, and the possibility that they had been followed from the Holy Land, now seemed a reality. But why?

Without alerting Adriana, Liam guided her back to her horse, intending to bring a group of men to sail out later.

When they arrived back at Laochre, Adriana was shocked to find out that her brother had been wounded during a skirmish with Kaall Hardrata, the Norseman she'd spoken with earlier. It seemed that the man was blind, and had been defending himself when Arturo had been caught between them.

She hurried into the castle and up the stairs where the healer Aileen had brought him. Liam shadowed her, but an icy fear gripped her heart. Arturo was not only her brother—he was also her friend. She was closer to him than anyone. He couldn't die. Not when he'd come all this way to escort her to her marriage.

Inside the chamber, her brother was lying upon the bed while three women worked to cleanse and stitch his wound.

Adriana couldn't see more than a bloody linen cloth upon his side, and she feared the worst.

'Will he be all right? How did this happen?' she blurted out.

'The wound wasn't deep,' Aileen reassured her. 'It's possible that he will be fine. But there is the risk of a fever.'

Before she could say another word, Brianna MacEgan interrupted. 'I'll stay with him.'

It was the woman her brother had been courting. Brianna took Arturo's hand, lifting it to her cheek. 'He was wounded because of me. He thought I was in danger.' Terror and regret filled up her voice, as if she couldn't believe it had happened.

'It wasn't your fault,' the healer's daughter interjected. 'It was an accident.'

Adriana lifted her gaze to Liam. He stood on the far side of the room, offering his quiet support. But she couldn't forget that he'd questioned whether or not she wanted to marry him. Was that how it had seemed? Had she made him believe that she didn't love him?

The healer stood from Arturo's side and said, 'He needs rest and time for the wound to heal. I believe Brianna should stay with him alone. The care of a woman can often bring a man back from the edge of death.' She blended wine with herbs, explaining, 'This will help him to sleep.' After she poured a cup and set it near Arturo's side, she rose and went to the door. Then she signalled for the others to leave.

Adriana had no intention of going anywhere, but Brianna promised, 'You have my word. I won't leave his side until he's healed.'

'I should be the one—'

'No.' Brianna cut off her words. 'I care about him, too.'

She didn't like the idea of leaving her brother's side, but

Arturo stirred at the sound of their voices. 'Brianna should stay.' At her doubtful look, he added, 'I've had worse injuries, Adriana.'

In other words, he'd rather be tended by the woman he was courting instead of his sister. She leaned down to kiss his forehead. 'I will keep you in my prayers.'

He squeezed her hand and she moved across the room toward the door. After she departed the chamber, she sensed a tension in Liam's demeanor. He took her hand and led her down the stairs to the Great Chamber. 'I'm going out for a few hours, but I'll be back before nightfall,' he told her.

'Where are you going?'

'I saw the ship my father spoke of.'

She didn't like that idea at all. 'Liam, no. Your father's guards can—'

'They'd only attract attention.' He cut her off, gripping her hand as he continued across the room. 'I just want to find out who they are and why they're here.'

'And if it is an invasion?'

'Then we'll know how many men they have and how well armed they are.' He pulled her into a darkened corner. 'I won't be seen, Adriana. I'll find out what we need to know and return to you.'

'Don't go alone,' she pleaded. Though Liam was good at remaining hidden, she hated the thought of the danger he might face. 'At least take a few men with you.'

'And get them killed the way I did the others on Crusade?' Vehemence lined his face, and she could say nothing to convince him that it wasn't his fault. He wouldn't believe it.

'There's no reason for you to go,' she said. 'Someone else could find out why—'

'I want to go.' He cut her off, and the impatient look in

his eyes bothered her. 'I've the need to spend a few hours away from here.'

Her throat closed off, for she suspected that he wanted time away from her. The darkening anger on his face and the frustration inside him were visible. And though Adriana had considered revealing everything to him, she retreated, fearing the worst of his rage. Now was not the time.

'I need you to be safe,' she whispered.

His grey eyes bore into hers, as if waiting for her to say more. He pressed her back into the shadows, seizing her mouth with his. In his kiss, she tasted the frustration and bitterness. Though it might have been a kiss of farewell, there was nothing gentle about it. And when he pulled back, she felt bruised, too afraid to ask why he'd been so rough.

'I'll return at nightfall' was all he said, not looking back at her.

There was no choice but to quietly alert his father and follow him with their own forces. Adriana wasn't about to let him be harmed, despite his claims that he would face no danger.

Liam left his horse behind and walked west, taking the coastal path down toward the strand. The sky was clouded, and much of the snow had melted, leaving patches of mottled green on the hills. He wanted time to be alone with his thoughts. Smaller fishing boats were anchored on the wooden pier the men had built, along the narrow channel that led toward an island fortress nearby. He intended to take one of the vessels and get closer to the ship he'd seen.

Adriana had cautioned him against going alone, but he didn't believe the ship had come for trading. Not from the look of it. And it was far easier to get in closer without others shadowing him. He could pose as a fisherman, and if there was no threat, likely the ship would ignore his presence. Sometimes, when the water was still, voices could be heard across the sea.

He gathered a few nets and pushed one of the boats out into the frigid water. Drawing a hood to obscure his features, he rowed out into the open sea. The water was grey and opaque, and he adjusted the mainsail until it caught the wind and drew him further into the waves. When he was still within visible distance of the shore, he dropped anchor, waiting to see if he could glimpse the ship once again. He shielded his eyes against the afternoon sun, trying to gauge where it might have gone.

Then, he spied it. The vessel was anchored beyond the island, west of Laochre. It was as large as any of Richard's ships, but Liam saw nothing to identify it. Drawing up his anchor, he sailed closer, casting out one of the nets. When he was as close as he dared to go, he anchored again, pulling up the net. He pretended to busy himself with choosing bait fish from within the net, but he heard voices shouting in a language he'd only heard among the Crusaders.

'MacEgan!' one of them shouted. He raised his head and saw a man standing at the prow. It was Frederic von Hohengrau, an emissary between Duke Leopold and King Richard. Liam had once believed Hohengrau to be a friend…until he'd caught the man eyeing Adriana with a hungry gaze. Though she'd been unaware of it, Liam had taken care to ensure that the two of them never met. He hadn't liked the man's blatant interest and had ended their acquaintance. It made him wonder why Hohengrau had come this far.

Liam finished untangling the net of fish, and unsheathed his sword beneath his cloak. In time, Hohengrau's men lowered a smaller boat into the water, and they rowed the man closer. When he was within a few feet of Liam's boat, a thin smile spread over Hohengrau's face.

'You have saved us a great deal of trouble, my friend. I was hoping to find you.' Hohengrau stretched out a hand, silently inviting him to board the small boat.

Liam ignored it, keeping his palm upon the hidden sword. 'What do you want from me?'

'A conversation.' He gestured again toward his vessel. 'We can discuss our business aboard my ship or back at your father's castle. And if your wife is there—'

'Whatever you have to say can be said without Adriana.' He didn't want her anywhere near the man.

'I presume you married her on your journey,' Hohengrau said smoothly, while one of his men boarded Liam's boat. 'Is she with child already?'

He had no time to answer that before Hohengrau's man attacked. Liam swung his sword, but three more men climbed aboard his ship, one moving behind him. He knocked one overboard, and his sword struck out at another. Though he tried to use the net to entangle their footing, there were too many against him.

Adriana had been right. He never should have come alone. That was his last thought before a vicious pain exploded in his head, and darkness closed over him.

Adriana tried to speak with the king, but the queen had taken ill, and Patrick refused to leave her side. With her brother wounded, she had no choice but to seek help from one of the other brothers. She recognised Trahern, the bard who had told stories the night before, but before she could say a word, he approached with his wife. The woman's long fair hair was tied back into a single tail, while her eyes were a deep blue.

'Liam and I spoke this morning,' Trahern said. 'He thought you would like to meet my wife, Morren. You might need a friend, since you've only just arrived.'

Morren offered a quiet smile, but there was something in her expression that held sympathy, almost an understanding. It disconcerted Adriana, as if the woman could see within her to the secrets that lay beneath.

'I would like that,' Adriana replied, 'but I came to ask for your help as well.' She explained what Liam had done, and the Irishman seemed to understand her concern. He glanced outside at the afternoon sun and agreed to help.

'I'll gather my brothers and we'll go after him,' he promised.

'He'll be angry with me,' Adriana warned. 'He asked to go alone because he didn't want to draw attention to himself or cause anyone to be hurt.'

'His pride might be wounded, but if it saves his neck, it will be worth it.' Trahern leaned in and kissed his wife, before adding to Adriana, 'You're not to follow us. Swear it.'

She hesitated, but offered, 'If he's brought safely home, I won't follow.' It wasn't a full promise, but it was all Adriana would give him.

Trahern nodded to both of them before hurrying to find his other brothers. After he'd gone, Morren offered, 'How are your skills with a needle?'

'Not as good as my knife skills, but they'll do.'

The woman smiled and said, 'Come, then. We can talk and if you've any mending, you can bring it along. Or I've some clothes belonging to Iain that need to be sewn.'

'Forgive me, but I don't know if I can sew just now.' Not

with Liam gone. Her mind kept forming images of him in danger.

'Keeping your hands busy will take your mind off your troubles,' Morren said.

That much was true. 'For an hour, then,' she agreed, following the woman inside and up the stone staircase.

Morren brought her into the solar and sent away the other women who were already there. A fire had died down to bright coals, but the chamber still held a slight chill. Adriana rubbed her arms, wondering why the woman had wanted them to be alone.

'I'd prefer not to speak in front of them,' she said, answering the unspoken question as she closed the door behind the others. For a moment, she lowered her gaze, as if searching for the right words. Adriana chose a chair beside the hearth, uncertain what this was about.

'Liam spoke to my husband a day ago, about what you both endured in the Crusade. He said you've been having nightmares about it. Trahern asked me to share with you my own story, in case it might lend you comfort.'

A coldness slid within Adriana. Liam knew nothing of her secret, but from the look in Morren's eyes, this woman seemed to suspect something.

'Years ago, a group of Norsemen attacked my home,' she began. 'I was caught in their battle, as was my younger sister.' She walked forward until she stood beside Adriana, facing the fire as she continued. 'They tried to…force themselves upon her. And she was hardly more than thirteen.'

In the woman's eyes, Adriana saw a mirror of her own pain. Morren's words were quiet, but in them, there was a strength. 'I refused to let them harm her.'

'You fought them?' Even as she spoke the question, she suspected the answer Morren would give.

'No. I gave myself in her place. I let them do to me as they wished, so I could save her life.' She turned her eyes to Adriana. 'And I would do it again, if I had to.'

A tightness stretched within her heart, the pain rising up. She said nothing, but her cheeks were wet with tears. Morren reached out and touched her hand. 'For a long time, I couldn't bear to be near any men at all. The smallest touch made me think of what was done to me. I lived in the shadow of my pain and every time I closed my eyes, I saw their faces.'

She knew. Adriana didn't know how, but Morren had guessed what had happened to her.

'When Trahern came into my life, he taught me how to love. How not to be afraid. But I had to trust him.'

The dark edge of guilt pushed past her shield until Adriana couldn't hold back any longer. Though she spoke not a word, her tears revealed the truth she couldn't say.

Morren knelt beside her and took her hand. 'Nothing said within these walls will pass beyond them. I only wanted to offer you my friendship and a listening ear, should you need one.'

'Liam doesn't know,' she heard herself saying. 'He can't ever know.'

'He won't love you any less.' Morren stroked her hair, the way a mother would. 'I've seen the way he looks at you. You belong together.'

Adriana took a deep breath, hoping she wasn't making a mistake by admitting the truth to Morren. 'They were torturing Liam, and I knew he would die unless I begged for mercy.' She stared into the young woman's face and saw no accusations, nothing but acceptance.

'I let the king…do as he wanted, so he would spare Liam's life.' She lowered her gaze, her skin prickling with remembered fear. For a time she waited for Morren to speak, but the silence only rested between them with understanding.

'It was terrible,' Adriana continued. 'And although the king promised to spare Liam and let us both go, I felt such shame, I wanted to die.'

Her eyes were dry now, the tears gone. 'Liam doesn't know why we were allowed to leave Acre, or why he was pardoned. But if I hadn't made that choice, he would be dead. I know the king wanted to kill him as an example.'

'You saved him.' Morren touched her shoulder, her words holding reassurance.

'By betraying him,' Adriana finished. 'I don't think he would forgive me if he learned of it.'

'You need to tell him. He needs to understand what you endured.'

'I'm afraid he'll turn away from me. That he won't want to have me as his wife.' She covered her burning cheeks with both hands. 'I can live with my decision if he still loves me.'

'It will come between you in the marriage bed,' Morren predicted. 'He won't understand why you're afraid, and he'll blame himself for your unhappiness.'

Adriana's lips tightened, for she knew it was true. Likely it was the reason he'd talked with his uncle.

'I don't know if I can,' she confided in Morren.

'It would be easier now than later. Show him your trust by revealing it to him. He's stronger than you think.' A maternal smile came over the woman's face. 'Even if he can't kill the king on your behalf.'

'I'll think about it,' she said at last. It surprised her that she did feel better after talking with Morren. It was clear that, although the woman had suffered, she shared a deep love with her husband and she'd made peace with her past.

But Adriana still wondered if Liam would ever be able to accept her as his wife, if he learned what she'd done to save him.

When nightfall came, her mood shifted to worry. Trahern had gone with all four of his brothers, and none had returned. After Adriana stopped to see how her brother was recovering, she joined the other women. From the grim looks on their faces, there was no news to share.

Queen Isabel stood by the window while the other women talked among themselves. From her stricken expression, Adriana worried about the older woman. 'Are you all right?' she asked quietly.

The woman shook her head. 'It's never easy, watching them go off to fight. Especially now.'

Whether or not it was right to do so, Adriana took the queen's hand in hers. 'They'll return. I'm certain of it.'

Isabel squeezed her hand. 'I hope so. Patrick and I recently learned that I'm expecting another child in the early summer.'

'That's wonderful,' Adriana responded with a smile.

'It might be, if I were ten years younger.' Isabel kept her hand in her grasp and took her back to the others. 'For so long, Liam has been my only son. But the years passed, and I never had another. We had always believed there would be more children.'

'And so there will be. It's a blessing,' Adriana reassured her.

'If we both live, it will be.' The queen frowned and sat among the others. 'I never thought there would come a day when I would not desire a pregnancy. But it's too difficult, as old as I am. I'm afraid of this birth, more than any other.'

The healer Aileen cut her off. 'Enough of this talk. You're alive now, and so is the babe growing inside you. It will do you no good to worry over it.'

'I've borne one child already, Aileen. I remember how hard it was the first time, twenty years ago.'

'Every birth is different. And the more you dwell upon it, the worse it will be.'

Isabel came to sit with them, her hands clasped against her middle where Adriana now noticed a slight swelling. 'I just don't want to leave Patrick,' she whispered. 'If the worst happens, I don't know what he would do. Liam has refused to assume the throne, and my nephews are too young.'

The women's eyes suddenly turned to her, and Adriana felt the invisible pressure. 'Liam has to make that choice, not I. I'll stand by him, whatever he decides.' Although the women seemed to accept her words, she understood the queen's fears. But when Adriana joined the others in sewing and conversation, one woman in particular was pacing.

She recognised her as Ewan's wife, Honora, a woman who was accustomed to fighting, like herself. Quietly, she approached her and asked, 'Should we go after the men?'

Honora took her toward a corner of the room, keeping her voice low. 'It's doing no good keeping vigil in the solar, is it? I'll go with you, if you want to find them.'

She gave a slight nod. 'Liam went to the coast, to investigate a ship he saw. That's all I know.'

Honora eyed the others and said, 'Isabel won't approve of us leaving.'

'And I don't approve of waiting around to find out if our

men are dead,' Adriana countered. 'I've been in battle before. I know how to remain unseen.'

'You can't wear that.' Honora glanced at her bright blue gown, and Adriana nodded her agreement.

'I have some clothing I wore in the Holy Land that would be more appropriate for riding.'

'Good. But we'll have to wait for dawn. It's only another few hours, and we'll have a better chance of finding them. I'll meet you at the stables, just before first light.'

Honora returned to the other women, claiming that she intended to join her children and go to sleep for the night. Isabel embraced her, but her gaze fell upon Adriana, as if she'd overheard their plans. Keeping her expression veiled, Adriana made her own excuses.

After she returned to her room, she opened her trunk and reached to the bottom. As soon as she touched the sand-coloured gown, she began to wish she'd burned the garment. For she remembered, too well, the last time she'd worn it. Her hands shook, the memories crashing over her until she let it drop to the floor. Her maid asked tentatively, 'Shall I help you, my lady?'

Adriana nodded, and forced herself to pick up the gown. 'I'll wear this tonight when I sleep.'

Confusion marred the woman's face, but she obeyed, helping Adriana pull it over her head. The linen lay against her body like a hair shirt, abrading her conscience.

'I'll be going out at dawn, and I'd rather not awaken anyone,' Adriana explained.

'It is no trouble to help you dress, Lady Adriana.'

'Not this time.' She stood still while her maid laced up the hated garment. When it was done, Adriana gathered up two daggers and laid them atop the chest where she could arm herself in the morning. Though she knew not what dangers she would face, it was necessary to have the weapons close at hand.

When she lay within the bed, a coldness drifted through her. She closed her eyes, feeling the familiar guilt tearing at her courage. The familiar nightmare returned, and upon the hated gown, she sensed the scent of a man. Not Liam.

Morren's claim, that she needed to tell him the truth, weighed upon her. And there, in the darkness, she made her own bargain with God. *Let me find him. Let him be alive, and if he is, I will reveal everything.*

Even if it meant losing him.

Liam tasted blood in his mouth. His hands were bound behind his back, and his head throbbed with pain. When he opened his eyes, his vision sharpened upon the face of Frederic von Hohengrau. The man was impeccably dressed in chainmail armour trimmed with gold, and his voice held a smug air. 'I thought we could have our conversation now.'

'Why am I bound?' Liam demanded.

'To ensure your full cooperation.' The man crossed his arms and regarded him. 'King Richard has gone missing since he departed Corfu. His Grace, Duke Leopold, is searching for him, and I've come on his behalf.'

Liam stared at the man, not understanding what he was implying. 'I left the Holy Land this past spring. I don't know where the king is.'

'But you were close to Richard,' he countered. 'You knew his plans and where he intended to go.'

Liam said nothing, for it wasn't all true. His friendship with the king had deteriorated since last autumn, until they had rarely spoken to one another any more. Even Adriana had appeared eager to avoid Lionheart, and they'd travelled inland from the Holy Land until they'd reached Italy, where they'd hired a ship and crew.

'If you've come all this way in search of the king, you've journeyed for nothing,' Liam said. 'You should have searched in France or in England.'

'Some of the duke's men *are* in France. Others have gone to England,' the man said calmly. 'But there is another reason that brought me here.'

When Liam said nothing, Hohengrau's mouth curved into a smirk. 'Aren't you going to ask me?'

Why should I, when you're going to tell me anyway? Liam thought.

'Perhaps I'll ask your pretty bride about Richard. She was close to the king in a way you never were.'

The slur against Adriana sent a flare of rage through him. Liam struggled with his ropes, wishing he could wrap the cord around the man's throat. 'You won't go near her.'

Hohengrau crossed his arms, steadying himself as the boat dipped against a wave. 'I'll send my men to fetch her. And we'll see what she knows.'

Chapter Three

They rode along the coast while the grey sky held a dark purple tint, revealing the coming dawn. Adriana remained close to Honora, praying she knew where she was going. The miles passed, and the ground was soaked from melted snow. When the light emerged over the horizon, a heavy mist cloaked the land, making it impossible to see very far in front of them. Once they reached the narrow channel, Honora pulled her horse to a stop. 'We'll have to go by boat across the water.'

Adriana eyed the rough tide, uncertain if it was wise to continue. 'Are you certain they've not gone by land?'

Honora shook her head. 'The tracks of their horses are there. And there's a torch that one of them dropped.' She pointed toward the water where Adriana could barely make out a fallen branch. 'Do you want to continue?'

Adriana drew her cloak tighter, half-afraid of what they would find. But she didn't want to remain behind, not when there was a possible threat toward the men. 'I don't see a choice.'

'If we're outnumbered, we'll go back for help,' Honora reassured her. 'I've no intention of dying.'

The two of them arranged to leave the horses with a fisherman and borrowed his boat to go out on the channel. As they worked together to row, Honora offered, 'I saw you fight the other night, on the solstice. You were stronger than I thought you'd be.' Her green eyes held approval, and she added, 'In that gown, no one would ever have guessed your skill.'

'My brother taught me to fight,' she admitted. 'I was the queen's guard for a time.'

'Then you won't be afraid to do what's necessary if the men need us.' Honora rested the oar on her lap, glancing around.

'No.'

The words gave her a honed focus, and suddenly it was no longer about her own fears or questioning what might have happened to Liam. It was simply the knowledge that she would do anything for him. She loved him enough to put her own life in danger, and the clarity gave her a sense of peace. 'We're going to find them and bring them home,' she told Honora and meant it.

'Aye, we will. You've an advantage I don't have. You can make a man believe that you're helpless.' A wry smile crossed her face. 'I can't say that most men would say the same for me.'

Adriana eyed Honora, noting her closely cropped dark hair and her lean arms. She moved like a warrior, though she was ten years older with children of her own. 'Any woman can disguise herself well enough.'

'Some better than others. Are you armed?'

'*Sí.*' Adriana showed her the blade at her waist and patted her upper thigh where she'd sheathed another dagger. 'And you?'

Honora revealed her own arsenal of hidden blades, along with a thin sword that she'd strapped to her back beneath the long cloak.

'Will your husband be angry that we've gone after them?'

'Oh, aye. Ewan doesn't mind my fighting, except when it endangers me. But neither of our men will care, once we've rescued them and taken them to our beds.' Her mouth curved into a smile. 'Ewan wants another child.'

Adriana didn't share her smile, for she'd never experienced anything but pain within a man's bed. And it was possible that Liam might spurn her, once she'd told him everything.

They continued rowing along the shore, until they spied movement atop one of the hills.

'It's our men,' Honora said. 'And look there.' She pointed to a large ship anchored in the harbor. The shape resembled some of the Mediterranean ships Adriana had seen, and from the size of it, the boat was meant for longer voyages. At least a dozen oars hung from both sides and the mainsail was tied up. In the morning mist, it had an otherworldly appearance, like a ship born from legends.

'We should join the men,' Adriana said. 'Perhaps they've found Liam.' Even as she spoke the words, she didn't believe them. If Liam were safe, they would have returned last night.

Honora helped her row toward the shoreline, where they stepped into the frigid water and hauled the boat ashore. The morning air was laced with the portent of more snow, and as they trudged up the hillside, the woman's steps slowed.

'What is it?'

'I've been thinking,' Honora said. 'Our men could use us as a decoy. Especially you, with the way you look. If we go together, we could be the distraction they need.' She studied Adriana, as if judging her worth. 'Unless you're afraid the foreigners might harm us.'

The idea of approaching a ship filled with strange men was enough to make her want to run the other direction.

'We'll talk to our men first,' she bargained. And, God willing, they would have another idea.

Liam's body ached, from where Hohengrau's men had beaten him, but he doubted if they'd cracked any ribs. Worse than the physical punishment were the threats Hohengrau had voiced against Adriana. His insinuation, that something had happened between her and the king, was undoubtedly a lie.

As the hours wore on, the man's words began to haunt him: *She was close to the king in a way you never were.*

What did he mean by that? Adriana had been the queen's lady, and on the rare occasion she was in Richard's company, she'd been with Berengaria.

Yet, her behaviour had transformed in the past few months since they'd left the Holy Land. She'd gone from a confident, strong woman…to one who drew back when he touched her.

Suspicion swelled within him like venom, filling him with suspicion. Had Richard hurt Adriana, after Berengaria had left? She could have been at the king's mercy without his knowledge. And if it were true, there was nothing he could do. He couldn't murder a king.

Liam tried to force the idle thoughts away, but there was enough evidence to weave a web of lies. The frustration and uncertainty fuelled his desire to escape, and he continued working against the ropes, trying to loosen them.

Until he heard female voices calling out.

In the darkness below the ship, he could see nothing. But he heard Honora's voice, and Adriana was with her. He heard the lilt of her Spanish accent as she spoke in low tones to Hohengrau.

Beneath the words, he heard her fear, the slight tremor in

her voice. And when someone lifted up the door to the hold, sunlight blinded him.

Adriana descended first, and when she saw him, she covered her mouth with one hand. 'Liam,' she breathed. 'Are you all right?'

'I've had better days.' But when she moved toward him, Hohengrau gripped her arm.

'Do you remember me, Lady Adriana?'

'N-no.' But there was enough confusion in her voice to make him wonder. The man stood back, crossing his arms as he regarded her.

'I was among Duke Leopold's men. I spoke with the king on many occasions. Surely you saw me.' The man's ego suggested that it was impossible for Adriana not to be aware of his presence. But from the blank look on his bride's face, she'd not recognised Hohengrau.

'There were many men who attended the king,' she said. 'I remained with Berengaria.'

'But you spent time in the king's presence,' he said smoothly.

'Only with the queen—'

'I am speaking of the time after she departed,' he interrupted. His gaze turned discerning, and Liam didn't like the way Hohengrau continued to stare at Adriana.

'I was there on the night you went to plead for MacEgan's life,' he said.

Liam frowned, for he'd not known Adriana had gone to Richard. Her face had gone white, and she took a step backward.

'Why have you come?' she demanded.

'Duke Leopold sent our ship, as well as many others, in search of the king. He will be held accountable for the murder of Leopold's cousin Conrad.'

'So you've said,' Liam interrupted. 'But as I told you, he's not here. You've no reason to hold me captive or to threaten my bride.'

'I would never threaten the Lady Adriana,' Hohengrau said. 'But I fear she has lied to you, MacEgan. Though she might deny it, she does know me. As I know her.'

In the Austrian's tone, Liam heard desire and interest. Jealousy ripped through him when he saw the man draw his fingers over Adriana's skin.

'I've never seen you before,' Adriana insisted. She started to move toward Liam, but Hohengrau grasped her arm.

'Your beauty fascinated the king,' he said silkily, 'and enchanted him.' He cupped her chin, and Liam saw his bride's hand move to the blade at her waist. No doubt it was not only the king who had been captivated by Adriana. From Hohengrau's tone, he'd developed an obsession with Adriana. There was a trace of madness in his voice.

'I must continue my search for the king,' the man said with an apologetic tone, 'but I had to stop in Ireland first.'

His hand slipped around her waist, and in one motion, Adriana unsheathed a blade and lifted it to his throat. 'You'll continue your journey without us.'

Hohenberg seized her wrists and twisted one until Adriana cried out. He slammed her against the back wall of the ship, and a curse tore from Liam's mouth. 'Leave her be. She's done nothing to you.'

'She's the reason I came this far, MacEgan. And I intend to take her back with me.'

Bile rose up in Adriana's throat. Her skin crawled as if a thousand insects were covering her. This man's scent was familiar to her, a choking odour that reminded her of the night she'd been violated.

'You didn't tell him what happened, did you, Adriana?' Hohengrau murmured. 'He doesn't know.'

She couldn't speak, for terror had seized her tongue, cutting off her air. No, she'd never seen this man's face before. But his touch…his scent…had filled up her nightmares.

'It was dark that night, wasn't it, Adriana?' Hohengrau said. 'You came to Richard, begging for him to spare Liam. He kept that promise, didn't he?'

Her teeth had begun to chatter, her body growing ice cold. *Oh God, oh God. Please, no.* Never in a thousand years had she suspected this.

And from Liam's silence, he was listening to every word.

It had been dark that night…and she'd known there was another man there to witness her shame. All this time, she'd believed it was one of Richard's guards. She'd believed it was the king who had demanded her favour that night.

Could it have been someone else? She'd never seen the face of the man who had stolen her innocence. She'd kept her eyes closed the entire time, trying to forget what was happening to her.

'It was against my will,' Adriana whispered, her mouth dry. 'I asked the king to grant Liam mercy, nothing more.'

The gleam in Hohengrau's eyes grew possessive. 'You gave yourself that night, didn't you? You came to his chamber, and you lay within his bed. Your virginity…for MacEgan's life.'

The words wove a spell of anguish over her. 'I—I never wanted—'

'You waited for him there and offered your body.' He cut her off, laying every truth bare. The tears were choking her, for she could feel Liam's hatred rising in the stillness. If he'd argued back or voiced his own protest, she might have a glimmer of hope. Instead, his lack of a response made her fear the worst—that he would blame her for the choice she'd made.

And she would lose him.

'It was not Richard who took you that night,' the man confessed. 'It was not he who claimed your sweet gift.'

His hand moved down to her breast, and revulsion flooded through her. Adriana reached for the blade strapped against her leg, slowly, so as not to attract his attention. 'He gave you to me as a reward. And he watched us that night.'

She unsheathed the blade, needing to avenge what this man had stolen from her. Denial caught in her throat, but when she raised up the blade, Hohengrau anticipated her impulsive move. He shoved her down, and Adriana struck her head against a barrel. Dizziness roared through her, but she managed to press her only weapon into Liam's bound hands. Before she could do anything more, two men seized her and dragged her above the stairs.

'Whether MacEgan lives or dies is in your hands, Lady,' Hohengrau stated. 'Give yourself over to me, and I'll let him go.'

His words were nothing but a crippling lie. But worse, was the knowledge that he'd destroyed whatever happiness she'd found with Liam. Her betrothed husband had not spoken a single word, and the silence was damning.

All she could do was murmur, 'I'm sorry.'

Liam gripped the knife Adriana had given him. Though he used it to free himself, a raw pain had hollowed him out inside. He might not have believed the lies, were it not for Adriana's apology.

The revelation cut through him worse than any tortures

he'd suffered in the past. He didn't know what to do now. A part of him wanted to kill Hohengrau, to eviscerate the man for daring to hurt the woman he loved.

Or had he harmed her? He'd claimed that Adriana had offered herself willingly to the king, intending to share his bed.

Only to be violated by a different man. The thought of her suffering beneath Hohengrau's hands, renewed his resolution. He would take the man's life, avenging Adriana.

But afterward…he didn't know.

Her lies of omission might have been to spare him. But now that he looked back on the moments they'd shared, he recalled the fleeting guilt, the unintentional flinches. The ghost of another man had come between them, haunting her.

And he didn't know if he could forgive her for it. Why had she made such a bargain with the king? Did she truly believe Richard intended to execute him?

It was possible. The king's rage at his disobedience had been terrible, and Richard had ordered a punishment that would have killed a lesser man.

But then, it had stopped. Without warning, Liam had been chained in the dark, his wounds left to bleed. The next morning, they'd released him, with no explanation.

Was it because of Adriana? Had she gone to the king and been led to believe that it was Richard who had claimed her? His mind tormented him with images of her being forced, of her weeping after it was done.

Or worse, her willingness. Of her surrendering to another man's touch. The rage sliced through him like a razor. She'd spoken not a word of it. Likely, she would never have told him. He gripped the blade in his palm, edging his way up the stairs.

'Not yet,' whispered another voice. It was Honora Mac-Egan.

Liam jerked around but could see no one. 'Where are you?'

Honora emerged from the darkness, admitting she'd hidden herself behind Adriana, in order to slip inside the hold. 'If you go now, you'll ruin all she's done to save you. Your brothers have the ship surrounded. Adriana is the distraction.'

'It sounds as if she was more than that to him.'

Honora softened her tone. 'She loves you, Liam. It was she who went to Trahern and asked him to gather the others. She would do anything for you.'

A harsh lump formed in his throat. Anything. God above, he wished it had been anything but that.

'And now she intends to sacrifice herself again.' The vitriolic fury undermined any sense of calm he might have had.

Honora's hand reached for his in the darkness. 'You can rage all you want when we're finished rescuing you. But save your anger for the one who truly deserves it.' She revealed the position of his uncles and their plan to take control of the ship. Though it would work, the danger was undeniable.

Footsteps approached, and Liam retreated, motioning for Honora to stay hidden.

When the trap door lifted, he was thankful for the darkness that kept the men from discovering that he'd freed himself from the ropes. Two men grabbed him by the shoulders and dragged him. Outside, the sun's brightness kept him from seeing clearly, but Liam thought he spied a fishing boat nearby.

'Your family, I presume?' Hohengrau nodded toward them. After Liam's eyes adjusted to the light, he saw three different boats surrounding them on all sides. Relief came over him, but he knew there were only moments before his uncles closed in.

'Unless you want to die off these shores, I'd suggest you release us.' Liam kept his back to the men, awaiting his father's signal. There were at least a dozen crew members manning the ship, and he took note of their positions. In his mind, the voices of doubt reminded him that the odds were not in his favour. He wasn't the strongest fighter here, and if he made a mistake, their lives were at stake.

But at the sight of Adriana held by Hohengrau, a coldness froze out all of his apprehensions. He felt dead inside, as if someone had emptied all of the emotions from his heart. If she had admitted the truth to him before this, they could have faced it together. But she'd meant to hide it from him. He didn't know if a strong marriage could be salvaged if she didn't trust him.

'Liam!' she shouted, pointing to the side.

He threw himself to the deck, while an arrow embedded in the wood where he'd been standing.

'A warning, MacEgan,' Hohengrau said quietly. 'You might have loosened your ropes, but the next arrow won't miss.'

'Don't hurt him,' Adriana pleaded.

Was that what she believed? That he had to hide behind her pleas for mercy instead of fighting his own battles? Did she think he was that weak? He regarded her with coldness. 'Would you rather stay with him?'

Her dark eyes held misery, filling up with tears. 'I need you to live, Liam. Please.'

'That wasn't what I asked.' He rose slowly, fully aware of the arrows aimed at him. 'Is he your choice?'

A single tear rolled down her cheek, but she shook her head. 'It was always you.'

Hohengrau crossed to the others, pulling Adriana to him. 'The king gave you to me, with his blessing. He witnessed the consummation.' To Liam he added, 'Before the eyes of God, she belongs to me.'

His words provoked a furious response from Adriana. When he reached for her, she snatched a dagger from one of the other men. The blade flashed in the sunlight as she aimed for Hohengrau's neck.

But the Austrian had predicted her response once again, and he spun, using his strength to overpower her. The blade rested at her own throat, and she flinched, a red line appearing against her delicate skin.

'It's time for you to go, MacEgan,' Hohengrau said. 'You may dive from this ship and take your chances with the sea. Or my men will shoot you in the heart. Either way, she stays with me.'

Adriana sent a glance toward the water, as if pleading for him to go. Liam raised a hand toward his father's ship, giving them the signal. He took one step forward. Then another, until he stood at the edge of the boat.

In her eyes, he saw the belief in his failure. Her eyes held goodbye and surrender to a life she didn't want.

'Go,' she whispered.

It broke Adriana's heart to see him standing there, poised to leave. She didn't understand why Hohengrau would go to these lengths for her, after she'd given herself to him for only the one night.

'Why?' she demanded of the Austrian. 'I never wanted you. I didn't even know it was you that night. Why would you come this far for me?'

'Because women don't refuse me.' He lowered the knife, drawing his arm across her throat. 'Any woman I desired could have shared my bed. And yet you ran away afterward.' His thumb grazed her jaw, sending a shiver of revulsion through her. 'You disappeared with MacEgan, as if I meant nothing to you.' Though she could not see his face, the idle caress tightened, like a man bent upon owning her. 'You chose an Irishman over me.'

'I love him.'

'In time, you will come to love me,' he said, returning the tip of the knife to the underside of her chin. 'And you'll learn to obey my wishes.'

The hunger for power and dominance underscored his words. Already she began to understand the truth. He didn't care what happened to Liam. This man's vanity bordered on madness.

'Did you truly come in search of King Richard?'

'I did. But first, I came in search of you.' His blade slid against her skin a whisper of pain. 'Admit that you made a mistake in coming here. Admit the truth…that you enjoyed the night in my bed. That you dreamed of me.'

'You were my nightmare,' she spat.

She saw Honora emerge from below, and she prayed the woman would make it to safety with Liam. But when she looked back, he was no longer standing there. He must have gone already, just before Honora.

A fiery arrow struck the ship, then another. Half-a-dozen flaming shafts embedded within the wood, spreading the fire across the vessel. Men were shouting, trying to put out the flames, but when they extinguished one arrow, another took its place.

'He'll never have you,' came Hohengrau's voice at her ear. Adriana fought against his grasp, struggling to free herself. 'I'll take your life now, and we'll go together into the sea.'

'Not if I take your life first,' came Liam's voice. He tore her out of Hohengrau's grasp, and Adriana fell to the deck.

Seconds later, she turned and saw her enemy lying facedown, a knife embedded in the base of his neck.

Fire raged before them, an inferno of choking smoke and burning flames. Liam took her hand but when Adriana tried to embrace him, he avoided it. Vengeance lay within in his eyes as he drew her toward the side of the ship.

'Brace yourself.'

Giving her no time to argue, he jumped off the vessel, taking her with him. Icy seawater struck her like a physical blow, and though Liam pulled her back above water, her limbs were leaden within the sea.

Honora was already swimming ahead of them, while the ship continued to burn. Liam remained at her side, helping her to reach the nearest boat. King Patrick lifted her inside, and Liam followed. Her teeth chattered from the cold, and Adriana shivered hard.

But it was Liam's coldness that frightened her most of all. He'd saved her life, but he wouldn't even look at her. And she didn't know what that meant.

Chapter Four

When they arrived back at the castle, Queen Isabel wept over all of them, and ordered hot baths to warm them from the sea. Adriana offered to tend Liam, but he refused. The distance seemed to magnify with every moment that passed, and she didn't know how to gain his forgiveness. Not in the face of such anger.

Isabel tried to ask what had happened, but Morren cut her off. 'I'll tend to her while you rest. All will be well, I'm certain.'

Grateful for the young woman's kindness, Adriana could only admit, 'He knows. And it was just as I feared.'

'It's not over yet.' Morren brought her back to the chamber Adriana shared with the other women, and ordered them out. She helped her to undress, but Adriana couldn't stop herself from shaking.

'He won't look at me or speak to me,' she whispered, spilling out all the details to Morren. The brutal pain cut her heart in half, but she admitted the worst truth of all. 'I don't think there can be a wedding any more.'

'MacEgan men have their pride,' Morren said, 'but if he loves you, he will forgive what was done in the past.'

'What should I do?'

'Confront him,' Morren advised. 'Fight with him and let him release all the anger.' She sent her a secretive smile. 'And then show him how much you love him.'

'I don't think I can do that. The last time I tried, all I could think of was what happened to me.'

'Sometimes a kiss is enough,' Morren advised. She handed her a drying cloth and helped her don a clean gown. Adriana went to sit by the fire, uncertain of anything. A knock sounded at the door, and Honora entered. The young woman's hair was wet, and her face was flushed with contentment, as if her husband had pulled her away and loved her thoroughly.

'I came to see if you were all right,' she said. Worry creased her face, and when she sent a questioning look toward Morren, the woman gave a quiet nod.

'She knows,' Adriana said. She combed her hair, wishing her life were as easy to untangle as these strands.

The two women spoke quietly, and Honora offered, 'Would you like me to arrange some time alone with Liam?' Though Adriana nodded, she doubted if he would want to talk with her.

'It must be tonight,' Morren insisted. 'The sooner the better.'

From the conspiratorial looks on their faces, Adriana understood their intent. But she wasn't at all certain it would work.

'I need to speak with you.'

Liam glanced up at Adriana, who had come into the solar. Her dark hair was braided and wet, and she'd changed into a green gown.

'Not now.' He kept his voice quiet, not wanting to shame her before the others. Talking was the last thing he wanted to do. He wanted to drive himself to limits, to break something or punish himself in a way where the physical pain would blot out the world.

Instead of listening to him, she moved past the others and stood before him, offering her hand.

He stared at it, but no longer did he feel the urge to cherish her, to enjoy a stolen moment together. A primal need was invading his senses, making him want to seize her, to drive out the memories of any other man but him. He wasn't feeling at all rational, and if he dared to go with her, she would bear the brunt of his temper.

But he took her hand and lowered his voice. 'I can't be alone with you right now, Adriana. I'm too angry.'

Crestfallen, she drew her fingers back as if uncertain what to do. He didn't care if his words hurt her. Inside, he was raw and wounded from the truths he'd heard this day.

Adriana touched her fingers to her lips, and nodded. 'I'll go and see to my brother. You can find me there, when you're ready to talk.'

But then, she leaned down, pressing her mouth against his cheek in a kiss. As if nothing wrong had happened between them. As if by willing it to be so, she could walk away from her past and not bear any penalty for it.

The kiss burned into his skin, tormenting him with the thoughts of the night she'd gone into Hohengrau's bed. It was a wonder he hadn't butchered the man instead of granting him a swift death. But he understood that this was Richard's greatest punishment for his disobedience. The king had known how much Adriana meant to him, and her betrayal was a never-ending torture.

But even knowing the truth, he still loved her. The question was whether or not he could forgive her for it. Or lay the past to rest.

The need to walk away and clear his mind was overwhelming. Liam murmured excuses to his family as he retreated outside. He spied Rhiannon walking through the fortress with the blind Viking, Kaall Hardrata, at her side. A dog trotted beside the man, and his cousin had created a harness so the animal could guide the man.

In her eyes, he saw love and happiness—the same feelings he'd held toward Adriana for so long. But now that his eyes were opened to her pain, he recalled every hesitation, every marked fear. She'd tried to force herself to be with him on the night of the solstice, as if that could heal her invisible wounds.

He walked across the castle grounds, endlessly circling, until afternoon turned into evening. When at last he returned to the Great Chamber, Adriana was waiting for him. 'You were gone a long time. Are you ready to talk now?'

'No.' He didn't know if he'd ever be ready to speak of it. Certainly not this night.

'All right.' She sent him an enigmatic look and went above the spiral stairs, her emerald skirts brushing against the stone.

All right? Her acceptance was clearly out of place, and he didn't know what to make of it. Without understanding why, he followed her. Instead of going to her own chamber, she walked into his. What was she doing? It wasn't a chamber that belonged to him, and at least four other men shared it with him.

He opened the door, thankful that no one was there. 'You shouldn't be here.'

'You said you weren't ready to discuss what happened. So I'll wait.' She sat down upon a stool by the fire, not looking at him. Though her demeanour appeared calm, he didn't doubt the storm of frustration building.

Her braided dark hair had a reddish gleam against the fire, and the gown clung to her slender form. His mind attacked with visions of Hohengrau touching her, of baring Adriana's soft skin. He turned away.

'You need to leave,' he said. Before he lost the fragile control over his anger and frustration. Though he'd killed the man who had hurt her, it wasn't enough to bridge the distance between them. She'd severed his trust, and it couldn't be repaired with words. Only time could do that.

'If I go, you'll only push me away,' she said quietly. 'The way you're trying to do right now.'

'It's not a good time, Adriana.' He kept his back to her, staring at the wall. 'You're asking me to listen when I'm too angry. I'll say things I'll regret later.'

'I can't stand back and let you give up on us,' she whispered. 'Not after all this.' She moved closer until he sensed her standing behind him. 'Don't close yourself off from me.'

'The way you did to me over these past few months?' he demanded, facing her at last. 'Do you think I didn't see your pain? That I didn't know how much you were hurting? But every time I asked, you made excuses. You behaved as if nothing happened, when the truth was, you wanted to hide what you'd done.'

The words were cruel, but he couldn't stop them. If she'd confessed the truth from the beginning, they might have pushed past this. But now...

Adriana raised defiant eyes to his. 'I would make the same choice again. Without hesitation.' She rested her hands upon his heart, where the pulse tightened inside him. 'You didn't see Richard's temper that night. He demanded your death. They were going to kill you, and I couldn't let that happen.'

'And so you offered yourself to him.'

'Yes.' Her tears broke free, sliding over her cheeks like the icy pieces of his heart. 'I begged the king for mercy. And I paid the price for it.'

His hands clenched at his sides, for the agony of imagining her there in another man's bed was a hot iron plunged into his chest.

'You lied to me.'

'No, I buried the shadow of that night inside me. I couldn't bear to speak of it, for I relived that vision, night after night. And the shame of what I did.'

She laid her head against his heart, in a silent plea for forgiveness. The scent of her hair allured him, making him want to touch it, to bring the strands to his face.

If these secrets hadn't been bared, he'd embrace her right now. He would feel the warmth of her arms around his neck, tasting the rich headiness of her kiss.

'I love you, Liam. My feelings haven't changed at all. I can only pray that you'll forgive me for what I did.'

It was an effort to keep his hands at his sides, instead of crushing her to him. His emotions were tangled up in a blend of frustration, anger, and hurt. A darker side of him wanted to punish her for what she'd done, by withdrawing from her. He thought of sending her back to Navarre so he wouldn't have to look upon the beautiful face that had ripped his heart asunder.

But then, to send her away, would only intensify the emptiness inside him.

'It's too soon. I have to think—'

'No, don't think.' She lifted soft hands to frame his face. In her dark eyes, he saw her love, a love he didn't want to turn away from. 'I'm the same woman you loved when we arrived here. And if you think I'll stand back and let you give it up, you're wrong.'

Inside, the coldness was twisting, transforming into a jealousy he couldn't control. 'You're asking too much, Adriana.'

'Possibly. But put yourself in my place. If I were about to die, would you have done anything to save me?' Her hands threaded into his hair, pulling his face closer. 'I would have taken your place, if I could have.'

'It might have been better if I'd died.'

'No.' Her voice was a half-whisper, her arms coming around his neck. 'Never that, *mi vida.*' Lifting her mouth higher, he felt the softest touch of her breath upon his lips.

'What are you trying to do, Adriana?'

'Do you still love me?' Her words whispered across his skin and a dark heat seized command of his body. She held him captive beneath her siren's spell, and he took her mouth in a rough kiss. He didn't care that it wasn't gentle or loving. Right now, he wanted to brand himself upon her, to dominate her senses.

A moan caught in her throat, but she opened to him, allowing him to taste her surrender. When her tongue slid within his mouth, his body hardened, his hips pressing close to hers.

'Do you think this will solve anything?' he demanded.

'I don't know.' She pulled back from the kiss, as if she now understood his anger. He didn't want her comparing him to Hohengrau. 'I think you should hear the rest. I want to tell you how it happened, so that you understand.'

'I don't want to hear it, Adriana.'

'And I didn't want it to happen,' she insisted. 'You seem to think I had a choice.'

'You did have a choice.'

'What choice? To let you die?' Misery lined her face as she took another step away. 'I couldn't.' She returned to the stool and faced the flames. His jaw tightened as he saw her shoulders slump forward, her wrists hanging upon her knees.

'He asked me what I would do to save your life,' she began. 'I told him I would do anything.'

Liam stood beside the bed, his hand curling around the bed post. She continued talking, weaving a story of that night. Of how the king had ordered her to go inside one of the tents alone.

'I couldn't see anything at all, but I heard the king's voice. There were two of them there, that night. I—I thought it was one of the king's men, there to guard him. I believed Richard was the one who touched me. Not Hohengrau.'

She wept openly then, and Liam moved closer, watching her lay open the pain. 'I shut my eyes, thinking I could close myself off from it. That I could lie there and let it be done to me, finding a place within my mind where I would feel nothing at all.'

'He hurt you,' Liam accused.

'He was rough, yes. I didn't like it at all, and it displeased him that I was not aroused by his body. He kept trying to make me feel something, and I didn't know what it was.'

Liam knew, and it gave him a harsh sense of satisfaction, that Hohengrau had not taken that from Adriana, at least.

Seeing her weep was bothering him, and he couldn't stand to watch her cry. Without knowing why, he gathered her into his arms, and she only wept harder. His own eyes stung while she released the terror and pain she'd suffered.

'That night, on the solstice,' she murmured, 'I really did want to make love with you. I wanted you to take away those memories and show me how it was meant to be.' Against the firelight, her skin glowed, while her dark hair fell softly around her shoulders. The deep green of the gown contrasted against her olive skin, while her dark eyes were wet and luminous.

Rising from the stool, she stood an arm's distance away from him. 'I still want to marry you, Liam. I want to sleep with you in my arms at night and bear you children.'

'I wanted that, too.'

He studied her, feeling as though his future was crumbling before his eyes. She was trying to reach out to him, to prove to him that her heart hadn't changed. But an invisible wall had come between them, and he didn't know whether he could still love her.

'It will soon be Christmas,' she told him. 'A time of peace.' She held out her hands to him. 'We could start again, Liam. And rebuild what was lost.'

The next morning, Adriana awakened, feeling as though a weight had been lifted. There were no longer any secrets between them, and though she worried about Liam, she held the steady belief that somehow she would gain his forgiveness.

The morning weather turned rainy, and outside, the mud grew thick and sodden. The children raced through it, while their parents scolded them. It was the eve of Christmas, and their excitement was tangible with talk of the feasting and the celebration that would happen this night. Greenery hung in swags throughout the castle, but there was still a great deal to be done.

Adriana searched the Great Chamber, only to discover that there was no sign of the king or queen. There was confusion about which animals were to be slaughtered for the Christmas feast, how many barrels of mead were needed, and what was to happen. More visitors arrived, but Adriana returned above stairs to seek out the queen.

'She's not well,' the healer Aileen said, her face solemn. 'She began bleeding this morn.'

'And the child?'

Aileen lifted her shoulders in a shrug. 'Thus far, she has kept it, but Patrick won't leave her side.'

'I'll keep her in my prayers.' She bade farewell to the healer and crossed through the Hall, thinking to herself. With so many visitors gathering, someone had to assign the tasks for the celebration. If Isabel was unable to do so, perhaps one of the other MacEgan wives could help.

She searched throughout the castle, but when she asked Morren, the woman appeared horrified at the idea. 'I'm sorry.' She clung to her young child as though the boy were a life line. 'I'm afraid I'm no good with large crowds.'

She had no better luck with Honora MacEgan, who was holding a screaming infant boy against one shoulder. With a rueful smile, Honora remarked, 'I'm not much good to you at the moment. But you could talk to the people and organise them. If you know how, that is.'

'It's not my place—'

'Liam will be king one day, and you the queen. Of course it's your place. You might as well start now, when you're needed.'

But she knew Liam did not wish to be a king. If she took on Isabel's responsibilities, it might make him uncomfortable. 'I don't know if I should.'

'It would be a great help to Isabel,' Honora said, 'and once I've settled down my nephew and found a place for my sister and her husband to stay, I'll join you.' She lowered her voice, asking, 'Did you and Liam mend matters between you?'

'Not yet.' But she intended to do everything possible to heal the rift. A blush covered her face, but she asked the question burning inside her. 'How can I...court his affections again?'

Honora thought a moment. 'You could tempt Liam. Leave him wanting you.'

The idea had merit, and Adriana strongly considered it. It had been a long time since she'd flirted with Liam. It might be good to return to the days when they'd first fallen in love.

'I'll try,' she promised.

The noise within the Great Chamber was deafening. Liam stood over by the dais, searching for the king and queen, but had not seen either of them. Before he could ask where they were, Adriana crossed through the people and approached him.

'Your mother isn't well, and the king is with her,' she said. 'I would like to help by assigning the tasks for the feast this night, if you'll get their attention for me.'

'What's happened?' he asked. She grew hesitant, and before she could answer, he touched her shoulders. 'The truth, Adriana.'

'Your mother is pregnant,' she admitted. 'The babe will be born in the spring, but it's been difficult for her. They fear she may lose the child.'

Whatever he had expected, it wasn't that. Isabel was nearly forty years of age, and few women had borne children so late in life. When he couldn't find the words to reply, Adriana insisted, 'Liam, we need to help them. Please.'

He understood what she meant. The people knew nothing of this, and if they did, it would cause unrest among the tribe.

It was better to go on with the Christmas celebration in the hopes that Isabel would feel well enough to join in.

Liam moved to the dais and stood before the MacEgan tribe. Raising his hands, he caught the attention of several men, and gradually the noise died down. 'We have come together this day to celebrate Christmas,' he said, 'and the king and queen will join us later, after Mass. For now, the Lady Adriana will assign you to your tasks, and when night falls, we will share in our feast.' He nodded to Adriana, and within minutes, she had divided up and given out tasks to all. Even the children were asked to help spread fresh rushes upon the floor, while beeswax candles were placed all around the castle, in every window. It was a luxury used only on special days, and it would fill the castle with light after the sun set.

Despite the mountain of work to be accomplished over the next few hours, Adriana remained calm and organised. He watched as the people came to her, asking guidance, and she held herself with confidence and ease…like a queen.

Liam had rejected the mantle of leadership, believing that no one would possibly obey his wishes, not when they were accustomed to his father. But to his surprise, most complied. As the hours passed, he gave orders, supporting Adriana as they found rooms for those needing shelter, food and drink for travellers arriving, and broke up disagreements.

At nightfall, she slipped away, just as the tables were set and the last candle had been lit. He spied her retreating to a corner far away from the others, sitting upon the edge of a bench. With one hand, she removed a shoe, touching her bare foot.

He moved past the others and sat beside her. 'You did well this day.'

Adriana sent him a tired smile. 'I'm afraid if I rest my head for a moment, I won't wake until morning.' But though he saw her exhaustion, there was a glint of satisfaction in her eyes. Together, they'd managed to bring order to the confusion, and now the food was nearly ready.

Liam reached for her foot and drew it into his lap. Her smile faltered, but she made no protest as he began to rub her feet. She leaned back slightly as he massaged the soles of her feet, his thumb moving upon the arch.

'That feels so good,' she whispered. A sensual tone lined her voice, as if he were touching another part of her body. His mouth went dry, and she closed her eyes, her mouth drifting open.

His fingers moved over her skin, and in this quiet moment, it was like before. In his mind, he silenced the hurt and betrayal, simply granting her comfort.

Liam moved his hand to massage her ankle, rising higher to her calf and then down again before he switched to the other foot. She inhaled a slight gasp before echoing her appreciation for his touch.

Her legs rested over his lap, and he supported her back with one arm. When he stopped rubbing her feet, she opened her eyes. 'Liam,' she whispered. She leaned in, touching his cheek with one hand.

His forehead rested against hers, and he struggled against the desires racing through him, not wanting to act upon them. But then her mouth reached for his, and she offered a single kiss. Only one, and she whispered against his mouth, 'Don't think right now. Just be with me.'

He kissed her back, savouring the familiar taste of her mouth and the way she responded to him by pressing her body to his. No doubt she could feel his arousal, since she was sitting on his lap, but she didn't move away. The pressure and heat of her hips against his shaft made him crave more than this kiss.

And when he stared into her sienna eyes, noting the flush of her cheeks and her swollen lips, he saw a hint of yearning.

'I'll always love you, Liam,' she whispered, just before she stood and retreated to her chamber.

Leave him wanting you. That's what Honora had advised, and Adriana had obeyed. Liam's gaze had followed her when she'd returned to her chamber. She took care in choosing her best gown, letting her maid arrange her hair while she imagined what to do next.

He'd come to her and rubbed her feet. Surely he must feel something for her. She took it as a grain of hope, a small step toward winning him back. But would it be enough?

When she was ready, she stopped to visit the queen. Isabel appeared tired and impatient. Her honey-coloured hair was braided over one shoulder, and she remained in bed with pillows propping her up.

'Are you feeling better?' Adriana asked.

'Come and sit with me a moment,' Isabel said, beckoning to her. When she did, the queen smiled at her. 'Patrick tells me that you and Liam organised the celebration for this night.'

She nodded. 'The priest celebrated Mass this morning, and all is in readiness for the feasting tonight. I hope there's enough food. I asked for the fishermen to bring in their catch, and we slaughtered some of the cattle—'

'I am deeply thankful for your help.' Isabel cut her off, squeezing her hand. 'And I am thankful that both you and my son are safe.' Her face held gratefulness and she added, 'I hope that I'll be well enough to attend your wedding.'

A knock sounded at the door, and Adriana went to answer it. When she opened the door Liam was standing there. He had washed, and his dark gold hair held droplets of water. One slid down his cheek, and Adriana started to reach out to touch it, before she caught herself. Transfixed by his handsome face, she could hardly think of what to say.

'I came to see my mother,' he told her, and Adriana stepped aside to let him in.

'I'll give you a moment alone,' she started to say, but Isabel raised her hand in protest.

'No, Adriana, stay with me.' To her son, she said, 'Judging from your face, I suppose you've heard about the babe. And you know what that means.'

'It means you'll have to be careful until this child is born.' Liam drew closer, and when Adriana returned to sit, he came up behind her, resting his palms upon her shoulders. The unexpected affection made her savour his quiet presence.

But Queen Isabel looked doubtful. 'Will you help your father and me during this time?' she asked Liam. 'I cannot perform my duties, but Adriana could take my place until…' Her words drifted off, revealing her uncertainty toward the future.

The weight of his hands on her shoulders suddenly tightened. But he said, 'Aye. We'll do what we can.' He went to kiss his mother's cheek and held out his hand for Adriana to follow him out.

After they left the queen's chamber, he released her palm. Adriana took a slow breath. 'Did you mean what you said to her? That we would help them?'

'I will help my father, yes.'

'And what of us?' she asked, almost afraid of his answer.

He stopped near the stairs, his expression shielded. 'I don't know, Adriana.'

She reached out to him, feeling her own frustration rising higher. 'Why do you still doubt me? Must I martyr myself for the choice I made?'

Liam leaned in to whisper against her ear. 'There is no greater torture, knowing that he took your innocence. And I could do nothing to stop him.'

'You hold me to blame for it.' It broke away the fragile hope she'd nurtured, believing that he might one day forgive her. 'I want to stay with you and be your wife, Liam. I believe we could be happy together. But only if you're willing to let go of your anger.'

She didn't know if it was possible, for jealousy was raging within him. He needed a way to release it, and she feared there was only one means. One that terrified her.

'We should go and join the others,' he said. He was avoiding the issue, and Adriana saw her chance disappearing. Taking his hand in hers, she led him back to his chamber. Once inside, she barred the door against anyone who might intrude.

'Sit down,' she ordered.

'What is this about?'

'You're not leaving this room until we've settled this between us.' She reached behind and struggled to loosen her gown.

Now she'd gained his attention, and he started to protest, 'Adriana, no.'

She fought to free herself from the confining garment, and finally managed to lift the bliaud away. In her silk shift, she took slow steps toward him, trying to behave with a confidence she didn't feel. Her heart pounded, but she forced herself to remove the shift until she stood before him naked.

Liam was motionless, his eyes drinking in the sight of her. In the frigid air, gooseflesh rose over her skin. She took one step toward him, then another, until her body was within close reach.

Taking his hand, she brought it to her wild heartbeat. 'I'm afraid, Liam. More afraid of this than anything in my life. If you don't want me as your bride or your lover, that is your choice to make. But I'm willing to face my fear if it means gaining your forgiveness.' She closed her eyes, then drew his hand from her heart, down to her breast.

'Make your choice, Liam.'

Chapter Five

Her skin tempted him, but Liam could only rest his hand upon her firm breast, knowing this was wrong. He didn't want her to believe that she had to offer herself in order to win his forgiveness.

The truth was, he still loved her, in spite of the terrible secret she'd kept from them. He could see the pain in her eyes, and it was a shadow of his own regret. No, he hadn't wanted her to sacrifice herself.

But he'd die for her without a second thought.

Seeing her here, humbling herself before him, made him feel like the lowest sort of man. He ought to help her clothe herself, to send her downstairs. Yet, if he turned her away, she wouldn't understand why. She would believe that everything was lost between them, and he didn't want to hurt her any more.

Liam stood. 'It won't be this way, Adriana. Not like this.'

Her eyes brimmed with tears, and she started to turn away before he caught her hand. 'You're worth more to me than that.' He removed his own tunic and covered her shoulders with it. 'If you want to lie with me this night, then do. But not because you feel you have to barter yourself.' He stood

before her, and the misery in her eyes made him understand
that he had to make the next move.

Liam wasn't a man accustomed to talking, but he forced
himself to find the words. 'I am angry about what happened
to you.' His hands clenched as he met her stricken gaze. 'I
wish to God you hadn't done it.'

She took the edges of his tunic, wrapping the fabric around
her as if she could hide herself. But he moved in closer. 'I
won't lie—this isn't something I can put aside and ignore.
Because he hurt you.'

He came closer and framed her face, bringing her near
to him. 'It's not you I can't forgive. It's myself for not being
there to protect you.'

She came closer, resting her cheek against his. 'I don't
want to lose you,' she whispered. Her arms came around his
neck, and the tunic slid off her body. Her cool skin pressed
against his, and at the touch of her breasts upon his chest, he
instinctively drew her hips to his.

The need to lie with her, to remove all memories of the
past, was an unquenchable thirst. But he gathered his control
and studied her. 'You don't have to give yourself this night.
I still want to wed you, regardless.'

She wiped away the tears, struggling to hold her feelings
together. 'And if I told you I want this night together?' Her
hands moved over his heart, warming his skin.

Liam took a deep breath, his pulse quickening at her offer.
When he caught her hands in his, he said, 'I won't use you in
that way.' He removed the rest of his clothes, standing naked
before her. Adriana's eyes averted in modesty, and he sat upon
the edge of the bed. 'But I'll let you use me any way you like.'

Confusion furrowed her brow. 'Liam, I don't know—'

'Touch me,' he ordered. 'However you want to.'

She took a tentative step forward, and sat beside him. 'What if you don't like it?'

'*A ghrá*, I promise you, I'll like it.' He rolled on to his side to face her. 'Touch me wherever you want to be touched.'

Her face reddened, but she reached out to rest her hand upon his cheek. When he did the same to her, she leaned forward to kiss him. Her mouth was warm, but there was hesitancy in her embrace. Her hand moved down his throat to his shoulder.

In turn, he did the same, noting the shiver that passed over her. 'Don't be afraid of me,' he said. 'If you need to stop, we will.'

'I want to face my fear,' she said. Her eyes held trepidation, but she drew her hand lower to the pectoral muscles of his chest. Liam brought his hand to her warm breast, and God help him, it was an effort not to caress her, to take the sweet bud into his mouth and suckle her until she cried out.

Her fingers opened, and she traced the ridge of muscle on his chest, her fingers grazing his flat nipple. Liam touched the underside of her curved breast, slowly passing his hand over erect skin. Her nipple was a darker tone, a rose colour that contrasted against her olive skin. Her gasp aroused him, making his body taut with desire. His shaft bulged against her stomach, and he ached to be inside her.

Adriana grew bolder, touching his nipple in a circular motion just as he did to her. The more he played with the tip, the more she grew restless against him. Her body jolted when he caught a sensitive place, and when she removed her hand from his chest, he did the same.

She continued her exploration, moving her hands over his ribs, and he moved her to straddle him so he could touch her in the same way. It drew her womanhood in close contact to his erection, and he could feel her growing moist.

It was a dark torture to lie still beneath her, to feel her awakening desire against him. Her touch was tentative, as if she were unsure of herself. He was glad that she'd never before experienced any pleasure and vowed that tonight, he would change that.

Adriana moved her hands down to his hips but then stopped, her gaze settling upon his shaft.

'You can touch me there if you want to,' he said. Her hand moved to the heat of him, and his hands gripped the coverlet as she did. She cupped his sac, moving her palm to his thickness, and he jerked with an instinctive thrust as her fingers caressed him.

'Slower,' he gritted out, and then remembered that he was supposed to be imitating her touch. God above, she tempted him. He reached between her legs, and when she shied away, he reminded her, 'I'm only touching you in the same place you've touched me.'

Her hand stopped moving, her fingers resting upon him. Against his own hand, he felt the damp curls, and waited for her to make a decision.

She lifted her hand away from him, and he did the same. 'You'll truly stop if I stop?'

He nodded. 'I swear it.'

His promise renewed her courage. Although thoughts kept invading, of the night when she'd lost her innocence, Liam's patience gave her the strength to keep going. Softly, Adriana drew her fingers over his manhood, startled at the way he responded. He grew thicker, harder as she stroked him.

And oh, God above, the way he was touching her. He'd

moved his hand between her legs, gently returning the caress before he slid a finger inside her. Her body had grown wet, as if ready to take him within.

With Liam, everything was different. She found herself leaning against him, welcoming the soft intrusion of his fingers. Adriana closed her eyes, and the sweet ache between her legs was starting to transform. He was rubbing her in a rhythm, and she echoed it against him, fascinated to see how he strained against her hand. A dark sensation was building within her, rising to a peak. She didn't understand it, and when her body began to tighten, she started to fight against it, stopping her movement upon his shaft.

'Let me touch you, Adriana,' he ordered. 'Let me give you this.'

She opened her eyes, staring into his stormy gaze, and nodded. He laid her back upon the bed, the sheets cool against her back. Though she feared the rise of sensation, she brought his hand back to her intimate slit. She didn't know what he would do, but she wanted to please him.

Instead, he pleased her.

His fingers stroked and caressed her while he spoke of how much he loved her. 'You're mine, Adriana. Now, and always.' She could hardly breathe as the burgeoning pressure took her higher, leaving her breathless at the sensation. He kissed her stomach gently, sliding his fingers inside her.

And then, without warning, she felt his mouth upon her. Over her intimate flesh, he feasted, sliding his tongue against her again and again. She arched, helpless to do anything except lean in to his delicious torment, crying out as he nibbled and sucked.

Adriana felt herself breaking apart, pressing against his mouth as a wave of shattering ecstasy roared through her.

She couldn't think, couldn't grasp anything save the rush of pleasure.

She gripped his neck, trembling as she pulled him close. 'I never knew. *Mi corazon*, I never knew anything like this.'

'I'm glad,' he said, catching her mouth in a swift kiss. Through her haze of satisfaction, she realised that he had not experienced the same pleasure as she. Her body was wet, craving more from him, but she wasn't quite ready to accept him inside her. She rested her hands upon his stomach, pressing him back onto the bed. 'Don't touch me yet. Let me tend to you.'

The intense fulfilment gave her the courage to touch him in the same way. She drew her mouth over his hardened muscles, kissing his skin as she drifted lower. She curled her hand over his length, exploring the smooth skin while his face transformed with need. His tight stomach was ridged against her cheek as she tasted the salt of his skin, moving her hand up and down. When she found herself close to his shaft, she hesitated, remembering what he had done to her. It had been a shocking rush, a pleasure like nothing she'd ever known. Would it be the same for him?

Softly, she took the head of him into her mouth, and Liam growled, his hands gripping her hair.

'Adriana, I— *Jesu*,' he nearly shouted. Encouraged by his wild response, she took him deeper into her mouth, caressing his length with her tongue and finding her own rhythm. But when she began to suck, he used his strength to pull her back, pinning her to the bed.

'Were you trying to torture me?' he demanded, his voice resonant with need.

Liam got up from the bed and drew her hips to the edge, raising her knees. 'It's going to happen again, Adriana. I'm going to join with you and do everything in my power to satisfy you.'

This time, she felt the thick head of him pressing against her. Slowly, he entered, welcomed by her wetness. There was no pain, no sense of being taken against her will. Only the need to welcome him, to make their bodies one.

'Come to me,' she said, her hands sliding into his hair as he gently penetrated and withdrew.

'Te amo,' she murmured, lifting her hips to meet his thrust. He lowered himself upon her, his heart resting against hers as he continued the gentle invasion.

'I love you, too,' he answered. At his words, she felt the tears returning, but they were tears of thankfulness, not pain. She wept as he came into her arms, whispering words of love, filling her with himself.

And when she gripped his hips, encouraging him faster, she let him take her as he wanted to. Over and over he plunged, his words falling into Irish endearments that captured her heart. She needed this man, and when he finished inside her, she held him tightly. Knowing she could never let him go.

When they returned to the Great Chamber, the room had been transformed, lit by soft candles. Swags of holly and other greenery were hung throughout the room, while the lilting sound of a harp filled the air with music.

Liam walked through the room with Adriana at his side. Her face held the flush of their recent lovemaking, and he brought her among his family, unable to let her leave his side. She sent him a secret smile, and it spread through him, warming his heart. Though the past still left a bitter taste in his mouth knowing the pain she'd experienced for his sake, he didn't want anything to come between them again.

'You look well, Liam,' came the voice of Honora. The woman sent him a knowing look, and winked at Adriana.

As they crossed through the crowd of people, his kinsmen smiled and offered greetings to Adriana and himself. She complimented them on the food and it was clear that she'd earned a place among them.

His father was still absent, so it fell to Liam to offer greetings to the people, beginning the celebration. And he found that he didn't mind it at all.

He climbed the stairs of the dais, raising his hands until the crowd fell silent. He spoke first in Irish, then in the Norman language so that Adriana could understand his words. On behalf of the king and queen, he offered them greetings and invited them to join in the feast.

As his gaze fell upon the familiar faces of family and friends, it felt right to have her beside him. Adriana was all that mattered. He embraced her in front of everyone, breathing in her familiar scent, wanting her to understand that he had not turned his back on her.

'You said once, you'd have done anything to save my life.' He stared into her eyes. 'As I would do for you.'

She traced his cheek, her hands trembling with emotion, and though the pain of the past was still there, her love for him shone through.

'You *are* my life, Adriana.' Despite the past troubles and all they had suffered, he loved her. They would work to overcome what had transpired before, until the horrors of the Crusade were a faded memory. 'God willing, we'll have many years together.'

She tightened her embrace, kissing him. 'May it be so.'

The MacEgans cheered and raised their knees in a gesture of respect. Liam gave the order for the mead to be poured and saw that his father had returned. Though King Patrick appeared weary, he climbed the dais and accepted his own cup of mead. Raising it high, he proclaimed, 'Blessings upon our people. And especially upon our future king and queen.'

Liam raised his own cup toward his bride, no longer feeling as if the kingship were a burden. Not with Adriana at his side. 'To the future.'

Epilogue

Winter passed and Adriana welcomed the coming of spring. Her wedding to Liam had come within a sennight of her brother's marriage, and her parents had arrived at last to offer their blessings. Although there would be many years before Liam would assume his father's place as king, Patrick had already begun to share duties with his son.

Until that time, Adriana had insisted that they live in a dwelling of their own, away from the rest of the castle. Liam had built her a small stone thatched hut, one where they could shut out the rest of the world and be together. They had spent many long winter nights in each other's arms, and there was no greater joy than to be with her new husband.

The snows had melted, and though Queen Isabel had wearied of remaining in her bed, the child within her continued to grow. This morn, Adriana was out walking with friends while a young girl was stomping within puddles.

With a heavy sigh, Rhiannon sent them an apologetic look. 'No matter how often I ask Emla to stop, she loves to get muddy and wet.'

Brianna smiled. 'She knows her father won't scold her.'

'Because Kaall can't see how much dirt is all over her,'

she moaned, picking up the child and holding her tight. Emla planted a kiss upon Rhiannon's cheek, snuggling close.

An ache caught inside Adriana, with the hopes that she would one day bear a child of her own. From the softness on Brianna's face and the contentment there, she suspected her brother would be a father soon enough.

A few moments later, Brianna's sister came running toward them, out of breath. 'Come quickly,' Alanna ordered. 'The queen needs you.'

'Is her babe about to be born?'

'I'll go and fetch the healer while you sit with her,' the young girl finished. Without letting them voice another question, she hurried off.

Though it should have been welcome news, none of the women looked happy about it. All throughout the pregnancy, Isabel had continued to suffer, and she was not alone in her fear.

Adriana exchanged looks with the others.

Rhiannon was the first to speak. 'I'll go to her. Adriana, have Liam take Patrick away from the castle. He shouldn't be there while she's in pain.'

'If he knows her labour has started, there's nothing that will take him from her side.' But she understood what the young woman meant. Patrick's fears would only multiply if he were there.

'Just try,' Rhiannon said. She handed her foster daughter over to Brianna, adding, 'Take her back to Kaall, will you?'

Just as Alanna had predicted, Queen Isabel was struggling against the pain. 'It wasn't like this the last time,' she claimed, closing her eyes as another labour pain struck her. 'These are…faster.'

'It's your second child,' Rhiannon said. 'Your body will remember what to do.'

Perspiration beaded across her forehead as the queen

fought to keep from crying out. The women kept vigil over the next few hours, and Adriana was grateful that Liam had removed his father from Laochre, telling him nothing about the queen's impending childbirth.

But by nightfall, everyone knew. Isabel struggled against the never-ending pains, and had nearly broken Adriana's hand from squeezing it so tightly. She'd been pushing for hours, but the babe refused to come.

Patrick had returned and was pacing the floors, his face grey with worry.

'Isabel,' the healer said, leaning in. 'The babe isn't turned correctly.'

'You're not cutting her to take the child,' the king insisted. 'I won't allow it.'

'Let Aileen try to turn the baby,' Isabel whispered. She reached out for her husband's hand, weeping openly. 'There's hope, Patrick. I haven't given up yet.'

Adriana saw the fear on their faces, and she considered retreating when the queen cried out in more pain. The king was speaking to her, words of encouragement and love. And she voiced her own prayers, that the babe—and Isabel—might live.

In the middle of the night, there came the cry of a newborn. Adriana's eyes were not the only ones weeping. She left the chamber and returned to the others who were waiting below. Within moments, Liam caught her in his arms. 'Is my mother all right?'

Adriana nodded, holding him close. 'I fear you'll still be the king one day. For you now have a sister.'

'Praise be,' he murmured, dropping a kiss upon her hair.

Her brother Arturo's face was pale, as if remembering the loss of his first wife. 'I am glad she is well. And I pray never to watch over such a birth again.'

He raised Brianna's hand to his lips, but she sent him a curious look. 'We'll know in the autumn, won't we?'

His look of surprise was replaced by his own joy as he kissed his new wife. 'Truly?'

She nodded, and Adriana congratulated them both. Liam put his arm around her and they walked outside where the stars glowed in the midnight sky above them.

'It was a blessing my parents never expected,' he said, his hand resting upon the small of her back. 'I didn't think I would ever have a sister.'

'Did you wish for a brother who would take the throne instead?'

He walked with her across the grounds, the torches casting shadows on the ground. 'No. If the people desire that I should be the next king, I will. Unless you object?'

'I would never stand in the way of your happiness. Whether you want to be a king or a shepherd.'

'It wouldn't matter, *a ghrá*. For all of my happiness lies with you.'

She drew him into her arms, holding him tightly. Inside, she sent up her own prayer of thanksgiving that there were no longer any nightmares of the past to awaken her. In Liam, she'd found forgiveness, and a love that had healed her invisible scars.

Just before they returned home, a star streaked across the sky in a silvery path. 'It's like a glimpse of heaven,' Liam said, stopping to marvel at it.

She cupped his face between her hands, letting him see her love. 'Yes,' she whispered.

And with a smile, she led him inside to where their own heaven awaited them.

* * * * *

REQUEST YOUR FREE BOOKS!

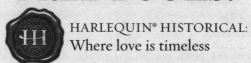

HARLEQUIN® HISTORICAL:
Where love is timeless

2 FREE NOVELS PLUS 2 **FREE GIFTS!**

YES! Please send me 2 FREE Harlequin® Historical novels and my 2 FREE gifts (gifts are worth about $10). After receiving them, if I don't wish to receive any more books, I can return the shipping statement marked "cancel." If I don't cancel, I will receive 6 brand-new novels every month and be billed just $5.19 per book in the U.S. or $5.74 per book in Canada. That's a savings of at least 17% off the cover price! It's quite a bargain! Shipping and handling is just 50¢ per book in the U.S. and 75¢ per book in Canada.* I understand that accepting the 2 free books and gifts places me under no obligation to buy anything. I can always return a shipment and cancel at any time. Even if I never buy another book, the two free books and gifts are mine to keep forever.

246/349 HDN FEQQ

Name	(PLEASE PRINT)
Address	Apt. #
City	State/Prov.	Zip/Postal Code

Signature (if under 18, a parent or guardian must sign)

Mail to the **Reader Service:**
IN U.S.A.: P.O. Box 1867, Buffalo, NY 14240-1867
IN CANADA: P.O. Box 609, Fort Erie, Ontario L2A 5X3

Not valid for current subscribers to Harlequin Historical books.

Want to try two free books from another line?
Call 1-800-873-8635 or visit www.ReaderService.com.

* Terms and prices subject to change without notice. Prices do not include applicable taxes. Sales tax applicable in N.Y. Canadian residents will be charged applicable taxes. Offer not valid in Quebec. This offer is limited to one order per household. All orders subject to credit approval. Credit or debit balances in a customer's account(s) may be offset by any other outstanding balance owed by or to the customer. Please allow 4 to 6 weeks for delivery. Offer available while quantities last.

Your Privacy—The Reader Service is committed to protecting your privacy. Our Privacy Policy is available online at www.ReaderService.com or upon request from the Reader Service.

We make a portion of our mailing list available to reputable third parties that offer products we believe may interest you. If you prefer that we not exchange your name with third parties, or if you wish to clarify or modify your communication preferences, please visit us at www.ReaderService.com/consumerchoice or write to us at Reader Service Preference Service, P.O. Box 9062, Buffalo, NY 14269. Include your complete name and address.

Are you ready for a thrilling adventure in the Wild West?

Read on for a sneak peek of
***REBEL WITH A CAUSE** by Carol Arens,*
available December 18, 2012, from Harlequin® Historical.

The woman's petticoat caught in the wind and whipped up to slap her chin. She struggled with it and tried to keep hold of the horse at the same time. Zane figured he must have dust in his eyes. It looked like a piece of her undergarment had come loose and begun to whip and whirl about the horse's hooves all on its own accord.

Wage, not one for missing an opportunity, took that instant to give the horse a hard kick. The pony lurched forward then galloped double-time toward the west.

With massive clouds dimming the light, Zane nearly missed seeing the woman's mouth form a perfectly pink circle of surprise when his horse, Ace, galloped past her.

Guilt squirmed in his conscience for hightailing on by like that. It couldn't be noble to leave a lady stranded so far from town in her underwear, not with one hell of a storm ready to strike the earth like a hammer.

Setting his sights on Wage again, he noted the outlaw was still a good distance in the lead, but losing some ground to Ace.

One fat, chilly raindrop smacked him on the cheek. It wouldn't be long until this whole area turned into a mud puddle. He could likely reach Wage before that happened.

He sighed hard. Heat skimmed his lips. He sat up slow and leaned back in the saddle. Understanding the unspoken command, his horse slowed to an impatient trot.

"Hold up, boy."

Zane watched Wage disappear over the next hill. His

whole body and soul itched to be on the run after the out-law. With a sour lump in his gut, he turned to look once more at the stranded woman.

Missy's mouth hung open in disbelief. It was surely an unbecoming gesture that her mother would reprimand her for if she could see it.

The hooves of his huge horse pummeled the ground. Clumps of sod, ripped from the soil, flew about. The earth trembled, bringing her hero closer.

In her whole sheltered Eastern life she'd never seen a man like this. The West rode wild in his smoky brown eyes. Black eyebrows slashed across his forehead like fired bullets. This was a man of adventure!

Dive into adventure with Missy and her rugged cowboy!

Look for
REBEL WITH A CAUSE
by Carol Arens.

Available December 18, 2012, from Harlequin® Historical.

HHEXP29719

Rediscover the Harlequin series section starting December 18!

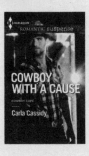